THE
SPIDER
CATCHERS

Marilynn Larew

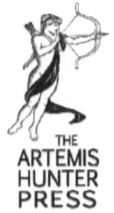

THE
ARTEMIS
HUNTER
PRESS

Artemis Hunter Press
20 New Park Road
New Park, Pennsylvania 17352
www.marilynnlarew.com

Publisher's Note: This is a work of fiction. Names, characters, places, and incidents are a product of the author's imagination. Locales and public names are sometimes used for atmospheric purposes. Any resemblance to actual people, living or dead, or to businesses, companies, events, institutions, or locales is completely coincidental.

THE SPIDER CATCHERS
Marilynn Larew—1st ed.
ISBN: 978-0-9910912-1-8 (pbk.)

For Karl

who has read every draft
without complaint

Acknowledgments

Despite the popular vision of a solitary writer working alone in a garret, every writer has a host of people helping her. I want to thank the following:

My husband, Karl, who has put up with it all, reading, helping, and proofing the numerous drafts. My son, Marvin Terry; grandson, Jeremy Terry; John Barry, and Adam Firestone for advice on guns. If I got it wrong, it's not their fault. My great editor, Lourdes Venard, for helping me shape the manuscript into something resembling a book, and Karen McCullough for designing a great cover. Granddaughter Samantha Terry provided artistic advice. Ellie Hofstetetter and Susan Burke read an early draft, Guppy Jodie Ball read the almost-final draft, and Guppies Kaye George and Diane Vallere gave me advice, aid, and comfort. Thanks also go to a guy named Nemo for guns, explosives, and general mayhem.

Any errors are my own, probably caused by my not taking their advice.

THE
SPIDER
CATCHERS

Chapter 1

I DRAPED THE strap of my laptop over the handle of my suitcase and climbed the worn stone staircase to the flat, my backpack heavy on my shoulder. Five centuries does a number on steps, even stone ones. I leaned the suitcase against the wall to unlock the Chubb lock on the thick oak door. A tall thin figure stood silhouetted against the French windows. A man. In my flat? Which one of the men who wanted me dead was he? I threw my pack at him and cannoned onto him, landing on his chest with my knees on his arms. I pushed hard on his windpipe with my right arm. He bucked and turned his head so that I could see his face.

"Well, if it isn't my esteemed mentor, Sidney Worthington," I said with relief. "What brings you to Paris?"

"Carruthers, get off of me! Are you trying to kill me?"

I leaned back and helped him to his feet.

"Would have if I'd been armed," I said. "How did you get in? Paul didn't say there was anybody here."

Sidney sat down on the sofa and rubbed his throat.

"I didn't stop in the café downstairs."

I put my hands on my hips. "There is no way you picked that lock."

"The Agency has a key."

I turned my back on him. "Why am I not surprised?"

The Central Intelligence Agency owns the fifteenth-century stone building where I live and work when I'm not out saving the world.

I turned back. "To return to my question," I pressed. "What brings you here? You've never visited me before. You don't visit your people. You summon them."

"I'm on my way to a money-laundering conference in Brussels."

Sidney is the head of the CIA unit that tracks the vast spider web of dirty money, the billions and billions of dollars that are the profits from crime. Money laundering is big business because crime is big business. From my office in Paris, I pursue the toxic spiders and seize their money. Arms merchants selling death, drug smugglers selling oblivion, slavers selling women and children. We unravel the international web of shady men and shifting entities that keep it all moving. Usually it just goes to enrich the usual suspects. These days it can also go to fund terrorism.

"Then you should be in Brussels." I went to get my suitcase and laptop from the hall where I had left them. "This is Paris."

"Don't be a smart-ass."

"I was a smart-ass when you hired me, Sidney. You didn't visit me for the sake of my beautiful green eyes. What do you want?"

"A cup of coffee would be nice," he said, crossing and recrossing his legs. He's uncertain about whatever it is, I thought. All he has to do is fold his arms across his chest. He folded his arms across his chest.

"So would an answer," I said.

He ran his hands through his short gray hair. "I need

you to go to Fez. You've got a reservation on the two o'clock Air France flight to Casablanca."

"Wrong answer, Sidney. I just got off the red-eye from Baghdad. Usually you let me do my laundry before you dispatch me to save the world again." I crossed to the window and looked out. There wasn't any sun in the street. My street never got any sun. "Why?"

"Alicia Harmon, the woman who runs the Femme Aid office in Fez, has vanished, and she's got to be found. You know the place and the people better than anyone."

Femme Aid is part of a network of similar offices the Agency set up around the world to monitor human trafficking. It's a cover, but it actually does provide help for women in distress.

"Nobody's seen her since the twenty-first of August," Sidney said.

"My God, Sidney, that's two weeks! Why didn't the station in Rabat do something?"

"They did. They couldn't find a trace."

"And I will? Why didn't you send somebody sooner? I'm not the only person on the payroll."

Sidney joined me at the window.

"I needed you to finish the Baghdad job."

I turned on him. "Yeah, right. That was real important. I found one and a half billion dollars, a fraction of what the contractors have stolen. The Swiss banks have had to jack their buildings up several feet to accommodate all the new dollars in their basements. It was all computer work; I could just as easily have done it from here."

"I needed you there to put the fear of God into them."

I snorted. "Sidney, they fear neither God nor man. There are too many of them. There are more contractors in Baghdad than there are flies."

"Look, Lee, you set up that office."

I would not take the dirty black suits out of my suitcase and put the clean ones in without a fight. I was too tired.

"So what? Why does it have to be me? This is a job for Clandestine."

"You know Fez and the people. Anybody else would have to waste time reading in, and that would take *time*, Lee. Time we may not have."

"Sidney, if you'd sent somebody else in the beginning, you would have had more time."

"That's not the point. I didn't. In her last—"

He didn't like the way that sounded. "In her most recent report, she wrote that she had found a link to terrorist money."

"Terrorist money!"

"Something she stumbled over, I suppose. I wrote asking her what she was talking about, but she disappeared before she answered me. I need you to go and find out if she really learned anything about terrorist funding."

"Who is she?" I asked. "I never heard of her."

"She's a contract employee about five years younger than you are," he explained. "She came on board right after she graduated from Wellesley. I picked her up at a meeting of the American Anti-Slavery Society. She's descended from generations of slave traders and generations of abolitionists, and she's passionate about slavery. That's why I hired her. But she hasn't got any street-smarts."

"She's not supposed to, Sidney. She's an analyst."

I moved to the sofa. Rather than take the wing chair facing me, he joined me there, and we sat stiffly side by side. He twisted a gold button on his Yale blazer and looked uncomfortable.

"You're an analyst, and you've got streets-smarts."

"I've developed some. That's why I'm still alive. You get me into things analysts aren't supposed to do."

He shrugged. "I need you to do things. Now I need you to go and find Alicia Harmon."

"What's so special about Alicia Harmon that tomorrow won't do? I quit."

"You can't quit."

"Sidney, this is not a good time to work for the Agency." He started to speak. I raised my hand to stop him. "I know. There's never a good time to work for the Agency, but my stay in Baghdad was not pleasant. It turned out to be downright ugly."

"Paris isn't Baghdad."

"That's not the point, Sidney. I'm tired of this. I chase money belonging to drug smugglers, gunrunners, slavers, and now terrorists. Sometimes I chase *them*. I put them out of business, and twenty-four hours later they're back, bigger than ever. Living in the slime gets to you after a while. I know a guy with a small IT business in Boston. He wants me to join him. Better salary, decent hours, no gunfights, and I could get out of this town."

"Lots of people at Langley would kill to be stationed in Paris."

"Yeah, so they say. They think I'm living high on the hog here. They should see this apartment with its three-inch stone walls and arrow slits for windows. Some nineteenth century tenant punched a hole in the wall for that window, bless him." I pointed to the French windows overlooking the sunless street. "I get light in here. Light, but not sun."

"Never mind. Carruthers, I need you to do this. There's no telling what she's gotten into."

"Why me?"

"I'm asking you to do it, Lee. Do I have to order you?" He sounded exasperated.

I was equally exasperated, but I know a losing fight when I see one. I sighed in resignation.

"All right. Tell me."

"Her reports were routine until about three weeks ago. You know. Who has new girls, which ones are abused, when new shipments may be coming in, who's got a new fast boat, women one way, cigars and brandy the other, the occasional passenger, that kind of thing."

I did. I ran that office for a while.

"The passenger sounds interesting," I said.

He ignored me. "The only unusual thing that happened recently was that she picked up a couple of sick women who were sitting by the side of the road, maybe Tuareg she thought. She took them to the house in the medina. Miriam got them a doctor and nursed them back to health. Alicia said they were thrown out of a slave shipment."

"If they were sick, they would be. The skin trade has no room for sick merchandise."

"But what was she planning to do with a couple of women who can't even speak Arabic?"

"I don't suppose she thought much about it. She just picked them up. I would have." I glanced at him. "So would you."

"She said they might be Tuareg. That's new. I didn't think they sold their kids."

"Sounds like the drought is really biting them. They'll sell their daughters, maybe even a son, before they'll sell their last few camels," I said. "I guess the recruiters are visiting the nomad camps now. They haven't before."

He shook his head and moved on. "Then this report about laundering money. She wouldn't know how to follow that."

"No, that's my job."

"That's why I need you to do this job."

"Sidney, I do money, I'm not a detective. I am obviously the only soldier you've got to send to Fez," I said, with more than a trace of sarcasm in my voice. "But, brilliant as I am, somebody else can do this."

"It's important."

"Why did you come all the way from Langley to get me to do this?"

"I didn't. I just stopped off on my way to Brussels," he said.

"And I've got a bridge I'll sell you. Why *me*?"

"While you were in Baghdad that Algerian group, the Salafist Group for Preaching and Combat, pledged allegiance to Al Qaeda and Bin Laden, and changed its name to Al Qaeda in the Islamic Maghreb."

"Bin Laden is dead."

"He wasn't when they changed their name. They began organizing all the little local groups in western North Africa into one big group allied with Al Qaeda. They have a lot of money, and we need to know where it's coming from. Maybe Alicia Harmon found out."

"If she did and she's disappeared, she's dead."

He looked stubborn. "I need you to find out what she learned."

"So I can get dead, too?" I asked.

"No. You won't get dead."

He was right, but I came damn close.

Chapter 2

ON THE WAY out the door, Sidney handed me a photograph and said, "You need to work fast, Lee."

"She may already be dead, Sidney."

He shut the door harder than I thought necessary.

The photo showed a slender woman with fine blonde hair, large blue eyes, and an oval face. Delicate, she looked delicate, like a porcelain cup. Her vital statistics were on the back. Five feet six and a half inches tall, 120 pounds. She looked like the girl I had seen accepting condolences at my father's funeral instead of me. That didn't dispose me to like her.

You have to fly into Casablanca to get to Fez, and I had to go to the embassy in Rabat to announce my existence to the station chief before I went there. During the flight, I mulled over the reasons I wanted to leave the Agency. The reasons I *had* to leave the Agency. I was not in Clandestine. I mean, I didn't go to Vienna and slink around the back alleys, but my time wasn't really my own. I don't work nine to five hours. The job's not like that. I work all hours when the money is jumping, and Sidney's always on my back. At thirty-three, I have no social life, because I can't predict when I'll be in town. How many times can I break a date or cancel a dinner party before people begin to ask questions? I might find people who could cope with my secret life at the embassy, but embassies are sealed hothouses of gossip and backstabbing. The vacuum in them sucks all the air out of you. After you've slept with everybody there, what else is there to do?

I don't live a quiet life, but sometimes my life is too quiet.

Depressing.

I need to get a life.

I picked up a car at the airport and set out on the short drive to the capital. As I neared Rabat I considered the CIA Chief of Station, Brad McNulty. Brad and I go way back, unfortunately. We were in training together. He hated me on sight, and I soon returned the favor. He thought that I was getting special treatment because my father worked for the Agency and because all of the instructors knew me by name. Some of them had even bounced me on their knees when I was a tot. I was getting special treatment. I was "rode hard and put away wet" every day. I was proud that I lived through it, but Brad and I were never going to be friends. I was going to have to swallow my animosity if I wanted to learn anything about Alice Harmon from him. A bad meal.

The embassy was a large rectangle with the first story set back behind pillars, built in the sixties when everybody was throwing rocks at US embassies. It looked like the Great Wall of China with windows.

The embassy receptionist was a pleasant woman wearing a headscarf.

"I have an appointment with Mr. McNulty," I said.

She called McNulty's office to confirm my appointment and had a recruiting poster Marine escort me to the station. Brad's reception room was pretty standard government issue, all light wood and mauve. The ice-blonde receptionist was not standard, however. She was a fantasy in well-filled blue. Eventually she looked up from her computer monitor.

"Yes?"

Not "how may I help you." Just "yes." The ice went all the way through.

"Lee Carruthers to see Mr. McNulty."

"Do you have an appointment?"

"Mr. Worthington made one for me from Paris."

She flipped open a book and ran her finger down the day's appointments. She looked at me again. Sidney Worthington did not cut much mustard in Brad's office.

"Mr. McNulty is in a meeting at the moment. Please have a seat, and he'll be with you shortly."

I took a seat.

Since the time of my arrival had been indefinite, I did not expect a busy man like Brad McNulty to see me immediately. If I knew Brad, he would make me wait at least fifteen minutes, just to emphasize how insignificant I was. You get points for every minute you make the visitor wait.

I improved my time by running down the list of Fez and Rabat informants from the Moroccan files I had copied to my laptop. My best bet in Rabat was Abdullah. He owned a pipe bar near the Guards' Barracks. And then there was Kemal. I smiled when I thought of him. A good kisser, Kemal. He also owned a pipe bar, this one in Fez. They were guaranteed to hear everything just before it hit the street. I knew two men in some branch of the security services as well. They would know whatever Abdullah and Kemal didn't. The others would be useful only if Alicia asked them something, and I wouldn't know if she did until I asked them.

It was only forty-five minutes before the Ice Maiden said, "Mr. McNulty will see you now, Miss Carruthers."

At that, the door to the inner office opened, and out bounced Brad, a toothy smile in place. He shook my hand and pulled me into the office.

"How are you, Lee? Long time no see. Have you been waiting long?"

"Hi, Brad. Oh, not long. How are you?"

I looked around. The office had only one door, so unless he did Spider-Man on the outside wall, his meeting was fictitious. Even more points for letting the visitor know the excuse was fabricated. He stood braced and bouncing up and down on the soles of his feet like the scrappy South Boston Irish kid he had been. He may have become the youngest Chief of Station in agency history, but he was still shorter than I was, always a sore point with him. His pinstriped Savile Row suit could not quite disguise the fact that he had grown portly from high living since I last saw him. He took his coat off, retaining his vest so he could fiddle with the Phi Beta Kappa key that dangled on a chain across it. He removed his large gold cuff links to turn the cuffs up one turn, office casual for a cozy talk with an old friend. How many Chiefs of Station wear bespoke suits to the office? It gave the message that he had arrived and was shooting higher. His thinning brown hair was combed over, which didn't hide his baldness any more than the suit hid his gut.

Postgraduate management courses taught government executives that a desk was a barrier to communication, so he ushered me to the settee across from his desk and took his place on the matching armchair beside me so that we could talk comfortably.

"Sidney said that you were coming in, but he didn't say why," he said.

"Alicia Harmon has gone missing from the Femme Aid office in Fez. Sidney sent me in to find her."

"We were notified. We looked around—hospitals, morgues, that sort of thing—and didn't find a trace of her." He passed his hand over the strings of hair to make sure they were still in place and laughed a good ole boy laugh. "She's gone off with a guy, Lee, count on it. Probably the first one who ever made her."

"You'd love that, wouldn't you, Brad? Every woman is June Cleaver to you, high heels, pearls, and a uterus."

"Don't tell me you've gone all feminist, Carruthers."

I declined to punch him in the mouth out of the goodness of my heart and said instead, "From her picture, she doesn't exactly look like a blonde bimbo."

"You don't know her?" he asked.

"Never met her," I replied. "Tell me about her."

"Oh, she's good-looking enough," he admitted. "She looks like a pretty little kitty, but she hasn't got kittenish ways, you know what I mean? And she's got no sense of humor. Serious, deadly serious. Always nattering on about slavery."

Sounds like she gave him the brush-off, I thought.

"Got claws, has she?" I asked.

He coughed.

"Go on," I said.

"She's a crackpot about human trafficking," he said. "I saw her at a party once. That's all she could talk about: slavery, real cheery."

Same old Brad, I thought. "Slavery's not nice, Brad."

"Yeah, I know, but the world is full of bigger problems."

"That's because it only involves women, except for the little boys who are going to die the first time they're penetrated."

He flushed. "There is no need for that, Carruthers."

"That office in Fez exists because women and drugs come through town. The caravan trail goes through Fez. It always has. They just don't use camels anymore. Knowing what's moving on the caravan trail is essential. You may be stuck in the Cold War, Brad, but Africa is the coming theater of conflict, and almost nobody is paying attention."

"Well, we do have a slight problem in Afghanistan."

"And Afghanistan is going down the toilet. We might as well leave now and let the Taliban get on with it. Besides, it will leave us free to invade Iran."

He shifted his argument. "All those offices are a waste of Agency resources."

"Total expenditure for those offices around the world is less than the cost of one of the war games we're playing in the Sahara, where we're training the next generation of terrorists," I retorted.

"As usual, you don't know what you're talking about!"

"About Alicia Harmon, Brad."

"She was here a couple of weeks ago."

"She was? What for?"

"A briefing. A briefing on terrorism."

"Why?"

"She didn't say," he replied.

I stared. "And you didn't ask? Terrorism is way outside her remit. I'd better talk to the person who briefed her."

Something about that amused him. He punched the intercom. "Karin, dear, will you take *Ms.* Carruthers down to 127?"

He was laughing when Karin came to get me.

Chapter 3

WHEN I OPENED the door to room 127, I saw the reason for Brad's amusement. The man behind the desk facing the door was Bill Kendricks, the man I didn't marry in Beirut. He looked up from his computer monitor, and his face hardened.

"What are you doing here?" he demanded.

Same old Bill—short brown hair, chocolate eyes I used to like to fall into, long-sleeved white shirt and regimental striped tie, in Rabat's heat yet.

"Hi Bill. Good to see you, too. Nice day isn't it?"

"What do you want?"

"That's right, Bill, let's get right down in the gutter and brawl," I said.

"I never brawl," he retorted and turned his monitor off. That was the only way to go since he didn't have any papers on his desk to turn over. I looked around.

Medium-sized office, as befitted his rank, all buttoned down, as befitted his character. No rug, or picture of the Director. He did have a visitor's chair. He didn't offer it, but I took it anyway. I almost laughed. His desk was empty except for a ballpoint pen and a pencil can that looked like a kid had made it. The books were lined up on parade on the shelves. In Beirut I always threw my jacket over the back of my armchair and went to fix the drinks. He always picked it up with an annoyed look and put it on a shaped wooden hanger to store away in the closet. I'll bet his blue blazer with the Harvard crest is on a shaped wooden hanger behind the door, I thought.

"Sidney send you out to save the world again?" he asked snidely.

Sidney sending me out to save the world was one of the reasons we didn't get married. In his world men did the dangerous things, and women stayed home and had babies.

"I'm here looking for Alicia Harmon. She's gone missing," I answered placidly. He hadn't liked it when I refused to rise to his bait.

He looked startled. "She was just here."

"That's what Brad said. When?"

He checked his calendar. "August 19th."

"For a briefing on terrorism?" I asked.

"For a briefing on terrorism," he confirmed.

"Did she say why?"

"No."

"And you didn't ask her?"

"No."

"Striking behavior for an analyst," I said.

"I assumed it was something to do with her job," he said crossly.

"Well, it wasn't. Her job is human trafficking."

"The groups traffic in humans."

"Let me rephrase that," I said carefully. "Her job was to monitor the traffic from Mali through Fez on the way to the EU. Women, mostly, although there are some boys."

He flushed. Bill had always been uncomfortable with sex unless it was missionary position in the dark. Perhaps he'd been uncomfortable with sex, period?

He rolled a pencil along his desk.

"She should have no connection with terrorists," I continued. "She's an analyst, not an agent. Her job is to observe and report."

"Is your job to observe and report?" he asked roughly.

"Let's not go there, Bill." I got up and walked to the window. "My job is to do what Sidney tells me to do."

My forays into the field were another one of the reasons we didn't marry. I'm tired of it now, but in those days I loved it, and I was good at it. The Beqaa Valley was dangerous right then, and he didn't like me going in harm's way.

"And this time he has told me to go to Fez and find Alicia Harmon." I leaned against the windowsill, hands in my pockets, ankles crossed. "Alicia Harmon seems to have developed some kind of an interest in terrorism. She told Sidney terrorism finance, but she told you terrorism?" I asked.

He nodded. "Just terrorism. She asked about Al Qaeda."

"And you told her about the Soviet–Afghani war." It was a statement not a question. Bill liked to reinvent the wheel.

"She said she knew about that. She wanted to know about recent events."

"What did you tell her?"

"About Zawahiri taking over after the death of Bin Laden. Drones searching them out in Pakistan."

"Al Qaeda Central doomed, thanks to Superpower."

He balled his fists and leaned toward my face. It was good to know I could still yank his chain after all these years.

"William?"

We turned to see a slight blonde woman standing in the doorway, a steely look in her baby blues. Bill blushed and stepped back. Blushed? Bill? I couldn't think what he had to be embarrassed about except possibly a desire to throttle me.

He ran his hand through his short hair.

"Uh, Claudia, this is Lee Carruthers. Lee, this is my wife, Claudia."

She came toward me, her hand out, a gracious smile on her face. "Lee Carruthers," she said sweetly, "I've heard so much about you."

"Nothing good, I hope," I replied.

I levered myself up from the windowsill and crossed to shake her hand. I had to go around Bill. He seemed rooted in place. Her gaze ripped me up and down. Cold baby blues. She transferred the look to Bill, and I saw him flinch. She came and sat in the visitor's chair, her hands clasped in her lap, her ankles crossed, and smiled. Really? Does Miss Porter's teach that kind of deportment anymore? Somehow I couldn't see today's kids without a cell phone clasped in one hand.

Bill rushed into speech. "I was just briefing Lee."

"I *am* sorry to interrupt." She stood. "I'll just run down the hall and talk to Karin."

I thought he was going to wring his hands. This was going to cost him when he got home. I decided that while it was fun for me to torment Bill, watching his wife do it was another matter entirely.

"I've come from Paris to find a colleague who is missing, Mrs. Kendricks. Bill briefed her just before she disappeared. I was asking him what he told her." I looked at Bill. "There's nothing secret about what you have to tell me, Bill. Go ahead."

She sat back down, and I retreated to the window, which left him standing in the middle of the room like something that had been left when the tide went out.

"Go on. You told her about Al Qaeda Central. Did you tell her about Al Qaeda in the Islamic Maghreb? AIQM?"

"I started to," he replied, "but she told me she knew about them."

"It would be hard to miss an outfit that carved out a

fief in northern Mali and held an Algerian gas plant hostage," I said.

He glared and went on. "There's a new group—the Pure Warriors of Islam."

"Never heard of them," I said.

"They emerged after the French threw AQIM out of Timbuktu. Some of the jihadists jumped ship and formed this new group, the Pure Warriors of Islam. They say that AQIM is nothing but a criminal cartel."

"Pretty much," I agreed. "Drugs, money, women, cigarettes, you name it, they'll move it. Belmansur is the worst," I said.

"They threw him out. They think he's a loose cannon."

"That was before the Algerian gas plant operation. He may be a loose cannon, but he can still plan a first-rate operation. Ask yourself, Bill, if they really threw him out or if he's just running a game for them in southern Libya. Even if he is skimming, he's valuable to them."

"He's skimming?" Bill asked. "It's a miracle he's alive then. Abu Zeid is emir down there. He likes to behead people."

"I wondered where he'd got to. Zeid probably doesn't know. I only know because I keep finding his bank accounts in Geneva."

He grinned. "Confiscating his retirement fund?"

"Every franc I can find." I grinned back. For a moment I remembered. It didn't last long. He looked at his wife, and the smile left his face.

"These pure ones. I love pure people who blow up women and children. Saints, every one of them. Are they pure because they don't engage in criminal activity or because they don't keep any of the proceeds for themselves?" I asked.

"The latter," he said. "They seem to restrict their activities to Morocco. The first operation we can trace to them is the theft of a gendarme payroll near Rissani. They thought it was a simple robbery, although the guys took the weapons. Then somebody hit the Midelt mine payroll, again taking the weapons."

"Weapons have a street value, Bill," I reminded him.

"I know that," he snapped, "but they also took the driver and guard, too."

"So they thought it was AQIM raising funds."

"Right, until they burst upon the scene in a spectacular way. They posted a manifesto on the gates of all the royal palaces."

"What! All ten?"

He nodded. "Yes, although I think it's eleven now."

"Cheeky of them."

"And they used an industrial glue. It was a hell of a lot of work removing it from those bronze doors at the palace in Fez."

I giggled.

His voice rose. "It's not funny!"

I always did have an inappropriate sense of humor. "What did the manifesto say?"

"The usual. Called for the overthrow of the 'apostate' government of Morocco, the establishment of Sharia law, the reestablishment of the Caliphate . . ."

"And regaining Islam's rightful place in the world, which is to say, dominating it. Not very original. Do you have a copy?"

He tapped on his computer keyboard.

"Come and see."

I leaned over his shoulder to look at the monitor, and Beirut came unbidden to my mind. Lime aftershave, hair lotion, and some indefinable scent, not unpleasant, that I always associated with him. Claudia cleared her throat, and he jumped, pushing his chair back into me and overturning his pencil can. He stooped to pick up the pencils, and I looked at his wife. She looked like the cat that ate the canary. I hoped she choked on it. I never did like watching somebody pull the wings off butterflies. He bumped his head on the desk coming up.

"Good calligraphy," I commented and stepped back.

"Looks like the Al-Azhar style, doesn't it? Somebody there is a scholar. They specialize in ambushes. They've hit army and gendarme convoys and raised their flag over border control posts. They haven't killed many people, maybe twenty-five, but they've taken ten people—tourists, foreign workers, and local government officials—and held them for ransom."

"It was paid?" I asked.

"Oh, yes, after they circulated a video of a village head being beheaded."

"Viral on YouTube, I'll bet. So they're not nicer than AQIM. Purer maybe, but not nicer."

He nodded. "That's about the size of it, and they're just getting started."

"And have to prove themselves to the big boys. How often do they strike?"

"The turnaround time isn't very fast, but they are original. They rarely do the same thing twice."

"How long has this been going on?" I asked.

"A little over a year." He tapped into his computer. "The first we can trace to them was a year ago in August."

"All in Morocco, you say."

"Except for one attack at the Algerian Space Program Headquarters in Hamaguir."

"Where's their headquarters?" I asked.

"We don't know whether it's in the desert in Morocco or over the border in Algeria."

"Needle in a haystack. Who are they? I mean, besides AQIM defectors."

"Some of them are veterans of the Iraq and Afghanistan wars and have plenty of experience. We think those are the guys running the desert training camps."

"Desert training camps? How do you hide a training camp in the desert?"

"They're mobile. They drive a couple of trucks to a remote oasis, set up shop for indoctrination and training, stay a couple of days, and then move on before any of the governments in the neighborhood get a fix on them."

He paused to take a breath.

"Bill, this is more serious than I thought. Morocco's the anchor."

"Yes," he replied.

Bill's wife looked at me with a curious expression on her face. "But it's only the desert," she said. "Nobody would want that."

"It's a whole lot of territory, Mrs. Kendricks."

"Oh, do call me Claudia," she said.

As if. Bill's wife sounded either thick as a plank or deficient in geography. Perhaps he found it restful.

"Morocco and the rest of the Maghreb in the north, Sahel in the south. If they succeed, Mrs. Kendricks, there will be Sharia law from the Atlantic and the Mediterranean to the Niger River," I replied. "Why should they stop there?"

Bill looked at me in embarrassment.

"But she doesn't go in harm's way," I reminded him.

He gave me a nasty look.

"I really thought the Palace had a grip on things," I said.

"The Arab Spring changed everything. When the demonstrations started, the King moved immediately to head them off."

"Yeah. I read. New constitution he promulgated—free elections, moderate Islamic party wins the new election, their leader, Abdelilah Benkirane now prime minister." I looked closely at him. "But?"

His shoulders slumped. "Nothing has changed, Lee. Nothing at all." He sounded tired. People waiting for change in the Arab world get very tired.

"So long as the King holds defense and foreign policy in his own hands, there will be no real reform. The Palace can't keep the lid on forever, though, and when it blows, it will be nasty. You told all this to Alicia Harmon?"

He nodded.

"She said, 'I thought it was something like that,' thanked me and left. She seems to be a very calm woman."

"It looks like it," I said.

"You don't know her?" he asked.

"Never met her. Bill, what's going to happen?" I asked.

"What do you mean, what's going to happen next?" he snapped. "I'm not a psychic."

"No, but you're an analyst. Analyze. I get the feeling—"

"I don't deal in feelings. I deal in facts."

I could see that he was cranking up to have the same old fight, so I changed the subject.

"Bill, I used to know a guy named Ouzzat in the gendarmerie. He seemed to get along with Western women better than most, I thought."

"Hakim?"

"Yeah. Have you got his number?"

He scrolled through his contact list and gave it to me.

I got up, ready to leave. This short time with Bill had made me want to run screaming. How could we ever have been lovers?

"Where are you going?"

I looked out the window. It was getting dark. Perhaps the worst of the rush hour was over.

"Bar hopping," I replied.

He snorted. "You are insufferable!" Perhaps he was remembering why we didn't get married, too.

"Always was."

I shook hands with his wife. "Nice to meet you, Mrs. Kendricks."

She responded in proper fashion. Very proper.

"Oh, Lee."

I turned at the door.

"Alicia Harmon said one more thing. She said she thought there was something new about the terrorism that was spreading inside Morocco."

Chapter 4

BEFORE HOPPING ANY bars, I called Hakim and made an appointment to meet in the Hamilton Bar at the Hilton at nine that evening. It was a place where a man and a woman could be seen drinking together without causing the *ulema* to issue a fatwa.

The first bar I intended to hop was a sleazy café in Salé, the grimy port across the river from Rabat. I needed a gun before I went there, so I left the new part of town that looked like any provincial town in France and went into the old quarter where I knew a grizzled pirate who would sell me a gun for a price. The Rabat medina was smaller than those in most Moroccan cities because the town wasn't a very big place before the French made it the capital of French Morocco, but it resembled all the others. It was walled, with narrow alleys through which you rode a donkey, unless you wanted to walk. The same plastered mud brick houses with large wooden doors and, like every other Muslim house, no windows facing the alleys. In such crowded conditions, people wanted privacy, and, given the history of Morocco, they wanted security, too. They never had to leave the old quarter unless they wanted to, for the souks sold everything a body could need and a great many things they didn't.

As befitted an illegal arms merchant, Achmed's prices were extortionate, but the neighborhood called him a pirate because he wore a patch over his useless left eye. Considering the scar that ran from his eye to his chin, he probably lost it in a knife fight. He lived in a shack down a dirty lane near the walls in a place where I needed a gun to go just to buy one. I checked the knife in my boot before I entered the hovel. Achmed was sitting cross-legged in his usual place on a ragged prayer rug wearing his usual dirty and ragged *djellaba*. A bright new turban was perched on his head. A nice contrast to his face, because he hadn't shaved in a while and probably hadn't bathed recently, either. The whole room smelled of sour old man. Not all Muslims are clean. His eye brightened when he saw me.

"Lalla Lee! I have not seen you in years!"

"No, you haven't, and I'm not paying extra for you to call me Lady Lee." I sat down near him on the small rug, careful to put my back toward the wall. "I need a Glock 26, a spare mag, and a box of hollow points."

He rubbed his hands and quoted me a price that would have bought a Glock factory. How he loved to dicker, that old man! I countered with a price about half what I thought an illegal Glock should cost, and after a few more rounds, we settled on a price only a little higher than my estimate. He yelled into the back of the room, and I took my knife out of my boot and held it conspicuously. He tutted and held his hands wide open, just an honest merchant, and why did I think otherwise? His lout of a son brought a box out, and gave it to me after his father pointed to me. I removed the gun from the box, and keeping an eye on both of them, stripped it and reassembled it. Fortunately, I could do it mostly by feel. The first time I bought anything from Achmed, the "new" gun had several parts missing.

I was young then. I had to go back and threaten to slit his throat to get a gun that worked.

I loaded the magazine and clicked it into the grip, racked a round into the chamber, and paid the old man. Then I had to get out. I backed toward the door, the gun down by my side. When I cleared the door, I spun around just as the lout came out after me.

"Tsk, tsk. Not good customer relations at all." I gestured him back into the room and ran to the next cross alley. I wove my way through the alleys until I knew I was clear. Visiting Achmed was always a delight. Visiting the café in Salè was even more fun.

Salè wasn't much of a port these days, but in the eighteenth and nineteenth centuries, it was the home of the "Salley Rovers," as the English called them, the most feared pirates on the North African coast. The Sultan took a cut of the swag to protect them, all the while issuing pious denunciations of their depredations. They had a long run of preying on the ships of all nations, until the British fleet destroyed them in their lair. After that, Salè became a sleepy backwater.

I intended to get in and out of the café before the real hard cases turned up. In my day it had been owned by Hassan. His manners and morals left something to be desired, which made him an easy purchase. I hoped he was still there.

Port areas the world over are not the nicest sections of town, and Salé was no exception. The café I was looking for was insalubrious in the extreme after the sun went down, and the sun was setting when I found a parking place. As I walked the short block to the cinderblock building, young men strolled along the cracked sidewalk behind me making kissing sounds. They began closing in. How tedious of them, I thought and drew the Glock from my hip, holding it down beside my leg. I heard a short intake of breath behind me, and the kissing sounds stopped. I walked at a steady pace, neither slow nor fast, until I went in to Hassan's. All talk stopped as I took a seat at a table near the door, sitting with my back to the wall. It was easy to see why it was traditional. It allowed me to keep an eye on the customers. Hassan, looking more used than I remembered, hustled up wiping his hands on a dirty towel.

"Oh, Madame, this is really no place for a lady."

I put the pistol on the table. "Who says I'm a lady?"

The silence was thunderous.

Hassan got a hit on his facial recognition system.

"Lalla Lee," he said in a nervous voice.

"Calling me Lady isn't going to get you anywhere," I said.

It did give the customers the idea that he knew me. A subdued mutter went from man to man. I moved the pistol a little and ordered an espresso in a soft voice. Hassan scurried away to make it. I wanted to finish my business and leave before somebody started tearing up either me or the café because a whore of a Western woman had invaded their sacred turf. I looked around the room. Ten men, some of them in jeans and some of them in traditional dress, and all of them with hard closed faces. It wouldn't take much to ignite them.

"Madame." He bowed as he served me.

I put the coffee to one side. "Will you join me?"

Hassan hadn't worn well in the decade since I had last seen him. He was a squat man of indeterminate age, swarthy with a pock-marked complexion and bags under his eyes from drinking *raki* for breakfast. He went away and returned with an unlabeled bottle of clear liquid and a pair of small glasses. He poured a healthy slug into each and sat down across from me. I don't drink raki if I can help it, but if it would lubricate his tonsils, I was willing to make an exception. I accepted a glass and took a wary sip. I had forgotten that he made the stuff out back. It tasted like gasoline with licorice added.

"It's been a while, Hassan," I said.

"As you say," he replied.

Assuming that he was still part of the network, I nudged a picture of Alicia across the table toward him.

"My friend was here recently looking for information."

He looked blankly at me. I had some dirhams ready in my pocket. With Hassan it was pay as you go. I put one on the table. He looked even blanker, if possible. I put down another.

"These have brothers," I said and sipped my coffee. It was good, but it couldn't remove the taste of raw raki from my mouth. "But only for information."

A chair scraped on the cement floor. I looked up. One of the blue jeaned men looked like part in the discussion. I moved the pistol gently forward, and he sat back down. I returned my gaze to Hassan.

"She was here," he agreed guardedly.

"And what did she want?"

"Don't you know?" He smirked, and I remembered how much I disliked him.

"I do. I want to hear it from you." I wrinkled the remaining dirhams in my hand. The sound seemed to move him.

"She wanted to know if there was trouble," he said unhappily.

"Trouble?"

"In the cribs."

I'm not sure that I hid my surprise entirely. How did trouble in the brothels relate to terrorism?

"And is there?" I asked.

"There was across the river."

"But not here? How is that?"

He shrugged. "Soldiers have more money than sailors."

"And Salè isn't much of a port these days, is it? What form does this trouble take?" I held his eyes.

"Heavies busting up the places." He shifted in his chair, but he didn't look away.

"You told her this?"

27

"Yes."

"Anything else?"

He reached for the money, which he had been unwise enough to leave on the table. I pulled it away.

"Hey!"

"Anything else?"

"Some bodies," he mumbled.

"I can't quite hear you," I said, my hand still on the money.

"Some bodies," he said a bit more loudly, looking over his shoulder at the listening men.

"Some dead bodies?"

"Yeah."

"Details?"

The words stuck in his throat, but he finally pushed them out in a rush.

"They were in the Chellah with their throats slit."

The Chellah was a cemetery laid out amid the ruins of Roman Rabat and surrounded by a high wall. The mausoleum of King Mohammed V was inside, guarded day and night by mounted troops of the Royal Guard. How did you arrange to dump corpses there?

"A bit public," I said.

"They'd be found quicker, wouldn't they?"

I acknowledged his point. Dumping your victims in a well-guarded place also made a point. I added some money to the pile on the table and stood. Abdullah in Rabat would know more and charge less.

The chair scraped against the cement again. Mr. Blue Jeans certainly was a determined chap. I raised the pistol and fired a shot between his feet. He jumped. I raised the pistol a bit and smiled. He sat back down. For a marvel, when I got to it, the car was in one piece and so was I.

Terrorism and now brothel violence. What had Alicia Harmon gotten herself into?

Chapter 5

I DROVE BACK across the river to Rabat and let the attendant at the Hilton park my car. It was just on nine when I walked into the Hamilton Bar. A cool breeze drifted into the open room from tinkling fountains in the garden. My quarry was in the shadows at the far end. I walked in his direction casually. He saw me, and, when he nodded, I moved to the table and sat down. We examined each other in silence. Slumped over an empty glass and pulling hard on an unfiltered Gauloise, he looked more than ever like a weary bloodhound. His white coat was rumpled and none too clean. It sagged on him, as if it had been made for a much larger man. I've never been exactly certain how I felt about Hakim. If being afraid had been in my job description, I would have been a little afraid of him. As it was, I treated him gingerly, like an unexploded bomb, although I think we'd almost been friends, off and on, while I was in Fez. When the waiter came, I ordered peach iced tea and he ordered another vodka.

"You've held up better than I have," he said.

"Not much."

Our drinks arrived, and he swallowed a third of his in one gulp. I looked at him seriously. These days he was drinking more than he had when I saw him last. At least he was drinking faster. Was the job getting to him? It got us all in the end.

"I gather this is not a social call," he said.

Had we really been friends once? Maybe. I could never tell for certain.

"No. I need some information."

"When did you not?"

I ignored that. "Have you met my colleague in Fez?"

"Alicia Harmon?"

I nodded.

"Haven't had the pleasure. Why?"

"She's disappeared, been gone for about two weeks, as near as I can tell."

"And?"

"I don't think she's the sort to go AWOL."

"Everybody is the sort to go AWOL if the attraction or the pressure is strong enough."

I knew he was right. "Hakim, she hasn't gone to Agadir for a dirty weekend and stayed two weeks. I don't know her, but that is not the act of a professional."

"I understand she's very emotionally involved in her work," he suggested.

"She is," I agreed.

"What do you want from me?" he asked.

"I'm not really sure. I thought maybe if I laid the bits out, they might make some sense to you or at least make more sense to me. She's recently developed an interest in terrorism and went to the embassy for a briefing. What's new?"

"The Chemist Saad al Houssaini. We picked him up a while ago."

"Who did?" I've never known what outfit Hakim belonged to. Gendarmerie Intelligence was my guess.

He ignored the question. "He's the bomb maker for the MICG, the Moroccan Islamic Combat Group. Where have you been recently?" he asked sarcastically.

"Baghdad," I said.

He grunted in sympathy.

"When?" I asked.

"March."

I shook my head. "He probably didn't tell her about that. She was interested in current events. In her last report, she said that money was going somewhere funny."

"Did she say where or how she knew?"

"No," I replied in frustration. "Hakim, how serious is this? When Bill briefed me, I got the idea that things are getting bad."

"They are, and they'll get worse. Until recently we've been able to keep the lid on it, break up cells before they went operational, but the cells are getting larger and better funded."

"Al Qaeda?"

"In the Islamic Maghreb, yes. We broke up a recruiting cell the other day."

"How did you get onto them?"

"Anonymous phone call."

"Oh, come on," I protested.

"Absolutely. It's the way we find out about most cells. Somebody with a grudge. Somebody who's trying to keep his kid from going on jihad. You know the drill," he said.

I did. More cases were solved using anonymous information than with brilliant detective work, no matter what the TV programs say.

"Before they changed their name, they had about a hundred men and were on the run from the Algerian security services. Now they're all over the place," I said. "What happened?"

"Kidnapping for ransom has made them rich, and that wealth has made them able to recruit hundreds of men. All they needed was some media hype. Al Qaeda gets big play on CNN and Al Jazeera. That's why they changed their name to Al Qaeda in the Islamic Maghreb, to piggyback on their publicity."

"Every time I walked down the street in Baghdad, I saw the TV sets tuned to Al Jazeera," I said.

"These kids have a little education, but they're not readers. A TV picture is worth—how many? A thousand?—a thousand words. A guy has got to see something to give him the idea of joining up."

"I would think hearing the Friday sermons in the mosques would be enough."

"Not in Morocco. The Palace makes sure of that. Remember, the King appoints the imams here. An imam steps out of line, he's fired."

"The Maghreb guys have been very active in the Sahel, in Mali particularly. Any chance it will spread to Morocco?" I asked.

"It will eventually, but the French in Mali slowed it down some," he replied. "Whether the French push it north from Mali or the Algerians push it west from the Kabyle, it will get here. The army has reinforced the border, but it's a long border, and it is disputed, one of the things that the French didn't settle when they left. There is a component in the Algerian Sahara just south of the Moroccan border."

"This new lot, the Pure Warriors? What about them?"

"They're trouble. They get a lot of attention because they're cute."

"Surely the Palace can keep that kind of news shut down?"

"Haven't you heard of instant communication? Somebody can have a video of an operation on YouTube before the Palace gets the report."

"Unh. To change the subject, do you know anything about trouble in the brothels here?"

"Only that there's been trouble. Not my turf."

We looked at each other.

"Is Driss still in Fez?" I asked.

"Yes."

Driss Bouchta was to Fez as Hakim was to Rabat.

"I need him."

He wrote a phone number on a napkin and shoved it across the table. He waved at the waiter and pulled out his wallet.

"I'll get it."

He shook his head. "Do you want the whole town to hear I let a woman buy me drinks?"

"Oh, God, not you too." I frowned.

He put the bills down on the check.

"Hakim, I don't know who has this Harmon woman, if anybody does."

"Or if she's still alive."

"Or if she's still alive," I agreed. "If you hear anything—"

He looked me in the eye in a most unIslamic way.

"Remember, anything you find out is mine."

I nodded.

"Before or at least at the same time as Langley," he said.

Chapter 6

ANOTHER REASON IT was fairly easy to be with Hakim
was that I didn't have to hide anything from him. Or from
Driss in Fez. What had Alicia Harmon gotten herself into?

I looked at my watch. Almost ten. I drove to
Abdullah's bar in the quarter behind the palace parade
ground where the Royal Guard liked to swagger and called
him on my cell.

"Lalla Lee! It has been a long time. Are you well?"

"Hello, Abdullah. I'm well and I hope you are. I need
to talk. Now. I'm outside. Do you want to come out and
sit in my car?"

"No. No. Come to the back door. You see the alley
beside the building? Drive down it and turn to the right.
You will see my car. Park and knock."

He must have been waiting for me, because the door
opened before I could knock. He hugged me.

"Lalla Lee, come in, come in. Peace be to you."

Abdullah's place was a pipe bar, a place to smoke
various substances in a water pipe, and the smell of
tobacco and kif, the premium marijuana grown in
Morocco, drifted through the bead curtain and down the
corridor. On a good night, you could get a contact high

just from breathing. There was a rumor that there was a back room where alcohol was served, but I'd never seen it.

He led me into a combination office and sitting room, and we sat on the rug-covered bench that ran around three of the walls.

"You're looking well," I told him.

The usual inquiries about his multitude of dependents and relations followed. His father had died since last we met, he had divorced one wife and was separated from her replacement. His oldest daughter had given him three grandsons. It had always astonished me how many individuals in that part of the world were dependent on one man's income.

A boy brought a tray with coffee, glasses of water, and a plate of little salted things and put it on the brass tray in front of us. My family news took less than half a cup of coffee, and Turkish coffee cups are small. He thought I was being modest, but I had only myself and my grandmother to account for, so it didn't take long.

"Abdullah, do you know Alicia Harmon?"

"Of course. A nice lady. She was here asking. She was worried about something," he said. "She said she would return, but she has not come back to ask again. And now you come, asking."

"She's missing, Abdullah," I said. "She has been gone for at least two weeks, and nobody knows where she is. I've been sent to find her."

That rocked him. "And so you follow her trail?"

"It is so," I replied. "What did she ask?"

"You know the job she did?" he asked.

"I do, I once did it, if you remember."

"I do. So she asked questions about things a lady like her should not know."

"It's OK for a lady like me to know about these things?"

He looked uncomfortable. "There was violence in the brothels of Fez," he said.

Who better to know what was going on in the brothels than a man who served the brutal soldiery?

"She asked if there was any here."

"And was there?"

"There was a little trouble here. There was more trouble in Fez."

"When was the trouble here?"

After a little thought, he said, "In early July."

"And Fez?"

"Late in the month."

"What kind of trouble?" I asked.

"Oh, brawls, violence, thugs breaking up the furniture, assaulting the customers and the women," he said. "It ended when the Big Man of Rabat and his bodyguard were found in the Chellah with their throats cut."

That agreed with what Hassan had told me.

"How did anybody get past the mausoleum Guards with two corpses?"

"I've been thinking about that. The only thing I can work out is a false funeral." He went to make some more coffee.

At first it seemed ridiculous, but after thinking for a while, I realized that it was quite feasible. All that would be required was a procession carrying the two corpses in shrouds. The Guards would pass them without asking any questions. If they carried the bodies far enough away from the mausoleum, they could unwind them and dump them and go on their way mourning.

When he returned, I said, "A nasty bit of work, requiring staff that wouldn't talk."

"Oh, they have that kind of staff."

"Alicia Harmon was concerned about something else as well?" I asked.

"Yes. She was asking about terrorism. Brothels I know. Terrorism I do not. She asked about Hassan in Salé, and I told her not to bother with him. He would not tell the truth though she paid him a King's ransom. He has not the truth in him," he declared.

"I know. I just saw him. I had forgotten what he was like. She did go to see him, however. He told her what you have just told me."

"Lalla Lee, do you think these questions are the reason she is gone?"

"I do."

"Then she is not alive," he concluded, his voice mournful.

I silently agreed with him.

"Why does a nice lady do such work?"

"Somebody has to do it, Abdullah." He didn't ask why I did it. I stood up to go. "Will you see what you can find out?" I said. "Carefully."

"You don't need to tell me that," he replied. "I will think."

"Do not ask questions," I cautioned him again.

"I will ask no questions, but if there is anything to hear, I will hear it."

I stood. "Call me," I said, giving him my cell number. "From a pay phone."

"It's that way, is it?"

"It's that way."

Chapter 7

IT WAS PAST one and a little over seventy-five miles to Fez. Abdullah's coffee had put some starch in me, but I knew I would be wasted before I got to Fez.

I don't like to drive at night in Morocco. The roads are full of *kif* heads, guys driving without lights under the impression that they were saving their batteries, and men in Mercedes the size of a small German state who have a right to drive in the middle of the road. I thought perhaps the superhighway would be better, but I soon found that it only gave them more scope. For a while, the challenge of driving among the mad made it impossible to think of anything else, but they thinned out a little after we left the Rabat suburbs, and I had time to think about the case.

Alicia Harmon had reported something about terrorist financing. She had been in Rabat asking about terrorism. Why was she interested in terrorism? Something she stumbled across. According to Hassan and Abdullah, they had told her something about violence in the local brothels. Brothels were something they would know about. Terrorism was not.

She had asked about brothels. Was there some connection between the brothel violence and terrorism?

What did I know about the girl? Woman. Facts: She was missing. OK. She had an obsessive hatred of slavery. She had recently (when?) acquired two black women who were sitting by the side of the road. Except for her message to Sidney, that was the sum total of my direct knowledge. I knew nothing about the woman or what she might be expected to do. I decided I needed to find out more about Alicia Harmon when I got to Fez.

Four flights of badly lit stairs. I wished Ibrahim could bring himself to buy brighter light bulbs. I could barely make out the lock. I managed to insert the key and open the door. I heard a click behind me, but when I turned to look there was no one there.

I had been tired and cross, but now I was tired and angry. It was the same flat I had lived in when I opened the Fez office. I had come prepared to pick the lock, but I had also brought my old key just in case, and it actually opened the door. Apparently no subsequent occupant had possessed enough sense to change the lock. It was a wonder that the lot of them hadn't gone missing. A bunch of people were going to have to take security training again.

I flipped on the light and dropped my things, stuffing the mail I had taken from the mailbox in the lobby in my pocket and looked around. Nothing disturbed in the living room. Alicia Harmon had gone native. Bright Moroccan fabrics, two bronze trays on turned wooden legs for a coffee table, a good Berber rug. Framed pictures of Moroccan women and Arabic calligraphy on the walls. Small dining table and two chairs. A small, basic kitchen. A microwave, a two-burner butane cooker, a few pots and cooking implements, four of everything of colorful native stoneware. The only thing in the refrigerator was a bottle of champagne. Nothing but a pair of pantyhose in the freezer.

The small bathroom had one of those delightful triangular French showers where you could not turn around without hitting the handle with your bum and getting scalded, a cupboard with a drawer and shelves below for necessities like toilet paper, a toilet. A medicine cabinet with aspirin and mouthwash. A more innocent medicine cabinet I have never searched. The cupboard drawer held two packets of birth control pills dispensed by a Paris doctor six weeks ago. If I have come all the way from Paris to find a woman who is still on a dirty weekend in Agadir, I am going to be seriously pissed, I thought.

In the bedroom, I looked longingly at the bed. I would have given a month's pay to get into that bed. Baghdad to Paris to Rabat to Fez in twenty-four hours was a bit much, even for me. I had stopped trying to calculate the last time I had been to bed.

The bedroom was undisturbed as well. Another colorful piece of fabric served as a bedspread. Multiple pillows were propped against the wall. The blue Princess phone was surely an antique by now. Some books on a two-shelf bookcase, *Culture Shock Morocco*, and two dictionaries, English-Moroccan Arabic, and a French-Arabic one. A couple of histories of Morocco, Marvine Howe's *Morocco: the Islamist Awakening and Other Challenges,* Peter Mansfield's old but still good *The Arabs,* Paul Bowles's novels, and a Lonely Planet *Guide to Morocco.* I riffled through the guide book and found some dog-eared pages. I threw that on the bed. God, but I wanted to follow it.

No suitcase anywhere. Should there be? If her suitcase was gone, that argued that she left willingly, didn't it? So why hadn't she returned? The wardrobe's contents were revealing: three pairs of jeans, skirts and jackets in navy and beige, flat heeled shoes ditto, and a pair of turquoise spiked heels that matched a spaghetti-strapped beaded thing that was either a very long blouse or a dress with a very short skirt. Three much more restrained dresses. No Western woman wore dresses in Morocco much. Islam preferred its women wrapped in impenetrable black. The beaded thing was for a disco. Combined with the birth control pills, that meant a guy. Find the disco, find the guy?

A blue blazer with a Wellesley crest on the pocket. I wondered if she ever wore it. I had stopped bragging about being a Yalie years ago. I picked it up and was going through the pockets when a quiet knock on the door made me drop it. A visitor after three a.m.? I turned off the light and looked through the peephole. I could just distinguish the distorted figure of a man. He tapped on the door again and waited. After a long moment, he disappeared. I leaned against the door and breathed deeply. Who was he? Was he expecting Alicia Harmon to answer the door at three in the morning?

After I got my heartbeat under control, I continued the search. The chest had two drawers. The first drawer held T-shirts in navy, beige, and white. The bottom drawer had white cotton underwear, five pairs of knee-high stockings and a pair of lace teddies in black and fuchsia with the price tags still on them.

A pair of lace teddies in black and fuchsia?

Champagne and racy underwear weren't much to find in a single woman's flat these days. Did a guy explain the apparent split personality of her wardrobe? A guy would explain the birth control pills. But the teddies still had their price tags, and the birth control pills. Did she have an open pack with her?

I did wonder how she snuck a guy past Ibrahim.

The reading material could wait until tomorrow. Well, maybe not.

The bank statement was not very enlightening. Paycheck in, checks mostly made out to cash out. Morocco was still very much a cash economy. I noted a couple of checks made out to local shops and marked them to run down if I had to. The credit card bill wasn't much better. She had spent the night in Rabat.

I'm missing something, I thought, and looked around the small room. Ah, the table by the bed. The drawer held her bank statements for the last six months and a stack of papers held together with a paper clip. I opened them out on the bed. A dozen notes. Individual letters cut from a magazine were pasted on cheap paper in a rough line.

STOP ASKING QUESTIONS OR YOUR DEAD!

I sat back on my heels. Alicia had collected a dozen death threats. Threats with the same misspelled word to make it look like the sender was only semi-literate? Had she reported that to Sidney? And, if so, why hadn't he told me? Was she dead? With no contact in ten days it seemed very likely.

Damn Sidney! I thought angrily. He should have sent somebody as soon as he found out she was missing! Save your breath to cool your porridge, I thought. Sidney Worthington is a law unto himself.

What had she discovered? Since Sidney didn't know or wouldn't tell me, maybe she had recorded it in her computer.

The phone on the stand rang, and I jumped. Alicia Harmon certainly got a lot of action after midnight. With my heart pounding, I picked up.

"Hello?"

I heard nothing but breathing for maybe thirty seconds, and then the connection was broken.

Welcome to Fez, I thought. We know you're here.

Death threats and threatening phone calls. Alicia Harmon had gotten herself into something heavy.

Chapter 8

MY TRAVEL ALARM didn't have a snooze button. That's the reason I bought it. When the alarm went off at eight, I thought briefly of throwing it against the wall as I always did but changed my mind as I always did and shuffled groggily into the kitchen. Where was Alicia Harmon? Why didn't Alicia Harmon have any coffee? In a former French colony, Nescafé was the equivalent of brown dust. I drank some of the coffee, to dignify it, and went into the bathroom to take a cold shower. That did more to wake me up than the Nescafé had done.

When I stepped out of the flat in search of breakfast, I came face to with a tall man whose untidy hair was bleached by the sun. Little Benjamin Franklin glasses made him look like an earnest dandelion gone to seed. He looked at me out of mild blue eyes, a puzzled look on his face, his hands in the pockets of tan linen slacks with a crease sharp enough to cut you. The tailored shirt covered quite respectable shoulders.

He stepped back and raised an eyebrow.

"Where's Alicia?" he asked.

"Just what I want to know," I replied. "Where *is* Alicia?"

He looked to make sure the door to his flat had caught and turned back. He had an attractive smile. In fact, all of him was attractive, particularly the dimple in his right cheek.

"Let's start over again. I'm Sam Glover." The blue eyes behind round lenses switched from bland to sharp and back again. "Who are you?" His winsome smile didn't reach those blue eyes.

"Ms. Harmon seems to have gone missing."

"Missing?"

"Missing. Nobody has seen her in almost two weeks. You know her, I gather. When was the last time you saw her?" I asked.

"It's probably been that long or longer since I saw her. We meet in the hall or at the mailboxes, you know, but I can't say I know her well. Who are you?" he repeated.

I started down the stairs. "I'm Lee Carruthers. I've been sent to find her. Have you any idea where she might have gone?"

He shook his head. "I can't. Perhaps Fatima knows?"

"I'm going to ask her."

We continued down the steps.

"Ibrahim must be losing his touch," I said. "When I lived in that flat, no men were allowed above the third floor. Now he's renting to a man just across the landing." I laughed as we went out the door.

"I have special privileges."

"Oh?"

"I work for the company that owns the building." He turned and flashed such an irresistible smile at me that the hairs stood up on my arms. "Would you like to have dinner with me tonight? We could talk about how your search is going. Maybe I do know something that would help."

Maybe he did at that. At least I could find out why the hair on my arms was standing up.

"All right, but it will have to be late. I've got a lot to do. Does 8:30 sound OK?" I asked.

"Sounds fine," he said.

He got in a white Land Rover and drove away.

Walking back from breakfast, I considered my fatigue. I had been wasted by the time I finished searching the flat. I'd been living on NoDoz for about thirty-six hours. If I took another my head would explode. I took another. If I had been sharper I might not have missed a major clue to Alicia's disappearance.

Coming back from breakfast, I eyed the apartment building. It looked like the 1890s buildings along the Boulevard Haussmann in Paris, all mansard roof and dormer windows, one of the better French imports during the colonial period. Too bad Alicia didn't leave me a clue in the flat.

Ibrahim, the concierge, looked up from sweeping the walk.

"Lalla Lee." He nodded but made no effort to welcome me.

"Hello, Ibrahim," I replied and began the lengthy inquiry about his family unto the third generation.

He swept faster, in short angry strokes.

"Ibrahim?"

He looked up. "Lalla Lee, you should not stay in Lalla Alicia's apartment. It is not right."

"It's not Lalla Alicia's apartment, Ibrahim. It belongs to Femme Aid."

"It is Lalla Alicia's apartment," he said. He looked me square in the face, a thing he had never done in all the time I had known him.

"Her things are there. You have no right." He pressed his lips into a thin line.

Instead of lowering my eyes as a proper woman should, I looked right back at him. "Ibrahim, I'm going to stay in the apartment."

He shrugged. "You will do as you please," he muttered and resumed sweeping.

Ibrahim and his wife, Fatima, were my friends when I lived in that apartment, and I couldn't understand his attitude. I went down to the concierge's basement apartment and knocked. Fatima greeted me with a severe look on her face.

"What's the matter with Ibrahim?" I asked. And what's the matter with you, I wondered.

She crossed her arms. "You should have come to see us before you went upstairs."

"Fatima, it was three o'clock in the morning. You were in bed."

She pursed her lips. Had I contravened some obscure rule of Moroccan etiquette?

"Still, he regards your behavior as improper."

Ibrahim was a stickler for propriety. He had been dubious about renting to a single woman when I came, and he kept a sharp eye on me. Any approach of a man to my doorstep, however slight, would have gotten me thrown on my ear. That had bothered me only intermittently.

Fatima went into the kitchen and banged the kettle to boil water for tea.

"I haven't time for tea, Fatima," I called into the kitchen.

"You have time for tea," she asserted and continued banging.

I surrendered. Nobody resisted Fatima for long, and I was going to have to tiptoe and apologize for entering a flat owned by my employers. I couldn't wait to return to Paris, where they don't care whether you live or die. I live alone, and I like it that way.

"Where is Miss Harmon?" I asked her. "Femme Aid has sent me to find her."

"Lalla Alicia has never been away this long," Fatima said as she poured the tea. "She goes on trips to Rabat and Tangier and places like that. I don't know why."

I did. She visited her informants.

"But she always tells us, so that we won't worry," she continued.

"And this time?"

"No. She did not tell us. We worry. We never worried about you."

She sat back and crossed her arms.

Apparently I was expendable. "How long has she been gone?"

"I don't know. Weeks, I think. Maybe two?"

That wasn't much help.

"Who is the man in the flat across from Alicia's?" I asked and prevented her from pouring me more tea.

"Sidi Sam, Sam Glover."

I raised an eyebrow. "Ibrahim must be losing his grip."

She smiled a little. Maybe the melt was beginning? Fatima was a cheerful woman and being angry with me was a strain.

"He works for the company that owns the building."

"Somebody new owns the building? What happened to Mr. Daoud?"

"He sold it and moved to Israel to be with his son. A company called Worldwide Entertainment Systems owns it now."

"What does Mr. Glover do?" I asked.

"He coordinates."

"Coordinates what?"

She shook her head. "I don't know. He has no family with him, poor thing. I can't tell you any more about him."

I might as well get it over with. "Fatima, I'm sorry I didn't wake you."

She smiled and hugged me.

"But I'm going to stay in the flat."

She stopped smiling.

The phone rang as I opened the door to the flat. I hurried to the bedroom. There is a cosmic law that states that you'll pick up ten seconds after the caller hangs up. This time the law failed.

"Hello," I said.

"Lalla Alicia! Lalla Alicia! We have been attacked! Attacked!"

"Wait a minute! Slow down! Who is this?" I asked.

That stopped the caller. "Lalla Alicia?" the woman asked in a tentative voice.

"This is Lalla Lee. Who is this?"

The woman began to cry. "Lalla Lee! Lalla Lee! This is Miriam. We have been attacked!"

Miriam and her husband, Abu Musa, cared for the safe house in the medina. Why would anyone attack the house in the medina?

Chapter 9

I RAN OUT of the flat, forgetting the door, careened into Glover, and sprinted down the steps. I tore down the block to the car, climbed in, and scratched off, blowing the horn to clear my way. Somebody was attacking the house in the medina!

I ran a red light and passed a large truck on the right. Naturally there was no parking space close to the Bab Bou Jeloud gate. I was tempted to park in a No Parking zone, but while I was dithering, a white Rover pulled out of a place next to the gate, and I slid into it under the nose of a guy in a Mercedes. He waved his fist as I locked the car door and bolted through the gate.

You can only drive to the edge of the medina, the old quarter of Fez. Then you have to walk, unless you want to ride a donkey. I ran down the hill, cursing the house for being so far from the gate. I cursed the crowd I had to shoulder through yelling, "*Balek, balek*! Get out of the way!" The people stared at me as if I were mad. I cursed a donkey driver because he was carrying a wardrobe loaded sideways. I ducked under one side, which shifted the load, and the driver cursed me back. It seemed forever, but at last I was running down the curving alley to the house. All

49

appeared quiet. Nothing to see but bare walls and the occasional heavy door. The door to the Femme Aid house was standing open. I drew my pistol and stepped over a pool of what looked like blood, edging slowly, following the trail of blood along the zigzag tunnel that led to the courtyard. All was quiet there, too, except for the plashing of the fountain.

Abu Musa, the household's caretaker, was sitting on the base of the fountain, his elbows on his knees, his head in his hands while his wife Miriam pressed a cloth against the back of his head. A bloody scimitar lay at his feet. She rinsed the cloth in the fountain, and the wound began to bleed again.

"It looks like you repelled whatever borders there were," I said.

Musa picked up the sword again. When he recognized me, he put it back down. I looked at his wound.

"Do you think he'll need stitches?" I asked Miriam.

She shook her head and lifted the cloth. The blood was already clotting. Miriam and I helped Musa to a chair by the table. Miriam said, "Tea," and bustled away.

I amended the order. "Coffee with lots of sugar," I called after her. The sugar would help Musa's body throw off the shock. By the time I had determined that Musa saw only one finger no matter where I held it, Miriam was back with a coffeepot. After he drank a thimbleful of hot, sweet Turkish coffee, his eyes were clearer, although I could see that somebody was beating a big bass drum inside his skull. I had a cup of coffee too. It was like mainlining caffeine.

"OK. Tell me what happened," I said.

Musa opened his mouth to answer, but Miriam shot him the look of a frightened and angry wife, and he subsided.

"You know about the girls?" Miriam asked.

I nodded.

"I had taken the girls with me to the market. It was the first time they've been out since Lalla Alicia brought them here. I was buying some cilantro when one of the girls pulled on my sleeve. She pointed to a man walking toward us. Both girls ran. I did not know what to think, so I ran too. Musa had left the door unlatched so we could get back in. The girls were screaming when they ran into the courtyard. I followed them, and the two men were right behind me. One of them grabbed the girls, and one grabbed me. By that time, Musa had his sword."

"I couldn't get at them. The girls and Miriam were in my way," he interjected.

Miriam continued, "The men saw him with a sword and dropped us. They rushed toward Musa . . ."

"I cut them," he insisted. "I know I cut them."

"You did. There's a puddle of blood in front of the door."

He smiled in satisfaction.

"Why did the girls run?" I asked.

"I don't know," she replied.

"Ask them," I ordered and started down the tunnel to the door.

"Where are you going?" she asked fearfully.

"To follow the trail of blood. I'll be back. Bar the door, and don't let anybody in but me."

I followed the blood drops up the hill toward the Bab Guissa. About halfway up the hill, I lost the trail and turned back and found it again. The trail turned into a pharmacy, and I followed it.

The pharmacist was an elderly man, stooped and nearsighted. His shop had the snake skins, tortoise shells, sea horses, and herbs that belonged to traditional medicine. He also had a small collection of modern medications on a shelf against the left wall. The courtesies took more time than I had, but I knew I would get nothing without them.

"Father, I am looking for a bleeding man. I see blood drops at your step. Has such a one been here?"

He looked over his glasses at me and thought about refusing to answer, but his habit of obeying Europeans was too strong.

"Yes, Lalla, such a one was here."

"What did he look like?"

"The one who was bleeding was a Berber, not old, not young, with a mustache."

That's a help. It was the description of half of the males in town.

"The one with him . . ."

"He had a companion?"

"Yes, Lalla, there was one with him. The bleeding one said that a knife had slipped and he had cut himself. I didn't believe him, but I bandaged his arm and gave him a sling to support it."

The pharmacist came from behind his counter and stepped down into the street, pointing to a café about a hundred yards down the hill.

"There they are. You see them?"

Two men were seated at a table there, one talking on his cell phone. The other one, the man with the bandage, was drinking coffee and cradling his arm as if it hurt.

I watched as the first man paid the bill, and they set off down the hill, the one with the bandage leaning on the other. I let a few people pass in the busy street and followed, keeping under the awnings of the shops. I was too tall and too European to miss if they turned around. They led me into the metal souk where artisans shaped metal into everything from cooking pots to car mufflers. Through the sharp odor of hot metal and flying sparks, I stepped around a man squatting in the street welding without safety goggles and continued after my quarry. The men stopped beside a tall man wearing a long coat. The man in the coat reached out to the one with the bandage, but a woman in a burka moved between us, and I couldn't see what happened next. They walked on faster, as if in a hurry, and I followed them. After going about a hundred yards more, they turned a corner suddenly. When I got there, I couldn't see them. I didn't think they had seen me following them, but they must have. When I hurried around the next corner, I didn't see them and knew that I had lost them.

I stopped at the first shop and asked the man, "Did you see two men go by?"

He shrugged and continued welding.

Suddenly there was a roar. I was picked up and slammed into one of the welders, knocking us both to the ground. I went blank for a few seconds. There was a moment of absolute silence, my ears popped; it began to rain bits of metal.

And then the screaming began.

Chapter 10

I ROLLED OFF of the welder and landed on my back in the alley on top of what he had been welding. Whatever it was, it was hot. I dragged myself away and fell back, my head spinning. It began to rain bits of metal, and I tried to turn over to protect my eyes, but my body didn't want to move, so I put my arm up to cover them. When the rain stopped, I shook my head to clear the ringing in my ears, struggled up on my hands and knees and wobbled there, my muscles trembling. The welder lay stunned. Shaking his head, he caught his breath, he sat up and looked around.

A propane explosion? They all used propane for cooking, and the men used it in their shops. Did propane have an odor? I wondered. Yes, it did. It smelled like rotten eggs. This wasn't like that. It was a sharp acrid odor. My face felt strange. I wiped my hand across it and came away with blood and tissue. I sat down. Whose blood? I wiped my face with a Kleenex. Blood and tissue. I wiped it again. No blood. Not mine then. I looked around. The first thing I saw was a human hand. I gagged.

I struggled to my feet. My legs shaking, I leaned on a nearby shop front and made myself stop looking at the hand, but shreds of flesh lay all around me. The acid odor was dispersing, but there was something that reminded me of the time I dropped a plastic spoon on a hot burner on the stove. There was something that smelled like roasting meat, too. I turned aside and threw up. I wiped my mouth and looked away from the strips of flesh.

My brain stalled.

In a chaos of junk, there were people down who weren't getting up. The closest one was a man with a white beard wearing traditional clothing. He was bleeding from a gash in his forehead. My brain kicked in. If he was bleeding, he was alive. I squatted beside him. He looked bewildered. I reached for his hand.

"Come, grandfather," I said, taking his wrinkled hand. I supported him as he tottered over to the steps of a shop. The shopkeeper's wife, a plump body in black with a colored scarf covering her hair, was confused, pale and shaking, but she rushed to his side.

"Oh, Sidi Bram! Sidi Bram!"

"Tea, *umm*. Tea with lots of sugar," I said and began to rip the soft cloth of his turban to make a bandage.

Looking around, she said, "We will need a great deal of tea."

Given something to do, her brain kicked in too, and she bustled away.

I looked around me. Several workshop fronts had collapsed, their interiors naked, reminding me of pictures of London during the Blitz.

Not propane. There was too much destruction, and it didn't smell right.

A bomb.

Laying among the rubble were a dozen or more people, some not moving, frozen into obscene shapes in the act of dying, others injured, bleeding, crying. It was a new circle of Dante's hell without beginning or end. We were going to need more than tea. Time blurred. I went on autopilot, moving from victim to victim. The next bundle of cloth was a woman in a burka with a jagged metal fragment lodged in her throat. She was dead, a look of surprise on her face. I could do nothing for her. A man's leg had been broken when the concussion threw him up against a post. I could do nothing for him, either, but wipe his face and give him sweetened tea. I wiped the sweat from my face and my hand came away gritty and red from the dirt and the blood.

In the next street, where the bomb had gone off, the screaming had stopped. There was only silence, here there was only moaning, death in both. How many other alleys had been wrecked? How many people were dead? Injured? Where were the medics? Could they get through? The next alley must be worse.

On to the next person, crunching glass and fragments of brick as I went. By then, other helpers were moving among the wounded, wiping their faces and giving sweet tea to those who could take it. A young man was bandaging a tear in a woman's shoulder with professional skill.

I held a cup of cold tea for him to drink and asked, "Are you a doctor?"

He nodded at me and sipped the cool liquid. "Medical student," he answered absently as he moved on to the next patient.

"Can ambulances get through?" I asked.

He looked up. "They could get through to the next street, but that is where the explosion was. We will have to carry our injured around that to the square."

"How far is that?" I asked.

"Maybe three hundred yards, and that way will be blocked, too," he answered grimly

Some of the men were trying to clear a path through the rubble, quietly moving the bodies of the dead to one side. Others were taking what doors and shutters remained intact from buildings to use as stretchers. They moved automatically, their usually volatile emotions as frozen as their faces. Men lifted the injured gently onto the improvised stretchers and began to walk carefully toward the end of the street, stepping carefully around chunks of wall and the bodies of two dead women. It was hard not to step on others in the carnage.

I heard a low keening sound and turned to see a woman in black cradling what looked like a broken doll in her arms and rocking back and forth.

You see news photographs of what's left after a bomb, but they're not worth a thousand words. They can give you no idea. Neither can a thousand words. I had always thought the pictures of tiny sneakers were cheap shots to manipulate the emotions of the viewers.

The stretcher bearers started through the dead on a long walk to help. Some of the people would be dead before they could get there. As far as I could see, all of the living had been attended to.

So long as I had had something to do, I was all right. Well, not all right, but functioning. I followed the stretcher bearers and glanced into the next street, the one where the explosion had taken place. The full force of the blast had dug a crater in the middle of the alley and ripped through everything and everybody in sight. In the middle. Not off to one side, but in the middle. Where a man might stand. A suicide bomber, I thought dully. A man blew himself up there.

Small fires burned in the ruined buildings where the second-floor living quarters had collapsed into the first-floor shops. The acrid odor was stronger there, as was the smell of roasting meat. I retched at the stench. There was little a medic could do there. There were only pieces to be sorted at the mortuary. Muslims were buried the same day they died, but there would be no burying today, only weeping. The violation of the body in death was almost as terrible for them as death itself, for they believed that a person's body must be intact for him to enter paradise.

No longer having anything to do, I sat down in the dirt beside the shell of a shop and watched the shop across the street smolder. I do not understand, I thought numbly. I cannot understand men who would inflict such suffering on their own people for an idea. Ideas had killed a lot of people down the ages, but with modern improvements in delivering death, this lot had achieved some kind of a record. Today, with a pound of C-4, they could take out as many people at one blow as several strong men could in the old days when they had to hack until their arms grew weary to kill a few dozen. Who says there's no progress?

There was a little pink sneaker on the lip of the crater. After seeing the broken doll in her mother's arms, it no longer looked like a cheap shot. It looked unbearably poignant.

I thought about crying. It seemed like a good idea, so I leaned back against the wall and wept. Then I dried my eyes on my shirttail. Nobody had seen me cry since I was twelve and somebody ran over my dog.

Who had carried out this—this abomination?

Stop blubbering, I told myself, and suddenly I was shaking with fury. Innocent women and children. Innocent men, too. I understood the urge to kill all the jihadists and let God sort it out.

I heard an engine. It belonged to the smallest ambulance I had ever seen, and it was backing carefully toward me down the narrow street. I wondered how many people in Fez died every year because the rescue people couldn't get to them in time. The Baron Haussmann was onto something, I thought, when he blasted those wide boulevards through medieval Paris.

A man put his hand on my arm. I shrugged it off and whirled. When I focused my eyes, I saw Driss Bouchta. He was in one of the security outfits; I'd never known which. He would be here, of course.

"Lee? Lee Carruthers. What are you doing here?"

"Being bombed," I said numbly. "Presumably by terrorists."

He took my arm and escorted me to a square full of ambulances taking on the injured and sat me down in a café crowded with pale emergency workers knocking back shots of raki. He bought me a shot, too, and I knocked it back with the best of them and coughed. I didn't like raki, but any port in a storm. Just think of it as gin with licorice, I told myself. After another one my hearing and vision improved. Remarkable. Perhaps I'll write the People's Pharmacy. I couldn't think they had much call for remedies for being suicide-bombed, but it's as well to be prepared. One of these days one of the guys is going to slip through the FBI net.

My anger did not dissipate, however. Welcome to the modern world, I thought. Bombs are going off all over the world, and you have been sheltered, safe in an apartment in Paris.

In the square some cop was directing traffic. After listening to a handset, he waved an ambulance out of the square. After another consultation, one came in. I looked at Driss.

"Who did it?" I asked.

"Just an ordinary lout determined to blow up everybody, including himself, on a one-way trip to Paradise," he said bitterly.

Chapter 11

"THE NEW LOT?" I asked. "The Pure something?"

"Warriors of Islam. I don't know," he answered. "So far they've only done smart-ass things like posting that manifesto on the palace doors."

"Payroll robberies aren't exactly smart-ass."

"I know, but I can't see it. They're just starting up. Why should they have suicide bombers in stock?"

"If they've got Afghan veterans, they've got anything in stock," I replied. "Have you got any book on them?"

"Who says they've got Afghan veterans?"

"Bill Kendricks at the embassy," I replied.

"Where did he hear that?" he said, a bit sharply.

"Dunno. Is he required to share information with you?"

"That's not what I meant. If he knows it, why don't I?"

"Dunno that, either."

He popped open his cell. When somebody answered, he made furious noises. He was speaking Moroccan Arabic, so I only got the gist. He was threatening to flay somebody alive if he didn't get him some information about the Pures. He used some words that were new to me, but I doubted that I would find them in the dictionary.

People kept coming up to him to report things. I only got the gist of that, too. Suddenly I remembered the guy in the coat.

"Driss, I saw the bomber!"

He looked at me in surprise. "You did? Why didn't you say so?"

"I just remembered. I saw a guy stop beside him."

"Who?"

"I was following these two guys—that's how I got here. I lost them in the metal souk."

"Why . . . ? Never mind. Go on."

I pointed. "About halfway down that hill they stopped for a moment beside a man wearing a long coat, sort of a raincoat, and one of them spoke to him, maybe the guy in the coat gave him something. A woman came between us, and I couldn't see, but it didn't look as if they were asking him for directions."

He looked as if his patience was wearing thin. "OK. Tell me what they looked like!" he ordered.

"Both Moroccan, I think. The pharmacist said one of them was a Berber. One light, another darker with a pockmarked face. The Berber had a mustache. Thirty to thirty-five. Dark hair, dark eyes." I looked at him apologetically. "Um. No distinguishing features. No scars, nothing like that. The only thing that might help: one had a bandage on his left arm."

"Bandage?"

"Yes. Abu Musa cut him with a saber."

"Abu Musa. Saber," he said, with a dangerous look in his eyes. "What were these men wearing?"

"One was wearing jeans, a gold-colored T-shirt with AFEJ on it."

"The Fez football team."

"Oh. And running shoes. The other, maybe taller, was wearing khaki slacks and a blue and white striped short-sleeved shirt."

"Shoes?"

"I don't remember."

"That's it? That's all you remember? You call yourself a professional?"

"I call myself an analyst, Driss. They were really ordinary looking. Probably hired because they were ordinary looking." I pulled myself together. "You might want to send somebody to a pharmacy just down the hill from the Bab Guissa gate. I think that's where he got bandaged. Maybe the pharmacist can tell you more."

He looked like TNT, dangerous and unstable. He'd had one of the worst days an intelligence man could have—a bomb on his turf.

"Driss, first send somebody. Then I'll tell you."

He saw the wisdom in that. Barely. He barked into his cell and a tired man with a shirt full of blood appeared at his left elbow.

"Rami! You're covered with blood."

I looked down at my shirt. It was covered with blood, too.

"Driss, three-quarters of the people in the square are covered with blood," I protested.

He rolled his shoulders the way a bull does after the picador has set the lance. He could never explain that he was as tired as everybody else, but his voice softened. "Rami, get a clean shirt from somewhere and go to the pharmacy just down from the Bab Guissa." He looked at me.

"Fifty yards? On the left side coming from the gate."

"And ask the pharmacist about a man whose arm he bandaged." He turned to me. "When?"

"Ten-thirty, eleven o'clock this morning. Another guy was with him."

"Get a description. Anything. He may have spoken to the bomber."

Rami tried to look alert as he walked off to an unmarked car and jumped the queue to the traffic cop.

None of us is alert, I thought. It's the worst day of our lives, and it's not over yet.

I had never known what security organization Driss belonged to. Morocco had so many that it hardly mattered. He was midlevel when I first met him, so he must be pretty high up by now. The complete opposite of Hakim, Driss was a cheerful man, one of nature's optimists, tall and tan, with a slightly bushy mustache over full lips on which a smile usually hovered. Today he couldn't have smiled for a million dirhams. I had forgotten how much I liked him. Most Arab men sensed that I would shove back if pushed, and they object to that in a woman. Even Hakim, and we'd known each other for years. Driss seemed to find it exhilarating.

He ordered some more raki and went on taking reports. I ordered a kebob. I don't usually like to eat while covered in blood, but I hadn't eaten since dawn, and today was special. Even if I had a clean shirt, my mind would still be covered with blood. I felt fragile, and I hated it.

Driss took reports and gave orders quietly while I ate. A Person of Consequence in an exquisite suit strode importantly up to the table and looked at me in disdain. I looked back. Driss rose and saluted sharply.

"He wants a report," the man said.

Driss looked at him steadily. "Shall I come?" he asked.

The Exquisite frowned in annoyance. "Report to me." He looked at me again. I thought of saying something smart, as was my wont with authority, but he looked as if he had the power to order me beheaded on the spot, so I pushed my chair back slowly and removed myself to another table. Driss spoke quietly for several minutes, the gent standing magnificently at ease. When Driss finished his report, the man turned sharply away and departed, a panther stalking, exuding masculinity from every pore.

"Fencing," I said aloud.

"What?" Driss asked wearily as he sat down and waved for a coffee.

"He's a fencer," I repeated and ordered the same.

"Probably." He shrugged off all fencers. "He's Palace."

That explained it. The coffee came. From Morocco around the Mediterranean to Turkey and Greece, the coffee is wonderful. The societies have other drawbacks, but the coffee is good.

"Now you get to tell me what's going on."

"It started when those two invaded the house in the medina."

"Lee," he said ominously. "Have you ever been inside one of our jails?"

Chapter 12

"SORRY," I TOLD Driss sarcastically, "I get bombed every other day."

He still looked ominous.

"OK. I went to the house ... No." Not all the synapses were firing yet. "Alicia Harmon ... No." I stopped, drew a deep breath, and started over. "We have a safe house here in the medina?" I looked at him.

"Yes." Brusquely.

"There are two Tuareg girls there that Alicia Harmon—"

"Who?"

"Alicia Harmon. She runs the Femme Aid office. She picked these girls up from the side of the road, probably thrown out from a human trafficking shipment because they were sick. Miriam, the caretaker's wife, took them with her to the souk today. A couple of guys tried to grab them, and the three of them ran home screaming. The guys followed them into the house, and Abu Musa, the caretaker, defended them with a saber, cutting one of them."

I looked at him again. "Yes," he said.

I took him through the rest of it, following the blood, and then following the men until I lost them in the metal workers souk.

"They have some relationship with the bomber, otherwise why would they stop and say something to him?"

"That's all?"

"That's all I . . ."

One of his men rushed up and handed Driss a radio. Together we listened to a spokesman for the Pure Warriors of Islam claim the bombing in the medina and threaten more punishment for the apostate government of Morocco. Driss pounded the table in frustration. The voice of the bomber reading his martyrdom message came next. Presumably the video was showing on TV. Viral on YouTube in half an hour, probably.

"He did hand something off," I said. "That video."

"And you can't tell me anything more about them?" he demanded.

"They're not that memorable. I can identify them," I answered.

"We've got to get somebody to identify first. I need to talk to the people in that house. Maybe they know something."

"Driss, that's not a good idea. The girls are terrified."

"They'd be worse off if the men had succeeded in kidnapping them."

He waved the café owner over to pay the bill, but the owner wouldn't take any payment.

Driss exploded. "You think I'm corrupt? I will pay for what we had!"

The owner looked surprised and defensive but still wouldn't take any money. Driss threw a fistful of dirhams on the table and stalked away with me in his wake trying to keep up.

I caught up with him. "Driss, they probably don't speak Arabic."

"The people in the house speak to them. So will I."

"Driss, I have no idea how to get there from here."

He put his hands on his hips and glared at me.

"Take me back to the Bab Bou Jeloud. I can get to the house from there."

He summoned a car to one side of the square, and we rode silently to the gate. He radiated anger the whole way.

"Don't take it out on me," I snapped. "I didn't do it. If the bomber was on that street, he came through the Bab Guissa."

He glared at me. I was teaching my grandmother to suck eggs. We got out of the car at the gate, and I led him down the hill to the house. I didn't know why people looked at us strangely as we went. Nobody answered the knocker.

Driss pounded on the door and yelled, "Police! Open up!"

I heard Abu Musa slapping down the hall in his slippers.

"Musa, it's Lalla Lee. Please open the door."

He slowly opened the door and peeked out.

"Musa, it's me. Please let us in."

We stepped over a patch of dried blood and followed him to the courtyard.

"Mother," he cried.

Miriam came out of the kitchen and saw me.

"Lalla Lee!" she screamed and ran to me.

I looked down and saw my blood-soaked shirt. Miriam clasped me in her arms.

"No. No, Miriam. It's not my blood. It's from the bomb," I said.

She stood back and looked at me. "Bomb!"

Could the Palace keep something that big out of the media? I wondered. I looked at Driss.

He shook his head. "I don't think so," he replied to my unasked question.

"There was a bomb in the metal workers souk this morning, Miriam. I was following the men who attacked the house and was nearby. I was not hurt, but many other people were. This is their blood."

She covered her mouth.

"Coffee, mother," Musa ordered. "The men who attacked us?"

I introduced Driss, who stood there looking thunderous. What a time for him to go black! He's not going to get anything out of them looking like that.

"Yes," I answered. "They may be involved."

Miriam returned with coffee and pastries. I performed brief social niceties while Driss drank his coffee. That done, he looked Musa in the face and started in.

"These men who attacked you. What do you know of them?" he asked harshly.

Musa glanced aside. "Nothing," he answered.

Driss pressed him. "You must have seen something."

Musa shook his head. Driss looked coldly at Musa. Musa, like all Moroccans, had learned to hate the security services during the "Years of Iron" when the old king had arrested and imprisoned without cause and without cease. I'd never seen Driss like that before. I shifted uncomfortably in my chair as he turned to Miriam. Moroccan women are made of sterner stuff.

"I saw them," she said stoutly. "They wanted the girls. They hurt my husband, but he drove them off with his sword. That is all I know."

"One of them hit him in the head." I pointed to the bandage on his head. Driss ignored me.

"What did they look like?" Driss asked her.

She shrugged. "They were men. Not tall, not short, not thin, not fat."

"Eyes?" he asked.

Two, I thought irreverently.

"Brown."

"Hair?"

68

"Black."

"Beard?"

"No, but one had a mustache."

"Dressed?"

"I don't remember," she said. "Western. Maybe blue jeans."

He looked at me in frustration. "Why would a pair of guys try to snatch a couple of girls?"

"I don't know. I know nothing of them," I replied.

"I'll ask them."

"They don't speak Arabic," I said.

"Get them," he ordered Miriam.

She stood silently, her hands crossed at her ample waist.

"Get them, *umm*, or I will," he threatened.

Musa stood and faced Driss. "You are in my house," he said firmly, "but you are not a guest. Do not speak to my wife that way."

I looked at him in astonishment. Driss moved toward him, and I stepped between them. Miriam left the courtyard and returned with two girls wrapped in severe black. They took one look at Driss and began screaming.

Chapter 13

MIRIAM PUT HER arms protectively around the girls, and Musa went to stand in front of them, setting his feet and glaring fiercely. So I had once seen a water buffalo stand to protect his wife and child in the middle of a road in northern Viet Nam.

Driss looked at me in frustration. I sighed.

"You need to let me do it, Driss," I said.

I looked around. Driss could hear the proceedings from the *mandara*, the large public room in the middle of the first floor. I led him to it. By this time he looked like a thundercloud, Zeus ready to throw lightning bolts. I had no idea if our friendship would last the day. He took one of the leather cushions to the door and sat.

"I have to do it my way," I said. "A strange woman is bad enough. A strange man after two men tried to snatch them is too much."

I returned to the courtyard.

"Miriam, I need to know about these men. Why did they want the girls?"

Musa and Miriam exchanged a look. "I don't know, " Miriam answered, truthfully, so far as I could tell.

"They don't speak Arabic," Musa warned.

They were Tuareg rather than black African, Alicia had said. More and more Tuareg girls were turning up in the brothels, where they were a novelty for a while, with a virgin bringing a high price. The boys were headed to the brothels, too, special ones with a faster turnover than the ones who had women for rent.

The drought in the Sahel had lasted for a decade or more, and the ancient wells were dry. Tuareg men were faced with a terrible dilemma: leave their nomad life in the desert for the city, where they faced unemployment and the contempt of the black Africans whom they had enslaved for centuries, or sell something to make some money. First they sold the camels that determined their status in the desert to dealers in town for a pittance, knowing they would be slaughtered for their meat. When they were down to their last few camels, they sold their daughters, also for a pittance, knowing they were headed for the brothels in North Africa or the EU. Then came the most terrible choice of all: sell the last camel or a son.

My interview was compromised from the start. Driss had terrified them. There was nothing I could do about that. The main thing was that they didn't speak Arabic. Musa spoke a traders' argot, and the girls understood some of it, but working through an interpreter was like making love on different sides of a blanket. It disturbed the connection I needed to establish with the girls. At two removes, it was almost impossible. They were still spooked by the attack, as well.

I managed to get their story out of them in fits and starts, with long silences while Musa worked to make what they said make sense to himself so he could relate it to me. He was horrified by their story, although he must have heard it before when he interpreted it for Alicia Harmon. While Musa was shocked, I recognized it as a fairly typical story. A woman labor recruiter toured the camps in Mali looking for girls and young boys. She paid their parents a fee to find the girls jobs in the city so they could send money home. The boys would go to trade school and then get jobs. Their parents wept as a big truck took them away. No matter what the recruiters said, they knew where their children were bound. By the time they left Mali, the truck was packed with women and children, many more than the slat seats along the sides could hold. The excess sat on the floor where they were hotter, if possible, than those sitting along the benches.

There the story departed from all the others I had heard. A truck full of soldiers joined them when they reached the highway. No. They didn't know what the men looked like. Their faces were covered except for their eyes by black-checkered *cheches*. But they had guns. That's how the girls knew that they were soldiers.

The soldiers led the truck north, for how long the girls couldn't say, except that they slept where they sat as the truck drove on into the night. The driver handed water bottles and food to them sometimes, but it was terribly hot, and there was never enough water. The driver wouldn't stop for them to relieve themselves, so the truck bed rapidly began to stink of urine.

On the third or maybe the fourth day, the trucks turned off the highway onto a sand track between two mountains of stones and met a barricade across the track. When the trucks stopped, men swarmed down the hills on both sides shooting guns. The soldiers in the trucks fired back, but the attackers shot them all. The new soldiers made everybody get out of the truck and stand in line to be counted. Then a different truck full of the new soldiers took the other soldiers' truck and led them out of the sand track.

They crossed another graveled track and began to climb through semi-desert and scrub. Finally, they stopped at a broad open space where they could see the ruins of a large gate and the remains of a wall by the light of a full moon. Sijilmassa, I thought, the end of the old slave caravan trail. There were people in city clothes waiting, but it was too dark for the girls to see them well. One of the soldiers made them get out of the truck to be counted again. The man examined them, smiling as he felt the women. They stopped talking and looked down at their feet. It took hugs from Miriam and persuasion from Musa before they would resume.

The soldiers watched the man give the city woman a bag; she gave the soldier some money from the bag, and everybody got back into the trucks and drove on. The two girls had developed a fever, and soon they couldn't sit up. The truck driver left them by the side of the road without food or water. When a car or a truck passed by they hid in terror, but soon they were too weak to hide. Alicia Harmon found them lying beside the road, barely conscious. She picked them up and gave them water and some chocolate she had in her purse. She went to the house in the medina and got Musa to carry them there one at a time. They were delirious when they arrived, and for several days Miriam thought they would die, but slowly they got better. At that point they fell silent, unable to understand the enormity of what had happened to them. I was sorry to remind them of the men, but I had to.

"Do you know those men—the men who tried to grab you? Why did they try to take you?" I asked through Musa.

They squirmed and looked at their feet.

"You do know them. Who are they?"

They whispered together and then to Musa.

"They are men from the truck."

"From the truck that brought them from home?"

He consulted them again.

"No. From the other trucks, the ones with the soldiers," he said.

Miriam took them back to the room they were using, and Driss returned to the courtyard.

"What was she going to do with them?" Musa asked. "They can't speak any Arabic. All they know is herding goats."

"I don't know, Musa, but would you have left them by the side of the road?"

"They do nothing," he grumbled. "They eat and sleep and sometimes they cry. They could at least help with the housework."

"I don't think they know anything about housework," I said. "They've probably spent all their lives in tents. Give them a break, Musa. They were sold into slavery by their parents. They were hauled several thousand miles in an open truck. They were thrown out and left to die because they were sick. And now they've been chased by men who were so determined to catch them that they invaded the house and had to be driven out at sword point. That was nice work by the way, Musa."

He looked gratified. He also looked as if he had a headache. I took the tray to the kitchen, and by the time Miriam was back, I had another pot of coffee on the table. I'm not particularly domestic, but I can manage what I need. Coffee is one thing I need.

Driss returned and sat at the table. Musa didn't look pleased. "So somebody thinks the girls can identify somebody."

"Well, yes," I said, "but where would they ever meet somebody connected with the trip?"

"Maybe it wasn't the trip. Maybe it was the man and woman. What is this about Alicia Harmon?"

I shook my head in warning.

Miriam asked, "Lalla Lee, where is Lalla Alicia?"

"That's what I want to know. Where *is* Lalla Alicia?"

They looked confused.

"When was the last time you saw her?"

I watched as Miriam counted in her head.

"Three Fridays ago," she said uncertainly.

"Four," Musa interjected.

"It was the *moussem* of Sidi Raman," she replied.

"No it wasn't. I remember. It was the day the street sweeper fell down."

It looked as if they would fall into a serious discussion. Sidi Raman was the local Sufi saint, and the neighborhood downed tools to celebrate his feast day. I wouldn't have any trouble finding out the date.

I broke in. "Why did she come?" I asked.

"She came to see the girls. She is looking for someone to teach them Arabic."

There can't be all that many Tuareg teachers of Arabic in Fez.

"She didn't tell anybody she was going away, and nobody has seen her for about two weeks," I said.

They looked astonished.

"Has she ever gone away like this before?" I asked.

They looked at each other and shook their heads.

"No," answered Miriam. "If she goes away, she always tells us. And when she is going to come back, she tell us that, too."

"The girls. Has she ever brought anybody here before?"

The house in the medina was a refuge for women in trouble—pregnant girls, abused wives, runaway prostitutes. They came to the house because they had heard about it from other women. Sometimes we could find them work or training, but jobs were scarce. The prostitutes got bored with the quiet life and went back to the streets. The wives began to feel guilty and went back to their husbands, who beat them again, sometimes fatally. At least we could occasionally keep the fathers or brothers of the pregnant girls from killing them to defend the honor of the family.

But even if the girls could identify one of the men, what did that have to do with Alicia Harmon?

Driss finished his coffee and thanked Miriam stiffly. She bowed her head graciously—stiffly, but graciously—and I meandered through the leaving ritual. I never did find out how Musa's aged father was.

As we started up the hill, people stared at my bloodstained T-shirt, until I stopped at a shop near the tourist hotels and bought a black shirt and slipped it on. It was the smallest black one they had, but I looked like a ragamuffin. I certainly felt like one. We pushed our way through the crowd of touts and bewildered tourists around the cheap hotels.

"We need to talk," Driss said.

Chapter 14

OF ALL SAD words of tongue or pen.

"Driss, we've been talking!" I retorted.

He steered me to a table outside a café by the Bou Jeloud gate.

"No more coffee," I pleaded

He bought me a Coke instead. It is usually against my religion to drink Cokes in foreign parts, and the local knockoff (in a bright red can with Arabic script) was hazardous to your health, but I was in need. I rolled the cool can over my forehead and thought about taking a nap on the table.

"We have to talk," he repeated.

"OK," I sighed. "Let's talk. What about?"

"Alicia Harmon. I didn't know she was missing until Hakim told me yesterday. She came into my office about two weeks ago looking for information. You may imagine that not many citizens do that." Despite all that had happened that day to sour him, he was genuinely amused.

"Where did she get the address?"

"Out of the telephone book."

Now I was genuinely amused. "I didn't realize you were in the Yellow Pages."

"We're not. She went to police headquarters and told them she had something about terrorism, and she refused to say more, so they finally sent her to me."

"She appears to favor the direct approach."

"She does. She told the receptionist she had some questions about the human trafficking ring we had broken up in Meknès a while ago and that she might have information about another ring. She waited patiently while we decided what to do with her. She sat looking around at the office with interest, as if being in the office of an intelligence outfit was a new experience for her. She intrigued me, so I let her wait for a while longer and then asked her in."

He lit a cigarette. Although it had been five years at least since I had last had a cigarette, I inhaled with him.

"She told me about the women she found at the side of the road. Near here?" he asked.

"I don't know. Musa had the impression that it was near Meknès. That would make sense. The trafficking route from the Sahara goes through there to Tangier and Ceuta, which would be the ports they would use for the EU."

He nodded. "Or Al Hoceima. She had heard about the ring we broke up in Meknès and wanted to know whether we broke it up before she found the women or after."

"And?"

"Before," he said. "Definitely before. That led her to suggest that another group had taken its place."

"Or perhaps there was a parallel group all along," I suggested.

"Umm. Possibly."

"You can't just wave a magic wand and set up a smuggling ring after one has been busted, Driss. It wants connections, logistics, personnel. The shipment the two girls belonged to must have left Mali before your ring was broken up. It's a long trip. How did you learn about the ring?"

He smiled at me. "An anonymous phone call."

"Ah."

"Yes. A woman."

"Who took the call?"

"Ultimately, it came to me."

"While you were trying to trace it. It wasn't Alicia, was it?"

"No, it was not. And we weren't able to trace the call."

"Still, it's interesting. The usual anonymous tipster is a man with a grudge."

"She pointed that out, as well. She had thought the whole thing through quite thoroughly before she came to me. She said something interesting. She asked me if I had ever thought about the proceeds from human trafficking going to fund terrorism. Where did she get that idea?" he asked.

I shook my head. "I don't know. Can you give me the precise date when she came?"

"Not off the top of my head. Why?"

"She went to Rabat for a briefing on terrorism on August 19. She is a specialist in human trafficking and abuse of women. She usually left the money trail to me or Sidney."

"Sidney?"

I ignored him. "Terrorism was a new interest, and she was definitely interested in the money trail."

"She knew or suspected something that led her to link the two," he said. "What?"

"I have no idea. She left no record of her thinking in the matter. Since she wasn't trained for clandestine work, her mind would have come fresh to the topic. She might see connections that we wouldn't, simply because they had never happened before. Constraints of the box on thinking. You heard the girls talk about their soldier escorts. Belmansur has been making a fortune for the Maghreb Al Qaeda by protecting slave convoys for years.

The attack the girls described sounded like a new group muscling in. A new terrorist group? The Pure Warriors?"

"I still think they haven't got it in them to challenge Al Qaeda."

"If their claim of today's bomb proves true, they've got it in them to challenge the kingdom of Morocco."

He grimaced. There would be a long night ahead of him, with the Palace looking over his shoulder every step of the way.

"Two other bits of information from her reports: about a month ago, she wrote a report in which she mentions "money going someplace odd," and she asked for information about the Rashid Family Foundation, specifically about its head, Omar. Hakim says he knows nothing against the Foundation or against Omar."

Driss shook his head. "I know nothing, either, but clearly she knew something."

"Or thought she did. Whatever it was, she didn't record it, but somebody may think she knows something. I found a bunch of death threats in the flat."

He sat up. "Death threats?"

"The old-fashioned kind. Letters cut out of a magazine pasted to a sheet of paper. 'Stop asking questions or your dead.' "

"I want them."

"They're yours. I suppose there must be somebody somewhere who hasn't heard about fingerprints."

Chapter 15

WHICH WAS WORSE—trying to sneak a man upstairs or telling Ibrahim that he was a cop? That wasn't true, but saying that was simpler than telling him the truth. I took him downstairs and knocked. Fatima answered the door and saw Driss with me. She disapproved instantly.

What was Driss' rank? Did it matter?

"This is Police Inspector Bouchta. He's going upstairs with me. I need to give him something I found in Alicia's flat."

She still disapproved. I took him upstairs anyway. As I was unlocking the door, Sam Glover appeared out of his flat.

"Oh, God! I forgot," I exclaimed.

"Not very flattering, especially since you're smuggling another man into the flat." He smiled that thousand-watt smile.

"Mr. Glover, this is Driss Bouchta. Driss, Sam Glover."

The men shook hands. Driss looked as if he wished he had told me to bring the letters to his office.

"Dinner?"

"No, no. I remember that." I tried to look as battered as I felt. "I really don't feel like it, Mr. Glover."

"Sam, please."

"Sam, then. I was in the bombing this morning, and my dearest desire is to take a shower and go to bed."

"That's terrible!" He looked closely at me. "There's blood on your face. You were hurt!" he exclaimed.

"No, but I was in the next street over. It was very bad, Sam. I need time to get over it."

"But you shouldn't be alone," he said, his smile soft with concern.

The hairs on my arms stood up, and I remembered that I wanted to figure out why. Driss cleared his throat.

"I'll be all right, Sam, really."

I opened the door, and Driss followed me in.

"That guy is interested in you," he commented as he followed me to the bedroom.

I got the letters from the filing cabinet. "It's just my native charm," I said modestly.

He looked at me. Then he looked at the letters.

"How many have you touched?"

"The top one, the back of the bottom one. I flipped through them. You'll need my fingerprints."

"Don't worry about it. We already have them." He grinned.

I stood with my mouth open as he returned to the living room and walked out the door. I didn't like the idea of Moroccan Security having my fingerprints.

In the bathroom, I shucked my clothes and threw them in the corner. A long hot shower removed the remains of the bombing from my person, but nothing would ever remove them from my head. I dried myself and crawled in bed. I couldn't believe it was still the same day.

There was a roar. I was thrown to the ground. There was a moment of absolute silence, my ears popped; it began to rain bits of metal.

And then the screaming began. I turned over to protect my eyes, and when the rain of debris stopped got up on my hands and knees. My face felt strange. I wiped my hand across it and came away with blood and tissue. Tissue? I sat down. Whose blood? I wiped my face with a Kleenex. Blood and tissue. I wiped it again. No blood. Not mine then. I looked around. The first thing I saw was a human hand. I gagged.

I struggled to my feet. My legs shaking, I leaned on a nearby shop front, and made myself stop looking at the hand, but shreds of flesh lay all around me. There was something burning that smelled like meat. I turned aside and threw up. I wiped my mouth and looked away from the strips of flesh. In a chaos of junk, there were people down who weren't getting up.

I struggled awake, my heart pounding. That hand! The smell!

The room was dark. I turned the bedside light on and sat up against the wall with the blanket wrapped around me. I was cold. Shaking. As bad as blubbering. I fought to control my breathing. After a while I lay back down. I lay there for a long time, stiff as a board. Then I slipped into sleep.

There was a roar. I was thrown to the ground. There was a moment of absolute silence, my ears popped; it began to rain bits of metal.

And then the screaming began.

I heard a pounding. I woke all the way up. Somebody was knocking on the door. I got up and slipped into a kaftan. My hair was a mess where I had slept on it wet. Slept! Through the peephole I could see Sam Glover. I opened the door resentfully.

The thousand-watt smile. This time the hairs on my arms ignored it.

"You should eat something," he said. "I brought a pizza."

Yes, there was a pizza box in his hands. He came in behind it and put it on the dining table. He stood looking at me, smile in place. Expectantly.

"You shouldn't be alone. You really need company after an experience like that."

All I wanted was for him to go away so I could go back to sleep. Perchance to dream? I got two plates from the kitchen.

"All I've got to drink is water," I said.

He carried the water glasses in from the kitchen and held the chair out for me as if I were a Victorian maiden who might faint. It seemed a bit much for pizza.

"You need to talk about it," he said.

"I don't need to talk about it. I've talked about it." I bit into a piece of pizza. It was good. I've had pizza in a dozen countries except for Italy. It was good in all of them, particularly good in Ankara.

"That guy who was with you. Who is he?" he asked casually.

"He's a friend," I answered, wondering why he wanted to know. "Let's talk about Alicia instead."

He put his piece of pizza down and licked his fingers. I went looking for napkins and found them on a shelf beside a can of Campbell's Tomato soup. I returned and handed him two.

"I don't really know her well," he said.

"I don't know her at all. Anything you can tell me will add to my store of knowledge." I sounded like a college professor. Maybe it was the bomb.

"I used to meet her on the steps, help her carry her groceries up, that sort of thing."

"Never chatted?" I asked through the tomato sauce.

"A couple of times. Once I helped her carry her suitcase up the stairs."

Ah. She had a suitcase.

"She'd been to Casablanca to a conference, something about women. Princess Miriam had given the opening address."

"The UN, probably. Women's rights is one of the princess's Good Works. And what did she think of the

Princess?" I asked curiously. I wondered if she had a Princess Diana fixation.

"She said that rather than just welcoming them, the Princess made a substantive report. She went on about how Moroccan women were trying to get the law about rape changed. Something about girls having to marry the men who raped them?"

"It's the custom in a number of societies," I said neutrally.

"That was the only time we had a conversation, and it wasn't really a conversation, because she did most of the talking."

His smile was back. He'd forgotten that I should be treated tenderly. It was amazing. He was definitely alluring, but he could turn it on and off. Right now it was going full bore. Why did he want to attract me? I couldn't see him fancying me. The hairs on my arms were waving him off.

"I do know that she had a boyfriend," he said. "I saw them together a couple of times." He pressed his temples in a theatrical way. "I just wish I could remember where."

Chapter 16

THERE WAS A roar. I was thrown to the ground. There was a moment of absolute silence, my ears popped; it began to rain bits of metal.

And then the screaming began.

"No!" I shouted and woke up. First blubbering and now nightmares, I thought. The next thing you know, I'll be wearing a pink frilly apron like my mother's.

I lay there looking at the flickering pattern the moonlight made on the ceiling. Sam Glover was a peculiar man. Sexy as hell, but, according to the hairs on my arms, he turned it on and off. The man he had seen Alicia with was European, with medium brown hair, eyes, and stature, from what he could observe of a guy who was sitting down. No beard or moustache. No scars. As Driss said, not helpful. Too bad he didn't have a strawberry mark on his cheek. Maybe Glover could remember where he saw them. I'd hate to take a picture of Alicia around all the likely restaurants.

I was thinking about going to the office to get into Alicia's files when I fell asleep. I woke moderately refreshed with no need to buy a pink apron.

The office building was a four-story colonial Beaux Arts confection, its proportions a little off, the local workmen's take on molding a little strange. I always expected it to burst into Arabic scrolls. The Femme Aid Maroc office was on the fourth floor, reached by a round metal birdcage of an elevator, large enough to take two if one of them was small. I knew that it rocked back and forth as it ascended, producing a queasy feeling like seasickness in me, so I took the staircase that curled around it, holding carefully on to the iron banister, because the wedge-shaped marble steps were slick. The fourth-floor hall was badly lit by large skylights which had not been washed in living memory. I avoided one tear that I remembered in the hall carpet lying in wait to trap me, but I caught my foot in a new one and stumbled against the office door. It was marked FEM AI MAR in tarnished gold letters. The Chubb locks I had installed on this door and the one to the computer room are designed to be hard to pick, but I had brought my old key with me, just in case. I was about to try it when I discovered a new lock, the kind you could buy anywhere in the souk. I was muttering under my breath as I prepared to pick it when the door opened, and a man hit me with his shoulder, knocking me on my rear, and sped down the hall to the staircase. I picked myself up and ran after him. I tripped on a broken step in the second flight and nearly jerked my arm out of the socket holding to the banister, which lost me precious time. I reached the door in time to see a white Rover speeding away too fast for me to catch the number on the plate except for the Fez prefix.

I bent over to catch my breath. What did anybody want in the office of an NGO as seemingly innocent as Femme Aid Maroc? For that matter, what did anybody want with a woman as seemingly innocent as Alicia Harmon?

Four flights of stairs again, carefully, still out of breath. What was FAM's enthusiasm for fourth-floor space? Then I remembered that I had rented both. I couldn't remember why. Bottom line, probably. I picked up my pack and laptop and entered. The first thing I saw was the open computer room door. Alicia's files! I dropped my stuff again, on the desk this time, and hurried to the computer room. My heart sank. The CPU was on the floor, smashed. I fished through the remains. The hard drive was missing. Much good may it do them, I thought. The Agency's encryption would slow them down a bit. However it didn't do me any good, either. It prevented my accessing Alicia's files, too. I hurried to the office door and jammed the back of the visitor's chair under the handle. That would slow them down, too.

I went back to the computer room and looked around. The keyboard had been slammed against the wall and was lying bent on the floor. The monitor was still on the workstation desktop, blinking blindly, in search of something to display. The chair was on its side, stuffing showing through slits in the cover. Just meanness, I supposed, when they couldn't get into her files. I kicked the computer bits out of the way and tugged the handle of the small safe in the corner. Still locked. Surely ... I got my pack and fished in it for the flash drive I had copied my Moroccan files to and went to boot the laptop. I copied the safe combination from my day on a piece of paper and went back to the computer room. I was not unbearably surprised to find that the combination opened the safe. Inside was a holster. I had a momentary vision of Alicia Harmon wearing one of those teddies, black lace stockings, and red high-heeled shoes, and a shoulder holster with a Glock. I shook my head. I have always had an inappropriate sense of humor.

It was no wonder she was missing. The wonder was that they hadn't carried off the apartment furniture and the contents of the office as well.

I had come to search the office. It looked untouched. If the computer room was any example, if the bad guys had searched the office, the contents of the file cabinets would be strewn across the floor and the desk turned over. There were two three-drawer cabinets, one each side of the door. I decided to start with the right hand one. In my day, it contained UNICEF, INTERPOL, and UNODC communications. Why would she hide anything among the UN anti-crime and drug smuggling posts?

The first drawer was jammed with INTERPOL stuff, mostly Red "apprehend immediately" notices. What was she doing on INTERPOL's mailing list? I was just beginning the UNDOC stuff in the second drawer when I heard a loud knock on the office door.

Chapter 17

I RAN TO slam the communications room door shut. The shadow on the window of the door might be that of a woman. With my right hand on my pistol, I used my left hand to pull the chair out from under the doorknob and opened the door. A woman in the hall with her hands on her hips looking as if she owned the place. I pasted a look of pleasant enquiry on my face.

She took her time sizing me up; I did the same for her. Arab, not Berber. She looked maybe thirty, but she could be any age above fifteen. I find it hard to estimate the age of Mediterranean women. She wore a black pantsuit just like mine, except hers came from a much better tailor. As if it had its own will, her long hennaed hair snaked around her face, accentuating her smoky black eyes, which were fringed with long, dark lashes. Nature can be very unkind in the matter of eye lash distribution. A hawk's beak of a nose jutted out above a pair of lips in no need of collagen. A square jaw no man would ever notice until it was too late peeked out through the tendrils of her hair. Tiger, tiger, burning bright. It was a distinguished face, just short of beautiful. The care with which she was turned out had produced a slick polish that distracted you from her cold eyes. She let out an explosive breath.

"Who are you? What are you doing in Alicia's office?" she demanded. She Who Must Be Obeyed. The problem with modern Muslim women is that they burst out of the harem with attitude, which gave some insight on why they were haremized in the first place.

I raised a cool eyebrow at her. "And who are you?" She had spoken in English, lightly accented with something that wasn't Arabic. From her tone, probably French. Moroccan Arabic has been debased by its contact with Berber. I replied in classical Arabic.

"Didn't your mother teach you any manners?"

"Who are you?" she asked, uncertainty creeping into her voice. "This is Alicia's office."

A crease appeared on her smooth brow. If she wasn't careful, she'd get wrinkles.

"I'm Lee Carruthers. Do you know where Alicia is?" I asked.

"Isn't she ... ?" She slumped in the doorway and shook her head. "Oh, God, I hoped ... I don't know. I haven't seen her for over two weeks. I've been calling and calling." She sounded close to tears. From tiger burning bright to helpless maiden in one leap.

"Not here, you haven't," I said neutrally.

"No. No. Not here. At the apartment."

There wasn't an answering machine at the apartment. "Come in and sit down," I said, retrieving the visitor's chair from beside the door and carrying it to the desk.

She followed me and sat tensely, as if ready to flee. We contemplated each other in silence for a while. Then she relaxed. Although she must have seen it dozens of times, she looked around the office with unconcealed disdain. The room was badly divided from a larger room, its egg and dart molding an egg short of a dozen. The gray furniture had not been new when I bought it ten years ago, and the years since had not been kind to it. I shrugged. Her problem.

"I work for Femme Aide. The Beirut office sent me here to find out what was wrong when we couldn't reach Alicia. Perhaps you know where she is?"

Something moved behind her eyes. I couldn't tell what it was. It left no mark on her face, but she sat back in the chair.

"My name is Zeynab. Zeynab Bentali. I'm an attorney. My office is across the hall. When I saw a light in here, I thought, I hoped, that Alicia had returned."

Her Arabic was good, at least as good as mine, probably better.

"How well did . . . How well do you know Alicia?" I had trouble remembering that I was looking for a living woman.

"I'm her attorney. And her friend, I hope."

She pointed to the photographs on the wall, to the pictures of battered women in a variety of Islamic costumes—a woman in a burka, with only her bruised and swollen face showing; a girl wearing the beige raincoat and coif of the modest Muslim woman, two lovely black eyes and four splinted fingers; a flashy thing in a red leather miniskirt, net stockings, high-heeled boots, a minimalist tank that showed full breasts and erect nipples, and a slash across one cheek that had nearly taken her eye out. The photos were all the more disconcerting for being the only color in the room.

"Her clients often need legal assistance." She stopped. "How could she work with those poor women staring at her?" She shuddered.

"Perhaps she needed constant reinforcement to keep her rage topped up? When was the last time you saw her?"

"August 20th? The 21st?"

"You sound uncertain."

She pinched the bridge of her nose. "I have been in court in Salé." She seemed to count backwards. "I went over to Salé on the 20th, and didn't come home that weekend. My colleagues and I spent the weekend sorting out our client's defense. Not that it did any good."

I raised an eyebrow again, and she shrugged again. "A newspaper editor in trouble with the government. He was convicted. They always are," she said bitterly.

"Jail?"

"No, just a fine. And he's prohibited from publishing for a month."

"That doesn't sound so bad," I said, to see what she would say.

"In comparison with the old regime, it's not, but the constitution guarantees freedom of the press."

"So many of them do."

She grimaced. "But the trial wasn't over until last Wednesday. Three days. Five years ago it would have been over in one."

"And he would have gone to jail or to the desert."

"At least," she agreed. "Anyway, I didn't get back until that Thursday, and Alicia hasn't been in since I got back. You think she's missing?" She played with a heavy silver band she wore on the middle finger of her right hand. "She could just be away. Surely the people in the medina know where she is."

That answers one question. She knows about the house in the medina.

"Did she tell you anything about the women she found?"

Again that slight movement behind her eyes.

"I know she was looking for places for two women, but that's all I know."

"Was she working on anything particular?" I asked.

She shook her head. "Other than that, not anything that I know of. Do you have any idea . . . ?"

"No," I replied. "I just got here last night."

"She'll be back," she said. "She's gone away before."

"For this long? Without telling anyone?" I asked.

"Well, no, not without telling anyone, but there's probably a reasonable explanation." She stood up. "I'm just across the hall if you need anything."

I scribbled my cell phone number on the back of one of my cards, the one with Femme Aide and the Beirut address, and gave it to her. We walked to the door together, and when we got there she turned and offered me her hand. I shook it. I didn't have any reason not to.

Chapter 18

I OPENED THE second drawer of the filing cabinet, the UN Crime Office documents, and realized that if she had hidden anything there, I would be eighty years old before I found it. I shut the drawer and glanced at the UNICEF stuff in the bottom drawer. Nothing visible. The only thing I had discovered from searching that filing cabinet was that institutions loved to send out newsletters, and I already knew that.

I started on the left-hand filing cabinet. My mind wandered to Zeynab Bentali. She was lush for a lawyer practicing in a Muslim country. She looked more like an Egyptian belly dancer out of uniform than a lawyer. The ulema could issue a fatwa just for not covering that hair. Perhaps she dressed more conservatively for court. I wore my hair in a respectable bun and covered it with a scarf, and I still got called a Western whore. There's no justice. There was something ... unsettling about her. I tried to think what made me feel that way.

The left-hand cabinet was full of Femme Aid files. The first drawer contained files of individuals in alphabetical order: A through L. I picked one at random. It concerned an abused housewife. I flicked over the tabs. Nothing else.

The second drawer had M through Z and was only half full. Shouldn't there be more? I sampled the dates in the first drawer. All in the last two years on Alicia's watch. The same for the second drawer. Behind the files in that drawer was a rusty paper clip with a minute piece of paper caught in it. It was a piece of flimsy, which nobody had used for office copies since the advent of computers Was it a clue? It didn't look particularly old. The third drawer was crammed with files labeled A-Z, some of them going back to the beginning, proof that nobody ever throws anything away. I pulled one. It was a case I remembered, that of a twelve-year-old girl who had been living on the streets. We placed her in an approved school with a training program for embroiderers. I thought at the time that she was an unlikely candidate for embroidery, but the UNICEF woman was enthusiastic. Predictably, the girl didn't like it. Her back hurt and all those little stitches gave her a headache, so she ran away and took the office petty cash with her. She then went to ground, and we couldn't find her anywhere, and when I suggested that we look in some of the brothels, UNICEF was outraged. It had not been a success. Not all of them were.

Zeynab. There was something about her eyes. She had looked me straight in the eye, odd for a Muslim woman and not reassuring. Some of the best liars I had known had looked me straight in the eye, and one candidate for Lover of the Week had continued to do so as I threw him out the door after coming home from a business trip and finding him in my bed with a blonde. I couldn't put my finger on what it was about Zeynab. Was it the eyelashes?

That left the desk. The in and out boxes were stuffed with what looked like the kind of miscellaneous stuff that all offices collect. I riffled through it. Nothing but ordinary Femme Aid stuff. There was actually a blotter. Nothing on it, and nothing under it. Should there have been? I was unfamiliar with her office procedures, so unless I found a body on the linoleum or bullet pocks in the walls, I would not know what was unusual. I flipped through the small Rolodex. All of the names were familiar from my time. There was no desk calendar or appointment diary. They're probably all in the computer, I thought. Great!

What do you do in case your hard drive crashes? You keep a backup, dummy.

I went back to the computer room and stood looking at the mess. She would keep her backup here. Where? There were two drawers in the workstation. They held the usual stuff we can't bear to throw away—spent ballpoint pens, paper clips, an Art Gum eraser. An Art Gum eraser? I didn't know they even made them anymore. There weren't any flash drives anywhere. What did she do with them? My office was littered with the things. I returned to Alicia's office and resumed searching the desk.

I began sifting through the junk in the center drawer, trying not to stab my fingers on more broken pencils, out-of-ink ballpoint pens, and paperclips. The desk was unlikely to hold anything of consequence with a lock like that on the door, although I did find a spare set of keys to the office and the apartment. I swore. On the other hand, why bother with keys? Any fool could just walk in. I put those in my pack as well.

The three desk drawers on the side held nothing of interest until I got to the bottom one. The top one had some yellowing letterhead. Did she sometimes use the electric typewriter on a stand next to the wall? There should have been a computer. There was a computer in the other room, of course, but it looked bad not to have one in the office.

The second drawer yielded a Fez telephone book. The bottom drawer held, at first glance, a sweater and a pair of pantyhose. I struck pay dirt under the sweater. Two packets of folded paper, each with a rubber band holding it together. I recognized the paper in the first packet and message as well. "STOP ASKING QUESTIONS OR YOUR DEAD." I counted ten of them. Added to the dozen in the flat, twenty-two death threats. I snapped the rubber band back on the packet. No dates, of course. I wondered how long it had been going on. From the number of them, based on one a day, nearly a month. I concluded that she had paid no attention to them. Why? Courage? Nonsense! That was not courage. That was stupidity. I would at least have mentioned it to Sidney if not to the local police. And they knew where she lived. From the phone call, they also knew that I was there. Nice thought.

The second packet was more interesting. The paper was fine, and the notes appeared to have been written with a genuine pen. They were love letters. Just short notes: "It was so hard leaving you last night. I can't wait to see you tonight." They were all in the same vein, courting letters, nothing erotic, nothing you couldn't show your mother if you had to, but they all ended the same way. "Destroy this note." Who would ask the beloved to destroy a relatively innocent note? A married man? Whoever he was, he knew little of women in love. They *never* destroy love letters, no matter how compromising. I put the love letters in my pack and was preparing to leave when the phone rang.

The caller burst into speech without waiting for a hello.

"Alicia, what do you think you're doing!?" a woman asked angrily.

Chapter 19

"ALICIA?"

"Who is this?" I asked.

"I believe I have the wrong number," she replied.

Hurrying to keep her from hanging up, I said, "No, you don't. Who are you?"

"This is Nadia. Where is Alicia?"

Nadia Talib worked for UNICEF in Fez.

"It's Lee, Nadia, Lee Carruthers."

"Lee. But what are you doing answering Alicia's phone?"

"They sent me in to find her."

"Find her?"

"She's missing."

"Missing!"

"Yes. She's been gone about two weeks, as far as I can tell. Do you know what she was doing?"

"She came into the office about a month ago asking about the Rashid Foundation, and now I hear talk all over town that there's something wrong with the Foundation. What did she tell people?"

"I have no idea what she might have done. I don't know her. What was she asking about?"

"Terrorism," she replied. "Terrorism! Foundation money going to terrorists."

At last, traces of terrorism. "Where did she get an idea like that?"

"She wouldn't tell me."

"What did you tell her?"

"About the Foundation. Omar Rashid's great-grandfather, Rashid, was a Sufi saint, a very holy man. Pilgrims came from all over to his tomb to acquire some of his *baraka*, his blessing. They still do. Their donations support the tomb and the family. You know."

I did. "How did it get to be a Foundation?"

"Oh, there was a lot of money, a lot of donations, some even from the Sultan. Omar's grandfather invested some of it, and then there was more. Omar's father came to Fez to attend Al Karaouine University and stayed on, practicing law. Another son and his family took care of the tomb. It was Omar's father who established the Foundation."

"A *waqf*?"

"Yes."

A bequest intended for a specific purpose, like a school. "Then it's regulated by the Ministry of Religious Affairs?"

"Yes, it is. The old man left the running of the Foundation to Omar in his will. He was the oldest son in that branch."

"What does the Foundation do with its funds?" I asked.

Nadia picked up on my neutral tone and replied in a determined voice, "The money goes to the care of street boys. They find training for them so that they will have the skills to make a living instead of becoming criminals."

"Sounds like a laudable enterprise," I said. "Why do you think Alicia asked you about it?"

"She said she thought I would know," Nadia answered.

Nadia knew the genealogies of local notables back to the Prophet, from whom her own family was descended.

"There probably aren't many people she knew she could ask."

"She said she'd heard rumors."

"Rumors about what?"

"I asked her that. She wouldn't be specific. Lee, what has happened to her?"

"I wish I knew. Is she the kind to go on a dirty weekend to Agadir and forget to come back?"

"No. No. Certainly not. She's a very serious woman, Lee. She's not the kind to go off on a dirty weekend anywhere, much less forget to come back."

"Do you think she might have gone to see Omar Rashid?"

"I don't know. She didn't say anything about visiting the Foundation, but you could call him."

She gave me his number.

"Thanks, I will."

Nadia remembered her original question. "Lee, what has she been doing? I never heard a single question about the Foundation until Alicia asked. Now I hear questions everywhere."

"If there's nothing behind the rumors, I'm sure it will blow over."

It took me some time to calm Nadia down but, after a while, she was resigned to countering every rumor she heard.

"And see if you can find out who started the rumors."

She agreed. "We must get together, Lee. We need to catch up."

"We do," I agreed.

"I need to talk to you about Abdul," she said.

"How is he? Last time I saw him he was into heavy metal."

"I don't think that's fashionable anymore," she said vaguely. "He's going to law school in Paris next term. I worry about him, Lee. He's so young."

"He'll be all right, Nadia. There's a large Moroccan community there."

"They're all terrorists," she said.

"You know that's not true, Nadia."

She sighed. "I suppose so. Will you look after him, Lee?"

I mumbled. Just what he needed. A friend of his mother keeping tabs on him. Why else go to school abroad if not to get away from your mother?

"Oh, before you go, what can you tell me about Zeynab Bentali?"

She sounded startled. "Why?"

"I just met her. She's Alicia's attorney. Has an office across from ours. I just wondered."

"I don't know her personally. She does a lot of *pro bono* work in the slums, helping the people navigate the system, you know?"

"What's her background?" I asked.

"Why?"

Just answer the question, I thought. "I don't know why. I just have a feeling about her. I can't explain it."

"I know those feelings of yours, Lee. She's from a very distinguished legal family. Her people have been in the Fez ulema since the end of the fifteenth century."

"Andalusian?" There were a lot of refugees from Ferdinand and Isabella about that time.

"That's right. Her grandfather was the first judge appointed by King Mohammed V after we regained independence. There are no male heirs. She's the last of that line."

We signed off with the usual involved ceremony.

No matter how distinguished the Rashid family was, I needed to check the Foundation's money. It would not be the first to use its funds for things that donors didn't intend.

Chapter 20

AS USUAL I needed information. Mike Donovan was my best bet. He was Sidney's head researcher, the best in the business and no slouch as analyst, either. I switched the office chair for the ruined chair in the computer room, shoved the last of the remains of the computer aside, and booted my laptop. I needed what there was to know about Zeynab Bentali, Sam Glover, Omar Rashid and his Foundation. The brothel violence. All ASAP, of course. I would have to buy him a bottle of single malt when this was over. I would do the Foundation's money myself. It's what I do.

According to its website, the Rashid Foundation did exactly what Nadia said it did—cared for street boys, put them in approved schools for training or as apprentices with artisans, and got them jobs when they finished training. The names of the schools where they place boys were listed, with links to the schools' websites. Those websites listed the King and Queen, his brother, sisters, and other royals as directors. Princess Lalla Miriam served on several of the boards. When I Googled some of the other names, I came up with a list of men and some women so elite that it made my nose bleed. I supposed that some of them might be funneling money to terrorists, but it looked unlikely. Morocco was not Saudi Arabia, where members of the royal family knew the Bin Laden family personally and staked Al Qaeda with no apparent objection from the King. Besides, Alicia had asked specifically about the Rashid Foundation.

The Foundation's primary account was a checking account in the Banque de Lyon since the days of the Protectorate. They kept only a small amount on deposit. The checks were mostly made out to cash, but the sums were small, probably for payroll and buying office supplies. There were larger checks made out to the approved schools for taking boys. There was also a small drawing account in the Rissani branch of the Banque Populaire, topped up monthly. The monthly sums were pretty stable, although for the last three months, larger than usual sums had been drawn. That account was probably for the support of the Rashids who took care of the tomb and *zawiya* near Rissani. The larger sums were probably for upkeep of the buildings. I made a note to find out.

Six months of activity showed deposits to the checking account from maturing certificates of deposit in a number of banks, including some online ones. When one CD matured, the money was deposited into the current account, which was not entirely used up before another matured. The certificates were timed so that one matured every month. That way they didn't have a lot of idle money in the checking account. It was an admirably smooth operation, put together by somebody who knew what he was doing.

The money from the estate and the donations to the Foundation would be the source of the money invested in the certificates of deposit. There was nothing unusual in the activity of the primary account, except for the larger deposits in the Rissani account. No large checks to unknown payees, no wire transfers to distant banks.

There were accounts with two brokerages, both French, which probably held investments of surplus funds or the Rashid money from Protectorate days. I'd see to them later. It was hard to imagine cleaner financial records, and I doubted if the investment accounts would show anything different. If Omar Rashid was financing terrorists, he was doing it off the Foundation books.

After lunch I started looking at the investment accounts and found another clean whistle. These guys were beginning to annoy me. Could any books be so clean? I was e-mailing Mike to dig deeper, when there was a knock on the door. Getting to be Grand Central Station, the office was. I opened the door and saw a Royal Guard standing as if he had a poker up his spine. Gorgeous guy, tall and a little darker than most. Saluting with a white-gloved hand, he presented me with an envelope bearing the royal crest. Since he stood waiting, I gathered that a response was expected. In a fine copperplate script, in an exceedingly correct formal style, somebody whose signature I could not read invited me to tea at the Palace.

"There is a car," he said in careful English.

"No time to wash my hands?" I asked.

"There is a car," he repeated. That seemingly exhausted his English.

I went into the computer room and hastily ditched the pistol and holster in a drawer in the workstation. Somehow I thought it would be regarded as unfriendly to try to take a gun into the Palace. I stashed my pack there too and was closing the door when I remembered the new lock. I shifted the gun to the safe and locked the computer room door.

"There is a car," he said reproachfully.

So I went to the Palace without a chance to pee or comb my hair. Palaces are like that. Hurry up! The wait would probably come later. He ushered me down the stairs and out to where a driver was restraining a black limousine with a small and tasteful royal crest on the door.

Conducting me into the back seat, he climbed in—no, he *inserted* himself elegantly beside me. I surreptitiously stroked the gray velvet upholstery, pretending that I rode in such luxury every day. Right. In my blue jeans and boots. We slid through the city, traffic slipping by on both sides as if the car was the prow of a ship. I was reminded of the middle bridge in the Forbidden City in Beijing. The Palace is not a single building like European palaces. It is a group of low buildings, each having its own purpose. After entering the compound, we drove slowly to a small square building and stopped under its porte-cochere.

The guard escorted me along halls over-decorated in the French manner, tapped once on a pair of doors, and opened them for me with a flourish. I stepped into a cozy little parlor about two hundred yards square. The elegant gent who had received a report from Driss the day before watched me walk the distance to a conversation group of settees and tables. In my blue jeans and boots. The son of a bitch would intimidate me, would he? My Scots Irish many-greats grandfather, mustered out of the revolutionary war army in 1784, whispered in my ear, "Girl, don't let me down." And I didn't. The Exquisite rose at my approach and bowed. I presented my hand, palm down for kissing not for shaking. He shot an appraising glance at me and bent over it.

Chapter 21

WE SEATED OURSELVES on a pair of Louis the Something-or-Other settees facing each other over a low table.

"Ms. Carruthers," he said.

I stiffened my spine. He knew my name, but he didn't offer his. OK, if that was the way he wanted to play it. No name, no pack drill.

A minion wheeled a tea cart up to the table.

"China or India," the minion murmured in a Thames-bred accent, vowels all carefully swallowed.

"China, please," I replied. "No lemon."

The butler handed me my tea in a delicate cup. Sevres? Probably. I could crush it with one hand. I didn't. The gent took China with lemon, and the butler provided each of us with a dainty plate holding three small triangular sandwiches. Was that Gentlemen's Relish I saw? I took a sip of my tea and, glancing at him over the rim of the cup, said, "Ah. Lao Tzu's tea, Dragon Well." I took another sip. "It is said to have been the favorite of Mao Zedong." I put the cup and saucer on the table in front of me before the cup gave me away by rattling in the saucer. I took one of the minute sandwiches, took a small bite—it was

Gentleman's Relish—and placed the rest back on the plate. Leaning back in the settee, I crossed my feet at the ankles, no easy feat in boots, and clasped my hands loosely in my lap in Miss Porter's inimitable style. I left the next serve to him.

"I hope you are finding your visit pleasant?"

He knew I had been bloodied by the bomb.

"I've always found Fez an agreeable city," I answered, "Although I must say I found yesterday morning's events a bit unsettling."

He conspicuously ignored the unpleasantness. "I seem to remember that you have been here before."

"Yes, I opened the Fez office of Femme Aid and worked here for some time."

"And have you found it changed?" he asked, ever the host to the traveler.

"Except for being more crowded, very little that I can see has changed, except for the slums, which have only gotten worse."

He put his tea cup in the table and sat back on the settee. "I believe one of your employees has disappeared?"

Now we get to it. "Yes, the manager of the Fez office has not been seen in two weeks. We fear for her safety," I answered, putting it mildly.

He nodded and tapped a well-shod toe. "I believe she was asking questions before she disappeared."

"I believe she was," I answered neutrally.

"About the Rashid Foundation."

I nodded. "Among other things."

"You must know that Omar Rashid is above suspicion."

I looked a question.

"He attended the Palace School with His Majesty."

As good a character reference as you were likely to get in Morocco. I nodded.

"Even though Sidi Omar be innocent, it is still possible that someone else in the Foundation who has not such . . .

an . . . impeccable character might use the Foundation for . . . unlawful ends."

He frowned and rose. "I regret that you suffered inconvenience yesterday," he said stiffly.

I rose, too. "I'm sure the forty people who were killed were much more inconvenienced than I was."

My Guard returned to escort me out, but I soon discovered that we were not returning the way that we had come. As we walked, the corridors got narrower and less elegantly furnished. Down a flight of utilitarian stairs, we entered a hall in painted cinderblock, and I began to get nervous. They didn't do oubliettes any more did they? Besides being the Commander of the Faithful, Mohammed VI was the absolute ruler of Morocco, so his servants could do anything they wanted to. The Guard opened a door and thrust me into a small square room with no windows and a table and two chairs on a concrete floor. I turned around as the door closed.

I took the chair facing the door and sat down to wait. A large brown stain on the wall to my right caught my attention. It was in the shape of Asia, and it looked like dried blood. The peninsula that was Viet Nam looked fresh. Just a little motivator. I shuddered and imagined myself thrown against that wall hard enough to leave a blood stain. Subjects with an imagination had the hardest time in an interrogation and were possibly the easiest to break. The interrogator didn't actually have to do anything. He just had to give a little indication of what he *could* do.

No rubber hoses, no thumb screws, no car batteries were in evidence. So far so good. No threat yet except the bloodstain. I sat there for an hour and a half, long enough for them to think I was sufficiently softened up. By that time, I felt fairly soft. I wondered what the topic of conversation would be.

Why had questions about the Rashid Foundation rung bells with Palace Security? Not just because Omar Rashid was a pal of the King. That was too simple. They don't teach conspiracy theory at the Farm, but if you hang around long enough, it rubs off on you. Analysts have to take everything into consideration, even the wildest ideas. Who would have thought a few Arab terrorists could bring down the World Trade Center?

What was the wildest thing I could think of? That Omar Rashid was laundering money for terrorists at the instruction of the King?

I ran my mind over what I knew of Mohammed VI's attitude toward jihadis. So far as I knew, his agents sought them out and arrested them. The court system threw them in the jug and mostly forgot about them. That probably radicalized some of their fellow inmates. The IRA built membership like that. So did the old Russian revolutionaries. The anti-jihad climate in Morocco was so fierce that Moroccans who wanted to take part had to go abroad.

His view of Salafist theology? He might be descended from the Prophet, but he showed no desire to return Islam to the seventh century.

The old King, Hassan II, had harassed and imprisoned conservative religious leaders, men who did not necessarily espouse the Salafist ideology, but who challenged him in any way. Sheikh Yassine spent years in and out of jail and in and out of mental institutions for proclaiming that the King had no right to call himself Commander of the Faithful because he had not been confirmed by the Fez ulema. He was nothing if not persistent. He went inside. He came back out and said the same thing. He went back inside and emerged to repeat his charge.

Mohammed VI, however, had appeared to take an easier line when he came to the throne. The Palace still controlled staffing of the mosques, however, and an imam who spoke out of turn was likely to be out of a job. The Sheikh was let out of jail for the last time and put under house arrest instead.

Why would the King want to support terrorists?

Eventually a stocky man with grizzled hair and eyebrows entered, threw a file on the table, and sat down. He's been watching too much television. He sat, unmoving, looking at me for a while. A good technique. After a while you wanted to confess to something—anything—just to break the silence. I waited passively and tried to control my breathing, my feet flat on the floor and my hands clasped in my lap. After a while he gave it up.

"So, Miss Carruthers. How long have you worked for the CIA?"

Chapter 22

I JUMPED, AND he saw it. If that file was mine and he'd read any of it, he would know that I did. I stared at him.

"Come, come, Miss Carruthers. We know you work for the CIA. How long have you worked for them?"

Baseline question. I leaned forward earnestly.

"I work for Femme Aid, an NGO which aids women in distress."

"Our sources say different."

"Your sources are incorrect."

"You have been in Fez before?"

I decided to stop talking. I sat passively and looked at him. He looked back.

"You have come here from Paris," he said. "Why?"

I sat silent, making my breathing deep enough and long enough to work, I hoped, but not long and deep enough for him to see. We sat silently for five minutes by my count.

"You are associated with the man who blew himself up in the metal workers souk yesterday."

I let the words slide by me. I wondered what Driss had told them. Driss was obviously the source of the information that I worked for the Agency. Driss or Hakim.

Nobody else knew. He concluded that I was involved because I told Driss that I had seen a man in a long coat before the bomb went off?

"Who are your contacts within the Pure Warriors of Islam? Come, Miss Carruthers, it will go easier for you if you tell me. Who are your contacts?"

More silence.

"They have foreign support. French support. Muslim immigrants in Paris."

Maybe, but probably not. If I was right about the jihadi naming practice, those who had international agendas gave themselves names in international languages: the French *Groupe Salafiste pour la Prédication et le Combat*, GSPC, morphed into Al Qaeda in the Islamic Maghreb. English, without even bothering with French. I'm sure I could find some AQIM members in Paris if I went looking. Those with only local ambitions gave themselves Arabic names. The Pure Warriors of Islam had an Arabic name, but it was particularly infelicitous. The English didn't scan very well, either.

"Who are your contacts?"

I continued mute. We went around a few more times. I was getting tired by then. Fortunately, he decided to go away and let me simmer for a while. He took my watch with him.

You want to know how many seconds there are in an hour? Thirty-six hundred. Count 'em sometime when you've got an hour to spare. After thirty-six hundred and forty-two seconds, the door opened to disclose another man, this one with the round head of the Sub-Saharan African and a grim face marked by smallpox scars. He slapped the file down on the table, and we started again.

"How long have you worked for the CIA?" He had a brutal voice to go with his brutal face.

"I work for Femme Aid, an NGO that helps women in distress," I replied.

"Our sources say you work for the CIA."

"Your sources are wrong."

I liked to vary my answers so the guy transcribing the tape of the interview won't go to sleep typing the same thing over and over. I wished he'd change his questions so I could find out what was really bothering them.

"Who are your contacts with the Pure Warriors of Islam?"

Silence. I wondered if they would try something other than questions. He looked like the type. Would they actually harm a CIA officer? I didn't know anything to tell them if I wanted to.

"Who are your contacts?"

Silence.

"You are associated with the man who blew himself up in the metal workers souk yesterday. Who are your contacts?"

Two sentences. Was this progress?

"Who are your contacts? They have foreign support. French support. Support from Muslim immigrants in Paris."

"You have come here from Paris. Why?"

I looked at him.

When he left, they turned out the lights. The back and forth, the chatting, the sounds from the hall ceased. I was alone in a dark cosmos, and nobody knew where I was. I sat there in the dark and felt the walls closing in. The walls with the bloodstains. I breathed deeply. I could hear them move. Soon they would crush me. Nonsense. I shook myself. The walls moved closer. My breaths came faster. I fought to control them. My heart pounded. I put my head on the table and breathed. The walls would crush the table first, and then they would crush me. I got up and began to pace. Anything to escape the walls. I touched a wall. I turned and paced the other direction and touched a wall. I turned and counted the paces to the other wall. And back. Ten times. The walls were not moving. Unless the other two were. I walked along the wall to a corner and turned it.

I marched across the room and ran into the table. I went back to the wall to the corner with the other wall. I marched along that wall counting paces. Back. Forward. Back. The walls were not moving.

Tell that to my brain.

I walked back and forth, turned the corner and walked the other direction, getting more and more upset. They wouldn't really hurt me, would they? Morocco was one of our oldest allies. The oldest, in fact. The Sultan of Morocco had been the first to recognize the independence of the United States, but who would know what happened in the Palace basement? Maybe even the King wouldn't know. My body would not be hard to dispose of. A body in the river, throat slit or possibly raped. Women tourists would go into No Go areas after dark, no matter how many times they were warned.

I counted turns. I was on the fifty-third when the light came back on. A new man. They were deep in pitchers and didn't have to tire anybody. This one was tall, thin, and morose. He looked at me sadly. I was a recalcitrant child who had been sent to the principal's office. He sat down quietly and placed the file on the table. I had an insane desire to snatch the file and see what was in it. If they were as good as I thought they were, they had records of every time I had been in Fez, maybe every time I had been anywhere. With a good IT man, they could find out the name of my last lover and my bra size. I know. It's what I do.

The questions were drearily the same. So was my silence. Then a new question.

"Why was Alicia Harmon asking questions about the Rashid Foundation?"

Alicia Harmon this time and the Foundation. Are we getting to the heart of the matter at last? Did I twitch when I heard Alicia's name? The principal switched back to the old line.

"Why are you here? Who are your contacts in the Pure Warriors of Islam?"

He kept at that for a while. Have you ever tried to stand mute for several hours? It's a strain.

He departed, and they turned off the lights again. I was alone again with the darkness. So tired. I put my head down on the table and drifted off to sleep. Just as I had gotten well asleep, the lights came on again, and I jerked awake. Nobody came, and I sat looking at the door. I decided I could sleep in the light, so I put my head down on the table and dozed off. I woke up hearing a noise. It was dark again. We played that game for a while. In one of the asleep periods, I jerked awake at the sound of the door slamming against the wall. I saw the Hulk outlined against the dim light in the hall. It was all I could do not to scream. When I get home, I'm going to scream my head off, I vowed. The Hulk switched the light on and was transformed into my first interrogator, the burly guy. He looked quite rested. He slapped the file on the table and started over again.

"Who are your contacts in the Pure Warriors of Islam?"

He went through the litany quickly, as bored with the questions as I. Halfway through the list, he slipped in a new one.

"Where is Alicia Harmon?"

It was all I could do not to say, "That's what I want to know."

He handed me my watch and smiled.

"Nobody knows you're here, you know."

Chapter 23

IT WAS ONE in the morning when they dropped me in a quarter of the new city I didn't recognize. The abrupt ending of the interrogation confused me. They tipped their hand with their questions and got zilch from me, but their questions were off the mark even if I had been talking. I had no contacts with the Pures and did not know why Alicia had been asking questions about the Rashid Foundation. So far as I could tell, the Foundation was straight as an arrow. More research was indicated. More research is always indicated.

I considered the juxtaposition of "Where is Alicia Harmon?" and "Nobody knows you're here, you know."

Did they know where Alicia Harmon was?

Did they have Alicia Harmon?

Why would they want her?

I walked slowly along the street where they had dumped me, knowing that it would eventually intersect with a boulevard, and I would know where I was. It was so late that there wasn't even a cat on the street. I felt vulnerable without my gun. Late-night streets are no place for a woman alone in any city. I could see lights ahead. Finally. A boulevard. Just then somebody grabbed my arm, and I turned and swung automatically. I heard an "oof," and knew that I had connected. I could see the silhouette of my assailant then. A thin guy. I could smell him, too. He smelled unwashed. Very unwashed. A street person? He reached for a better hold on me, and I went for his eyes. He drew back, and I whacked his throat. I heard a rattle in his throat as he tried to breathe. I kicked him in the stomach for good measure and ran. I turned into the wide boulevard and found myself on the Avenue Mohammed es-Saloui across from the Public Gardens, another good place to get mugged that time of the night. I jogged on and eventually came to a roundabout I recognized. The apartment house was nearby, but I had to go to the office. My stuff was there. I was breathless from jogging. Let's face it. I had been out of breath for several blocks. Only the fear that somebody was behind me had kept me going for that long. I stopped and bent over to catch my breath. A passing car slowed, and I braced myself, but it drove on. I finally got to the office building, and it had never looked so good.

I dragged myself wearily up the stairs to the office. Nobody threw himself out of the door at me, which I took as a good sign. I replaced the holster on my hip and tucked the pistol into it. With the pack and the laptop, I was ready for home and bed. I walked as wearily down the steps as I had up them and out into the night, trying to remember where I had parked the car. I saw it half a block away and trudged toward it. I was so tired that I didn't have two brain cells to rub together.

The street had that late-night feel when everybody who was going to die had already died. It was a short walk to the car. When I reached it, a dark form came out from behind it and grabbed me. Seriously? Again? He was trying to get at my backpack. I fell back on my assailant and pushed up into his chin with my head. He let go of me. Before he could get a good grip on me again, I spun around and whacked him in the head with the laptop. I heard a satisfying "thunk." He grabbed the strap of the laptop case, pulled it away from me, and shoved me to the ground. He turned and ran, taking the laptop with him. My thunks need work, I thought. I wondered if the Palace had muggers on its payroll. What did anybody want with my laptop? Why wasn't he out mugging tourists?

I heard a vehicle engine start, and a white Range Rover swept past me. Putting off shaking for later, I got in the car and followed. We were the only vehicles on the road, so it wasn't difficult to follow him on the wide streets of the Ville Nouvelle, but when he left that for thirteenth-century Fez el-Jdid, the King's Quarter, it began to get hairy. The streets were dark and narrow, and I didn't know them, at least not as well as my assailant did. I lost him somewhere in the Mellah, the old Jewish Quarter, and it took me a while to get out of the tangle of streets and back to the Ville Nouvelle.

The apartment house wasn't hard to find but a parking space was.

As I wearily stumbled toward home and bed, I passed the mouth of an alley, and this time, tired and encumbered as I was, there was no way I could fight. I pulled the pistol from its holster and held it down beside me. Anybody who touched me was going to get shot, and damn the consequences. I ran to the apartment house door as fast as I could. I had lived a lifetime since I climbed those stairs two days ago. I felt old and cold. The flat smelled stale, so I turned on the air conditioner to move some fresh air in. Pack on the dining table. I had seen a jar of tea bags on the shelf. Alicia ran to herbal tea, which I normally thought tasted like grass, but, in the absence of gin, a cup of chamomile and mint tea might do, so I nuked a mug of water and dropped a tea bag into it. As I sat on the divan watching the tea steep, my hands began to tremble. Bombs and Palace interrogation rooms will do that to you. The tea was ready before my hands were quite finished shaking. I threw the tea bag at a brass bowl on the table in front of me, missing it by several inches. When I lifted the mug to my lips, it rattled against my teeth. I put the mug down and leaned back against the pillows, trying to calm my spirit.

Slowly I gained enough control of my hands and my breathing that I could begin to drink the tea. It soothed me a little. I closed my eyes and ran the time I had been in Fez through my mind like a film. The death threats and an anonymous phone call before I could unpack my toothbrush. The attack on the house in the medina. What could the girls know that would be worth snatching them? OK, maybe they could identify somebody, but they never went anywhere. Who could they see?

Their attackers and the man in the coat. Did he give them something? If they just spoke to him, did they know him? Were they linked to the terrorists? Had they seen me following them? Was that why I lost them? And what did that say about what the girls knew?

I made another cup of tea and continued. Who destroyed the office computer? He took the hard drive. He didn't need to smash everything. Or did he? Suppose he tried to open Alicia's files and found them encrypted. Did he smash everything to hide the fact that he had taken the hard drive or just out of spite? Was that why they took my laptop? Because they found Alicia's files encrypted and thought I would have them in my laptop? If they couldn't get into them, how could I?

The bomb. My mind shied away from the bomb and its aftermath.

The Rashid Foundation. Why did Alicia think they were laundering money for terrorists? And the Palace. What had they wanted? The only clue they had let slip was the question about Alicia and her interest in the Rashid Foundation. The Exquisite was disturbed by questions about the Rashid Foundation, so the Exquisite gave Omar Rashid the best character reference a man could have in Morocco. Or was it a threat? Did the boys in the basement have the same agenda as he did? Who else could have ordered me detained?

My mind circled back to the bomb and shied away again. I grabbed it firmly and hauled it back. My hands began trembling again, and the trembling was threatening to spread. I had to get a grip on myself. I had to look that horror in the face if I was ever going to sleep quietly again. Being bombed is like losing your virginity. Nothing is ever the same again.

I sat on the floor in the lotus position and struggled to control my trembling and my racing mind. Struggling is not the path to meditation. I sat back on the divan. I tried to relax, but struggling didn't help there either. I took a deep breath and gradually eased every muscle in my body one by one, starting with my toes. It took a while. I wondered if I was going to have to do that every night before I went to sleep.

I started again. A long list of things I didn't know. What did I know? That I'd been hot ever since I got to town. The only reason I could think of was that I was looking for Alicia Harmon, and she had been asking questions about brothels and money laundering before she disappeared. I took the tea mug to the kitchen and washed it. I took a long shower and put myself to bed, the familiar little things adding to the eventual peace that allowed me to sleep.

I don't think I'd been asleep long when I heard something. Something at the door? I listened and heard wood splintering. I scooped up the Glock from the floor beside the bed, racked a round into the chamber, and ran into the living room. The door had been kicked open, and a man was inside, the gun in his hand glinting in the dim light from the hall. I aimed, fired four times, and watched as he fell. Another man was silhouetted right behind him. Moving forward, he asked, "What is going on?"

"Stop!" I yelled. "Who are you?"

He had the good sense to stop.

"It's Sam. Sam Glover."

"Then put your arm inside the door *very carefully*, and turn on the light."

He did as I said. When the light came on he stared. The man I had shot was a short, swarthy guy dressed in miscellaneous clothes. Nothing distinctive about him. A miscellaneous man. I kicked the gun he had been holding away. No pulse in the carotid artery. He was comprehensively dead, and so he should be with four nine-millimeter hollow points in his center. I leaned down and nudged his wallet out of his back pocket and used my forefinger to open it. No ID. Using both forefingers to open the wallet, I discovered that it was empty. I sat back on my heels to consider the sanitized man lying dead on my living room floor. I heard a gasp and looked up. It was Ibrahim. He couldn't decide whether to be more shocked at the dead man or me. He decided on me and turned his gaze away. Sam Glover was still staring. I looked down and realized that I didn't have a stitch on.

Chapter 24

I REALLY MUST learn to wear a nightgown when I'm out of town. Retreating to the bedroom, I stashed the gun in the chest of drawers under Alicia's teddies and returned wearing a caftan and carrying my cell phone. Sam Glover cleared his throat.

"I've called the police," he said.

I nodded and turned the dead man over to photograph him.

Ibrahim was still in distress.

"Lalla Lee, I will not have this in my house!" he exclaimed.

"Ibrahim, it is not my fault that somebody broke into my flat!"

I glared at him. It was unkind of me. I knew he had been scandalized to his very core, but somebody kicking his way into my apartment in the middle of the night tended to make me testy.

Two cars of police arrived shortly, flooding the apartment with big bodies and bigger voices. One spoke to Ibrahim, who said something and looked over his shoulder at me. The cop took him out onto the landing to talk to him. I'll bet he got an earful. Why had a dozen uniforms responded to a call? They stood around talking loudly, and eventually I was pressed into the kitchen by the size of them. They cut the noise down after a plainclothes man arrived. He traced me to the kitchen, where I sat on a stool, my hands shaking. With a grimace, he put my gun on the table. Already searched the bedroom, had they? Apparently it was not the done thing for a woman to have a pistol in Fez.

"All right," he said, pulling up the other stool. "What happened here?"

I put my hands under my arms to stop them from shaking. "I heard him kick the door down. I shot him."

It seemed simple, but he wasn't satisfied. He asked again. I answered again. What was it with Moroccan cops? Were they deaf?

"Who is he?"

"I don't know."

"You photographed him." I could see that he was considering confiscating my cell. Kaftans have no pockets, so I put it in my lap and covered it with my hands.

"I thought somebody might know him."

"Who?"

"I don't know. Somebody." That sounded thin, even to me.

He moved on. "Why would he want to break in here?"

"Robbery?" I replied. It was not a convincing reason.

He looked disgusted. "He climbs four flights of stairs and kicks in your door to rob you? When he could just go down the street and mug a tourist? Why are you here?" he asked, branching out.

I kept it simple. I explained about Femme Aid and told him about being sent to find Alicia Harmon.

"That's not enough to explain a dead man in your living room."

"It certainly isn't," I said with a show of indignation.

"Get dressed. You'll need to come with us."

I stepped out of the kitchen and pressed my way to the bedroom, where two bulky uniforms were standing around talking. Time to ask for a phone call.

"I'd like to make a phone call, please."

They got the detective.

"The embassy can wait until morning. They won't do anything at this hour anyway."

Which is why you're taking me downtown now, I thought.

"Not the embassy. Driss Bouchta."

That startled him. Driss wasn't a cop, but they knew him. He gave me a flat look.

"Bouchta?"

I tell you they're deaf. "Bouchta."

He weighed the benefits of taking me down to the station right then against the possible ire of Driss if he did. Then he shrugged. Driss was not pleased at being awakened at that hour, and for a moment he couldn't figure out who I was.

"Sorry to wake you, Driss," I said to his grumble. "I need you."

More grumbling.

"Driss, I just shot a man in the apartment. *I need you.*"

"It can wait until the morning."

"No it can't. You need to see this guy."

"Let me talk to whoever's there," he said groggily.

The detective told him what he knew and gave my phone back.

"So why can't this wait until morning?"

"Driss, *you need to see this guy before they take him away.*"

His sigh would have blown down a small building.

"OK. I'm on my way. Let me talk to the lieutenant." I gave the lieutenant the phone and heard him agree to what Driss said several times. He closed the phone.

"Get dressed," he snapped and handed it to me.

I found it was easier to face a room full of cops when I was wearing blue jeans. Driss wasn't long in coming. He looked at the corpse and nodded to the waiting men to take it away. I took him in the bedroom.

"All right, what's this all about?" he demanded.

"Driss, I swear to you I will never set foot in Morocco again. Since I arrived I have been threatened, bombed, attacked, hauled off to the Palace to be interrogated by some heavies, and now this! This creep kicked his way into my apartment!"

He was almost distracted by the Palace heavies.

"What has the Palace . . . ?" He changed his mind. "Never mind. Tell me what happened."

"The lieutenant already told you," I said.

"Tell me again," he replied.

I told him again. He asked me again.

"Driss, do you have a short attention span? There is nothing more to tell. *He kicked his way into the apartment, and I shot him!*" I was close to shouting.

"OK, OK. Why did you call me in the middle of the night except as a character witness?"

"Did they tell you that he was carrying no ID?"

"So?"

"And had nothing else on him?"

"You searched him?"

"Yeah, I did. His wallet was empty. He had nothing else on him."

"So?" he repeated.

"Driss, he's one of the guys I was following yesterday before the bomb went off."

Chapter 25

"YOU'RE SURE?"

"Driss, I might have called you just to protect me from the cops, but why should I tell you he's one of the men I followed if he wasn't? Why would one of them break into my apartment?"

"Maybe they saw you following them and wondered why?"

"Having burned me somewhere in the medina, they doubled back through the debris of the bombing and followed me—where? We went to the house in the medina together. Perhaps they know you?"

"Of course not," he said stiffly.

"If they're associated with the Pure Warriors, they may very well know you by sight. We were still together at the Bab Bou Jeloud. Then having decided that I was important for whatever reason, they followed me to my office, because that's where I went, where I stayed until that Guard picked me up and took me to the Palace. Maybe they followed me to the Palace and panicked at what I could tell them? Which was what, by the way? What I know you could put in a thimble and have room for your finger."

I glowered at him.

"Don't glare at me," he said. "I can't see any link between you and the men from the medina."

"Nor can I. So what was he doing here with a gun in his hand? And how did he find out where I'm staying?"

"Followed you home."

"From the office at one a.m.?"

"What were you doing at the office at one a.m.?"

"That's where I found my way after the Palace dumped me in the middle of nowhere," I said bitterly. "I had to go there to get my stuff."

"Palace?"

"Palace. Did you rat me out, Driss?"

"What does that mean?"

"They wanted to know how long I had worked for the CIA. Only two people in Morocco know that I work for the Agency, you and Hakim. So which of you told them?"

"Why would I tell anybody that?"

"Yeah. You just keep the information handy in case you need to blackmail me," I retorted.

"Why would I want to blackmail you?" he repeated, exasperated.

"I don't know. For the fun of it? Look, Driss, I work for an intelligence agency. Intelligence agencies blackmail people."

"Why should I want to blackmail you?"

I was mad by this time. "I don't know. To turn me into a penetration agent? I could tell you all the secrets the Agency has."

He laughed at me. "You have access to—what did you call it?—enough information to put in a thimble and still have room for a finger. You think we don't know what they run through this country?"

"Yes, I do," I said hotly. "But you don't care about the slave trade, do you?"

"We don't need to," he retorted. "You keep us updated on that, don't you? Why are we fighting?"

"Because we're both tired. I'm sorry. Let me tell you about the Palace so we can both go back to bed. That terribly handsome chap from the Palace you reported to in the medina yesterday made me an offer I couldn't refuse. He sent a Guardsman to collect me and take me to the Palace for tea."

"Khalil el Hadid?" he asked.

"He didn't introduce himself, although he seemed to know all about me. He gave me a cup of China tea and a plate of terribly cute little sandwiches. I took a bite out of one."

He sat up straight on the stool and became intelligence officer, instead of my friend Driss Bouchta.

"Lee, you're not taking this seriously."

"Driss, dear, I assure you I am taking this quite seriously. Between 4:30 p.m. and 1 a.m., I was at the Palace, first with the elegant Mr. Hadid, if that's his name, and then being grilled by the boys in the basement until after midnight."

"But what . . . ?"

"Don't ask me. Actually, do ask me. Hadid wanted me to know that Omar Rashid is a Friend of the King. Downstairs they wanted to know about my connections with the Pure Warriors. Repeatedly. For hours. They also wanted to know why I was asking about the Rashid Foundation."

"Why *were* you asking about the Rashid Foundation?"

"Didn't I tell you that Alicia thought somebody at the Foundation was laundering money for terrorists?"

"That's right, you did. They didn't . . ." He looked slightly anxious. The boys in the basement were tougher than his lot? Or was it because I was a friend?

"Didn't lay a hand on me, thank you. Nothing any reasonable adult could complain about. Perfect gents. Not a water-board or a car battery in sight. They did leave me in the dark a lot, and I think they were contemplating introducing rats to the room, but they suddenly tired of the game and let me go. Driss, what does the Palace have to do with any of this?"

"Unless you haven't told me everything . . ."

"Driss, I haven't had time to get into any trouble. I've barely had time to search the apartment and the office between threats, attacks, and bombs. I tell you, I've been hot ever since I got here, and I haven't got the faintest idea why. To top it all off, some guy stole my laptop."

"Stole your laptop?"

"After the Palace dumped me, I got my stuff from the office and was walking to my car when a guy grabbed my laptop and ran."

"Why?"

"How do I know?" But I did know. They took the hard drive from the office computer and found they couldn't get into the files, so they thought they'd see if I had them. I decided that Driss didn't need to know that.

It was quiet now in the living room. The cops and the body and all of the scientists had gone, and peace reigned, if you didn't count the front door hanging by one hinge.

"You're not staying here tonight," Driss told me.

"I wouldn't dream of it. I wouldn't sleep, much less dream. I may never stay here again. Ibrahim was outraged at the disturbance. As if I invite men to break into the apartment once a week and twice on Sundays. He was angry with me for staying here in the first place. He regards it as Alicia's place. Now I have introduced not only a dead man and a pool of blood that somebody's going to have to clean up, but police. *Police!* And this a respectable house. Et cetera." I stuffed my hands in my pockets and slouched on the divan. "And that lieutenant took my gun. I need a gun, Driss." That last was too plaintive for my taste. "I would be meat cooling on a tray in the morgue if I hadn't had a gun tonight. I certainly didn't invite him for a drink. He came to kill me."

He took my gun from his pocket and gave it to me.

"Don't shoot anybody else."

I was about to make a rude remark when his cell rang. He checked the caller ID and groaned. He looked resigned when he answered it. After a few squawks from the caller, he sat up straight.

"What? Are you sure?"

The caller told him just how certain he was several times. Driss cut sharply across him.

"Don't tell anybody. I'll be right there."

"Get your things together. I've got to go."

"But . . ."

"The man you shot? The man you say you followed in the medina yesterday?"

I nodded.

"He worked for the Palace."

Chapter 26

DRISS WAITED WHILE I packed my stuff. I finished and reached to turn off the lamp on the table by the bed. When I did, I turned over a jug with pens and a pair of scissors in it. Stooping to pick them up. I found a flash drive among them. I turned it over in my hand. Funny place to put a flash drive. I tucked it into my jeans pocket and turned out the light.

He walked me to my car carrying my suitcase and my pack, tucked me and my things in my car, and hurried away.

I needed a safe place to stay. Where could I go in the middle of the night? A European hotel would be the best bet. I set course for the group of hotels on Mohammed V Boulevard. I was tired and drove on autopilot, so it was a while before I noticed headlights behind me. I sped up. They sped up. I slowed down and turned left. They slowed down and turned left. I was being followed. They must have been waiting for a second chance at me after the cops went away.

I ran down the limited number of safe places I could go at that hour and decided to go to Kemal's. It was a bit late even for a pipe bar, but a Guardsman or three would probably still be smoking. The area behind the Guards' Barracks was iffy in the daytime, since off duty Guards cruised the area looking for action. At night it was worse, and a dinky pistol, however nine-millimeter it was, was not going to impress them much, but the fact that I was European might.

I spent no time in evasive action, I just drove as fast as the road would allow. I saw Kemal's place was still lighted and rocking. I slammed up to the curb and jumped out. I was running for the bar when a vehicle double-parked beside me, and two men jumped from it. One of them grabbed me by the shoulders, and the other, quite mistakenly, tried to grab my legs. I kicked out as viciously as I could, missing any vital parts but giving him a good crack on the thigh, all the while yelling my head off. I sagged against the man holding my shoulders and strained up sharply. I heard a rewarding thunk. My thunks are getting better with practice. The first man was almost upon me, but I had time to draw. I was off balance when I fired, but I pinked him in the shoulder. Both of them were bleeding when they jumped into their vehicle and pulled away.

Men and some working girls poured out of the buildings along the street, attracted by the fracas. I backed against the nearest wall, prepared to shoot, although what good that would be against a mob of soldiers I couldn't think.

I heard salvation at hand. "Back off," a man yelled at the crowd and joined me at the wall. "Back off!" It was Kemal, and I have never been so glad to see anybody in my life. Despite Muslim custom, he put his arm around me, and the crowd began to disperse.

He didn't seem surprised to see me. I wondered what would surprise him. He looked at the sidewalk. "Is that blood I see?" he asked.

"It is. I broke one's nose and winged the other," I responded.

"Always were a violent girl," he said as he escorted me into the bar.

Kemal's place was a pipe bar, like Abdullah's, a place to smoke water pipes, tobacco and kif, as usual, being the major substances. The men in the room stared as he ushered me across me room and through a bead curtain. Down the corridor was a basic office—a desk, two chairs, and a filing cabinet.

I had put it off as long as I could, but once I was safe, I began to shake. I gritted my teeth, but the shaking continued. Kemal put his arms around me, and I sagged against him. He held me until the tremors stopped, and then he kissed me. He always was a good kisser.

He put me on one of the chairs. The murmur of voices from the bar had returned to normal. Live Arabic music was playing in the background. I could tell it was live, because the oud player kept getting his fingers stuck in the strings. Too much raki, I thought, which did not bode well either for his music or for a long life.

In the palate of Moroccan colors Kemal was a very light beige tending to white. He was broad-shouldered and tall. Think Omar Sharif without the mustache. Like Abdullah, Kemal was a veteran of the Royal Guards and still stood as if cast in iron. He didn't have to prove anything, which was why he could hug me in public. Like many hard men, he had a sweet smile, and the scar that ran from his eyebrow to his chin didn't contradict it. He said that he caught a saber slash in a fight while on camel patrol, and for all I know it's true.

We looked at each other. It had been at least five years since we had met.

"A gray hair here and there," I said.

"And a few pounds on me," he replied.

He clapped his hands, and Turkish coffee and Turkish delight and cold water appeared as if by magic. Dispensing with the formalities, he asked, "What was that all about?"

"I don't know. I think they may just be trying to snatch me."

"Who?"

"Perhaps the men who have Alicia Harmon? If she's still alive."

"Who is Alicia Harmon?" he asked.

"You don't know her?"

He shook his head.

"Abdullah in Rabat does. She runs the Femme Aid office."

"Perhaps she thought one disreputable pipe bar owner was enough? Why do you think somebody might have her?" he asked.

"She's been missing for almost two weeks. She's been asking questions around town about violence in the brothels, among other things."

"She has a death wish, this woman?"

"Both a death wish and a number of death threats. That's why I'm here. As soon as I got to her flat, I got a phone call from a heavy breather. Since then somebody's stolen my laptop, somebody kicked his way into the flat, and I had to shoot him, and somebody followed me here and tried to snatch me. And that doesn't count the bomb. Fez is not treating me kindly, Kemal. I need a place to stay."

He stared at me for a moment. "The bomb. You were near the bomb?"

"Next street over. Worst day of my life, so far," I said.

"Yes, it would be. The aftermath of a bomb is horrible." He spoke from experience. "I had forgotten you and your little ways, Lee." He took a sip of coffee and then a sip of water. "You can stay here. It's the last place they would think to find you."

"It's the last place they saw me."

"They're going to get through me?" he asked, offended. "In addition you get my company."

"Now that is a motivation." I smiled.

Chapter 27

"I THINK YOU need to go to bed," he said and took me and my suitcase to one of the rooms upstairs.

I looked around the room. The traditional bench around the walls and bed mats had been replaced by Western furniture, French, of course, a chest, double bed with silk canopy and spread, Louis the Something chairs upholstered in similar fabric but a tone darker. A luscious silk carpet—Isfahan?—was on the floor, instead of the wall.

The pipe bar didn't do much business until dark, but the upstairs rooms coined money in the daytime. There, Kemal offered a service much in demand in the gender-segregated world of Morocco. The back door of the bar opened to an alley across from the back doors of a beauty salon and a dressmaker. Men went into the pipe bar, ladies into one of the shops, and they met upstairs over the bar.

"Gone upscale?" I asked.

"European clients," he replied.

"Either they have imperial fantasies or a lot of money."

He grinned. "Both," he said.

"I feel unworthy of all this splendor." I laughed. I thought I had forgotten how.

Kemal was standing close behind me. I turned.

"The last time you slept here, you didn't sleep alone."

"The last time I slept here I had gone thirty or so hours without sleep and required protection."

"You require protection again."

I began to take off my T-shirt but stopped. I looked up at him. He was tall and strong, and somebody had just tried to snatch me. And I had just shot a man from the Palace. And I was cold and hungry. I reached over and began to unbutton his shirt instead. He shrugged and the shirt fell to the rug. I stepped closer and ran my hands over his shoulders and down his spine to the end. I pushed that spot and he shivered.

"I'd forgotten how lovely you are," I said.

"Men with saber scars are not lovely," he replied.

I traced the scar from his temple to his cheekbone.

"I won't tell."

"It would ruin my reputation if you did. You, however, *are* lovely."

He removed his pants and began on my shirt. I shivered in my turn. He ran his palm across my breasts and down my side. He stopped abruptly when he reached the pistol.

"Take it off!" he demanded.

"Kemal, you knew I was carrying. I just shot a man."

"I do not embrace women wearing guns," he said firmly.

Smiling, I removed the pistol and its holster and took them to the chest across the room. I bent and took off my boots. I didn't feel obliged to tell him about the knife there.

"Do you meet many?" I asked.

"Only you, lady, only you." The way he said it was peculiar. Sorrow? Acceptance? I couldn't tell.

When I turned completely around he was standing with his hands on his hips, lips tight in disapproval. His saber scar wasn't the only thing that was sexy.

I lingered uncertainly just outside his reach, suddenly shy. It had been a long time since we'd been together.

"You never used to object to the gun."

"I've forgotten you."

He stepped forward and his arms went around me. He ran his hands down my back and sides then held me back and ran them over my breasts and stomach, making me catch my breath.

"Now I remember you," he said,

He had always been a great kisser and an even better hugger. He set about proving it.

"Cold and hungry," I whispered.

He laid me on the bed, and after a while I wasn't cold.

"Hungry," I whispered again before I surrendered to sensation.

We lay back on our pillows, temporarily content. Kemal lit a cigarette and blew a smoke ring. It had been five years since I last had a cigarette, but I snatched it from his hand and took a deep drag. My lungs rebelled. When I had stopped coughing and Kemal had stopped laughing, I wiped the tears from my eyes, and he lit another cigarette.

I said, "I'm thinking of leaving the Agency."

Carefully casual he asked, "Oh? Why?"

"The territory." I pointed to the gun on the chest. "After a while it gets old. I used to set great store by the skills I have that most analysts don't acquire. Now I can count the scars, some of them physical, most of them not. I'm tired."

"What are you going to do?"

"I don't know. A friend in Boston has a small IT business. He keeps asking me to come to work with him."

Casual turned serious. "Fez has IT companies."

I looked away. "Can't stand the climate," I replied.

He reached over and turned my face toward him. "I know you too well to believe that's the reason, Lee. What is it really?"

I sighed. "Kemal, I'm tired of being called a Western whore when I walk down the street. I've spent nearly twenty years wearing a black suit and covering my hair with a scarf in deference to the sensibilities of Muslim males." I sat up in bed, the sheet falling to my lap. "I want to wear a short skirt, I want to wear a tight sweater, a bikini. Muslim men are lustful." He shifted his weight. "Lustful," I said, "And your women cover themselves from head to toe in bleak black gowns to control those lusts." I was breathing heavily, and my voice rose. I had wanted to say this, no, yell this, for a very long time. I *needed* to say it. "Why the hell can't Muslim men control their own lusts?"

Kemal jumped out of bed and swept up his clothes. He looked at me in fury before stalking out of the room, slamming the door behind him.

So much for truth in advertising, I thought and pressed the cigarette butt into an ash tray. I lay back on my pillow, flushed with the satisfaction of finally saying it, but gradually my satisfaction turned to something else. Kemal had never treated me badly. We hadn't been lovers for years, but when we were, he had always treated me with kindness, with tenderness, and, yes, with respect. His masculinity was another thing he didn't have to prove.

I began to feel guilty. Muslim men might harass any female not swathed in black, but that was no reason to take it out on Kemal. I turned over and tried to go to sleep. God knows I was tired enough. I turned back over and punched my pillow. I was cold. I pulled the quilt up. I was still cold. If I hadn't been such a pig, there would have been a warm body next to mine.

Oh hell. I thought. I'm going to have to apologize to him. I hate apologizing.

I pulled on my T-shirt and padded down the hall, trying to remember which room Kemal slept in. After a few false tries, including one room occupied by a pair of men, I found Kemal's room at the end of the hall. He was lying on his side on a bed mat under a quilt. I pulled off my shirt, slipped in behind him, and put my arm around him. He turned over on his back, lying stiffly. I was going to have to work for this one. I ran my finger down the saber scar.

"I came to apologize."

He grunted and relaxed a little.

"You have always been good to me. I shouldn't have said what I did."

He relaxed all the way and rolled over to face me.

"Please forgive me."

He put his arms around me and forgave me.

I opened my eyes at a call to prayer. The sun was high. Kemal was watching me. He kissed me.

"You taste of sleep and cinnamon."

"Cinnamon?"

"Cinnamon kisses."

It was a while before I thought to ask which call to prayer it had been.

"Noon," he said.

"Noon!" I sat up. "I have to get up! I've got a lot to do."

"Important things?" he asked and pulled me back down.

"Well . . ." I settled back down to enjoy some more cinnamon kisses. It's a flavor I don't get every day.

Chapter 28

I RAN OUT of cinnamon at breakfast.

A barefoot boy in ragged jeans brought a pot of coffee and hot milk, bread, cheese, and olives to us in the bar, and I filled the large cups three-quarters full of coffee and added hot milk. France in the morning, Turkey the rest of the day. The coffee was still too hot for me to drink. I pulled off a piece of flatbread and wrapped it around some cheese. It wasn't too hot for Kemal. He drank his thirstily and held his cup out for more. I raised my eyebrow at him as I refilled his cup. I was in danger of becoming domestic.

"What are you going to do today?" he asked as he rolled some flat bread around some cheese.

"I'm going to Madame Verney's."

"Are you out of your mind?" he asked curiously.

"I need to go to Madame Verney's, Kemal. There's something going on in the brothels of Fez."

My answer didn't please him. "And you need to know about this why?"

I told him about Alicia's interest in the brothel troubles in Rabat.

"What's been going on here?"

He rubbed his chin, and I heard a faint rasp.

"I didn't know about Rabat. Somebody new took over here, I think. Brawls, thugs breaking up the furniture, assaulting the customers and the women," he said. "Several customers were seriously injured. One died."

"When was this?" I asked.

"Oh, late May?"

"Earlier than Rabat."

"Oh, yes?" He raised an eyebrow. "Two of the madams attempted to protect their girls and had acid thrown in their faces. One lost her sight. Several of the girls disappeared. Nobody knows whether they fled or were killed. The Big Man in Fez wound up among the Merenid Tombs with his throat cut, and there wasn't any more trouble."

The Big Man's men protected the houses in Fez, for a good-sized fee.

"A cemetery again. They found the Big Man in Rabat in the Chellah."

"The Chellah!" He was outraged that somebody had gotten past the Guards at Mohammed V's mausoleum. He had guarded it himself in the past. "Brazen."

"As you say. It was earlier and worse here. Why the difference? Fez resisted, and Rabat didn't?" I asked.

He finished the coffee in the pot and called for more. "Possibly."

"Is anything known about who they are?" I asked.

"Nothing," he replied. "No one has felt inclined to ask."

"I'm not surprised. Other towns?" I asked.

"Not that I know of, but I didn't know about Rabat. The Palace doesn't like to see things like that in the newspapers."

"Rabat and Fez. That suggests a big outfit."

Both of us were on familiar terms with violence, were or had been professionally concerned with it, if you will. Whoever was doing this was hard, vicious, and very, very professional.

He agreed. "And a bad one."

"Who were the smashers?" I asked.

"Nobody anybody had ever seen before. Maybe Moroccan, maybe not. Several spoke in what one of the girls thought was an Algerian accent."

I nodded. "Once heard, never forgotten."

"She is from Constantine, so she would know. There were at least ten men in the wrecking crew. It took fewer to deal with the customers and the girls. Maybe four, five. They just waited for the customers to arrive, grabbed them, and beat them, put the boot in. The one who was killed died of a ruptured spleen. With the girls it was different. They don't go out much, you know?"

I did. The girls weren't trusted not to run away.

"Four of them were shopping with the madam as chaperone when they were attacked, acid thrown on the madam, the girls slashed. It was very bloody. The other madam got hurt trying to protect her girls inside the house during the first attack."

"The police ever catch anybody?"

He shrugged. "Who could identify them? Who *would* identify them?"

He was right. Identifying people working at that level of violence would get you dead in a hurry.

"Anybody know who they are?"

"Nobody who's willing to talk has ever seen them," he answered.

My coffee was now cold, but I drank some anyway and ate four olives.

"Madam Verney?" She ran the most exclusive brothel in town.

"Madame Verney's was the first to be attacked."

"If she surrendered the rest would follow?"

"Yes."

"What happened?"

"You know her place?"

"Not intimately," I said, smiling.

"This is not funny, Lee!"

"I never said it was, Kemal," I retorted. "I just wondered how I would come to know the place."

"It was a rhetorical question," he said stiffly. Kemal would take almost anything from me, but he had his limits.

"You know it's the most expensive in town?"

"So I've heard."

"It used to be furnished in antiques," he said.

"Antiques in a whorehouse?"

"They gave a certain elegance to the place."

"I'll bet they did."

He ignored me and pressed on. "At least downstairs. Upstairs was more . . ." He stopped.

I grinned at him. "Utilitarian?"

He ignored me again. "Now the place is furnished with similar pieces, but they are reproductions. The invaders smashed the antiques. Then they went upstairs and mistreated the girls. Some they beat. Some they raped. Gang-raped. One of the girls died."

I shuddered. The thought of rape pierces a woman's core, tears her up inside as if it had happened to her.

Kemal went behind the bar and held up a bottle of raki. I don't usually drink it for breakfast. A chill had settled over me. He poured a healthy slug into each of two glasses and handed me one. The first sip burned all the way down. The second was OK. The first had paralyzed my throat.

"Madame Verney held out?"

He nodded and poured us another small glass.

"And so did the rest of them."

"Yes. The violence spread. There were deaths, two in a place down by the dyer's souk. Some of the girls were kidnapped, and the owners had to pay a ransom if they wanted to see the girls alive. Two refused, and the girls were found in the river the next day, raped and with their throats cut."

"Ugh," I said.

He nodded. "Their girls walked off the job, saying they'd rather he shot them than be raped and have their throats cut."

"And Madame Verney's?"

"Her place was attacked a second time to emphasize the point, and the clients were beaten badly. That was when the man died. After that, she submitted, as did everyone else."

"Which is why I need to see Madame Verney."

"You think she will tell you anything?" he asked with his chin stuck so far out that you could hang a coat on it.

"Maybe not, but what she won't tell me might tell me more than what she does tell me," I said.

"I'm sure that makes some kind of sense," he retorted.

"What happened next?"

"All is quiet now, but talking to Madame Verney could be dangerous. The new men don't want anybody asking questions."

"Especially a foreign female? You're right, they wouldn't want any publicity. There has been nothing in the media?" I asked.

"Nothing. The Palace sees to that."

"Palace. I forgot to tell you about the Palace," I said.

"What about the Palace?"

"Never mind. I'll tell you later." I mulled it over as I finished the raki. "Her protection didn't work. Did the old mob not fight back?"

"Yes they did, but several of the troops wound up in the river with their throats slit, and then the new men did the Man. That ended their resistance."

"And now she's protected by somebody else. Where were the cops in all of this? Sitting on their hands?" I asked.

"Pretty much, although nobody would talk, so there wasn't much they could do."

"I wonder if they raised the price for the protection."

"Probably. It is not known."

"Then I need to go and ask her."

He bounced the crockery when he slapped the table.

"Didn't you hear what I just said?" He scowled.

I gritted my teeth and glared.

"I'll tie you up."

"The last man who tried tripped over his boot laces and wound up down a flight of stairs." I rose. "Time to go to Madame Verney's."

"Wait!" he said furiously. "Somebody out there wants you."

"I need to do my job, Kemal."

"You need backup."

"I need to go to Madame Verney's."

He scowled.

"You need backup."

"Kemal . . . ," I objected.

"Don't argue." He made a phone call, and shortly two large men appeared. They had the look of Guardsmen.

"You will stay with Miss Carruthers."

"Yes, sir."

They saluted and ushered me out. They were a tight fit in the car.

How was I going to get rid of them?

Chapter 29

I PARKED IN front of the dirty video store across the street from Madame Verney's.

"You stay in the car," I ordered.

"The captain said we should protect you," the tall thin one said.

"We can't protect you unless we're with you," said the taller thinner one.

"The captain will have our balls if we let you get hurt," said the first tall one.

"Worse," said the second.

Like Heckle and Jeckle. I tried to reason with them. "If I go in there with two large Guards, I'll never get anything out of the madam."

Kemal probably would have their balls if anything happened to me, but what could happen? The two of them looked as if they could tear a man apart. Even one alone could probably do it. After some more discussion in two-part harmony with me singing counterpoint, I convinced my security detail to stay in the car.

Madame Verney's house was one of the domestic jewels of New Fez, a house which in France would have belonged to a prosperous merchant. It was a classical stone building of three stories topped by a delicate mansard roof. A short flight of semicircular stairs with curved iron railings led to a pair of paneled doors, both sporting heavy knockers. I dropped the knocker on the right-hand door and waited for a response. Feeling eyes on my back, I turned in time to see four men who had come out of the dirty video shop across the street and were staring at me in wonder. The taller of my guards was leaning on the roof of my car looking at them with cold eyes. The four men went back inside, but they stared out of the shop window. Why should they miss the most interesting thing that had happened in the neighborhood since the mayor was arrested in a police raid?

The door behind me was opened by a European man in a black suit, white shirt, and black tie. A butler, for heaven's sake! The United Brotherhood of Serving Men would faint.

"Please ask Madame Verney if she can spare me a few moments." I handed him one of my many cards, the one with only my name engraved on it. The man raised his eyebrow with a look that only a well-trained butler can achieve, but I didn't shrivel. CIA employees don't shrivel. At least not because of an unarmed butler. When he saw the peanut gallery across the street, he let me in rather than leave me on the steps. What would the neighbors think?

"I shall enquire whether madam is at home," he said loftily in what sounded like a genuine British accent and left me standing on the black and white marble floor in the foyer. The haute bourgeois theme was continued in a series of portraits in oil of what looked like colonial officials and their wives. On the right, an ornate floor-to-ceiling mirror flanked by Louis the Something-or-other chairs stood between two heavily paneled doors. The chairs looked both delicate and uncomfortable. Those doors and those of two rooms on the left of the staircase were closed. A formal staircase with wrought iron banisters swept up to the second floor, almost obscuring passages on each side that continued to the rear of the house. The place looked more like Lady Windermere's town house than the best little whorehouse in Fez.

The butler returned and led me down the hall to a back parlor. Waiting in the doorway of a room furnished in comfortable contemporary furniture was a woman nearly as tall as I. She was slender with a long aristocratic face arranged in the hauteur that only a Frenchwoman can achieve. She held my card with two fingers as if touching it with more would corrupt her.

I almost laughed. She wore a tailored black suit like mine. Her silk blouse was white to my cream, but the gold chains and earrings were near duplicates. Only the color of the scarves we had twisted through our hair was different. If I'd had French blood instead of Anglo-Saxon, we might have been sisters. There was a lesson there if I cared to take it.

"How can I help you?" she asked coldly.

I can imagine that she was not accustomed to asking that of a woman in her parlor. I moved farther into the room. She followed me, moving so that she stood between me and the sofa. I had only a few moments before she called the bouncers. I handed her my iPhone with a picture of Alicia Harmon.

"Have you seen this woman?"

She flicked a look at the picture and something shifted in her eyes.

"I have not." A cold and definite no.

"She has disappeared," I said.

Madame Verney stiffened. "And you think she might be here? That I am, perhaps, operating a white slave ring?"

"No, no, madam, such thoughts never crossed my mind. I'm sure your place is—um—well-conducted."

She sniffed, another thing a Frenchwoman does better than anybody else in the world.

"She was investigating a wave of violence that has swept Fez's brothels. I thought she might have come to you for information."

"I have neither seen Miss . . . Harmon, did you say? . . . nor heard of any violence here."

Curious. I hadn't given her Alicia's name. Would a madam lie? She walked around me to the door. I stood my ground.

"I have it on good authority that your place was seriously damaged, as were several of your girls. Twice."

"There has been no trouble here, I said!" she replied through gritted teeth.

"Why would you lie about something everybody in town knows? A number of houses suffered much more. A number of madams were themselves injured. Seriously. You sustained no personal damage. Only your girls suffered from more than usually . . . ardent clients, but your house was invaded and damaged twice."

She turned back to me, her haughty face a mask of fury.

"Get out! Get out before I have you thrown out!"

I strolled toward the door wondering if I could goad her to indiscretion.

"Bentley!" she called.

I guess not. I arrived at the door in time to see a slight European man with sandy hair and metal-rimmed glasses hurry by carrying a briefcase. He wore a three-piece suit more suitable for Threadneedle Street than for a Fez brothel. Madame Verney stepped between us but he saw me, and I saw him. He snapped his eyes forward again and continued rapidly down the hall. I began to follow him when suddenly Madame Verney became chatty.

"What made you think your friend had come here?" she asked, blocking my way.

I tried to dance around her. "Your name was in her computer files," I lied.

"How extraordinary!" she said.

"Not at all," I replied sourly as I heard the front door open and close. "Your establishment would be the first place anybody enquired."

Her black eyes narrowed.

Then I realized how to get rid of Heckle and Jeckle.

"Madame, I wonder if I could ask a very great favor?"

She looked as if the only favor she would do for me was to throw me under a bus.

"Would you let me leave by the back door?"

I saw her think about it suspiciously. The neighbors were already talking. What was I up to? Then she decided. If going out the back door would get rid of me that made it a good thing. She rang for the butler.

"Show Ms. Carruthers out, Bentley," she said. "Use the kitchen entrance."

Suitable for servants.

As I left, I wondered again how she knew Alicia's name.

Chapter 30

I CAUGHT A cab a couple of blocks away from Madame Verney's. The list of things I needed to know exceeded the list of things I knew by a wide margin and was continuing to grow. I needed information. While Mike was rattling the archives and the Internet in search of information about the people in my investigation, I could do something on the ground. Last time I was in town, there had been a fey old gossip named Marcel Voix, who wrote a column for the Moroccan version of *Tatler* called simply "Le Causeur," The Gossip. If he was still alive he would he about 103, but he would know the dirt about everybody and everything. I fetched his address from my iPhone and directed the cab driver to an apartment house in the Ville Nouvelle, not forgetting to stop and buy a bottle of Pernod to loosen his tongue, although I suspected that he had switched to cheaper raki a long time ago.

The building was as old as Marcel, and it had never been handsome, a Stalinist Realist five-story structure of preformed concrete with scabrous plaster and casement windows whose metal frames wept rust down the front of the building. According to the faded card over a bell in the small entrance, Marcel still lived there. I pressed the bell, and nothing happened. I pressed it again and heard *attention!* I stepped out of the entry and saw a man's face in the window on the third floor. He dropped a key tied to a large ruler down to me. I couldn't hear his instruction, but I tried the key in the door and it worked. Near the inside door was a small lighted light switch, another gift of the French to Western civilization. You pressed it and the light came on for a brief time. You ran as fast as you could to the next switch, but the light always went out before you could get there. I ground my teeth and started up the steps. The light went out just before I reached the landing, and I pulled myself up the last steps by the banister to the next light switch. My theory is that the thing was invented by a committee of ambulance companies and orthopedic surgeons. As I started up the next flight, I heard a yoo-hoo and looked up. A small tortoise face appeared over the next banister.

"I'll turn this light on, shall I?"

"Yes!" I yoo-hooed back and puffed up the stairs.

I followed the small man into an apartment almost as dark as the stairs.

"Come along, come along," he encouraged in a thin, reedy voice, leading me into an extraordinary room furnished with furniture from around 1900, heavy as to feet and thick as to cushions. All around were piles of magazines and newspapers yellowed by time, enough to make a fire marshal blanch. The man in front of me was a gnome, a wrinkled gnome with badly fitting yellow false teeth, a badly fitting and unconvincing black toupee, and a mustache dyed to match the toupee. He had not changed a bit, except for the mustache. It had once been a finely waxed affair, a Hercule Poirot mustache, but now it had given up and drooped disconsolately.

"But it is Mademoiselle, Mademoiselle . . ." He snapped his fingers in vexation. "Ah. Mademoiselle Carruthers of the CIA! But my dear, it has been simply ages!" He drew me to a purple settee, its velvet rubbed and worn.

Here was a third person who knew I worked for the Agency.

"Ages, *mon Causeur,* ages," I agreed and handed him the Pernod.

He placed it in a cupboard on the far side to the room and drew out another bottle. He poured minute amounts of a dark green liquid into two minute glasses and returned to give me one. I had forgotten the *crème de menthe.* I wasn't sure how the breakfast raki was going to like it, but I sipped the sticky sweet liquid and held the tiny glass in my hand.

"But you are looking wonderful. If I were a century younger, you would not escape me!"

I simpered as I was meant to do. The things I do for the Agency.

"What brings you to the old Causeur?"

"Gossip, of course," I replied.

He drank off the *crème de menthe* and poured himself another. I had no idea how old Marcel Voix really was. He liked to pretend he was the last of the old Tangier rogues, a remnant of the gay community that flourished there in all its purple glory right after World War II. He was certainly gay enough, although I suspected that he exaggerated, playing the fag to his heart's delight.

"OK, Marcel," I said. "Enough with the limp wrist."

He laughed and rearranged himself into the role of a hyper-heterosexual male. I laughed, too.

"Be serious, Marcel!"

"But why? Life becomes a burden if one does not laugh."

"This is true, but I need some information."

"When did you not?" he asked mischievously.

Did all the men I knew in Morocco say that? Probably. I realized that I had sources in Morocco but no friends. Except for Kemal. Except for Kemal.

"My colleague, Alicia Harmon, has disappeared, and I have been sent to find her."

"The little anti-slavery girl?"

"Neither so little nor so young, I think, but yes," I replied.

"True, she is as tall as you and nearly as old, but she gives the impression of great youth, of vulnerability and naiveté. She is lost?"

"She has not been seen for two weeks, at least. I would like to know something about her, we've never met, and perhaps about the people I have come across while searching for her."

He settled back in his chair with a look of satisfaction. There was nothing he liked better than a good gossip. He steepled his fingers and tapped his lips.

"All great reformers are naïve, you know. They must be. If they knew anything about history, they would despair. She was naïve in that manner. She really believed that the slave trade could be destroyed, a trade that has flourished throughout human history. Of course, it's different now. People are trafficked mostly for prostitution and not for general labor. She was frustrated because she couldn't attract as much attention to stamping out the trade as she thought was necessary. I believe that she was often in despair over it." He cocked an eye at me. "She had recently taken a lover, you know."

"Yes I do, but how do you? Did you see them together?"

"By no means. I saw *her*. She was glowing. She had the burnished look of a woman well loved. As you do now, my dear."

I laughed. Burnished. I did feel burnished, at that.

"Kemal always was a good kisser," I said.

"Is his house of assignation prospering?" he asked mischievously.

"It must be. The furniture in the European room is very lush," I answered. "At least the bed is very comfortable."

"More comfortable than a bed mat on the floor?" He laughed merrily.

The dirty old man, I thought. "And how do you know that?" I asked.

"You just told me, my dear. I'm afraid your friend was being very unwise in the questions she asked. We have had a little trouble in our *maisons*, you know."

"I do know, and I wouldn't call it 'a little,' " I replied.

"Well, perhaps not. She was asking questions that should not have been asked."

"Such as?"

"Oh, who the new men were, of course. Someone new has taken over the protection of the houses. They will know that Miss Harmon is not just a child wringing her hands over a deplorable business, but that she works for an organization capable of making a good deal of trouble for them."

I turned the liqueur glass in my fingers. "I had not thought about it in those terms, largely because I know that the Agency would make no trouble at all for them, but perhaps they do not."

I took a sip of the liqueur and coughed to give myself time to think. He looked brightly at me as if to encourage a favorite pupil. I decided to change the subject.

"What do you know of Omar Rashid?"

He nodded his head. "Yes, that does, of course, follow."

I refused to give him the satisfaction of asking him why.

"I remember Omar as a boy," he continued. "A dreamy, introspective child, given to the poetry of Rumi."

"Yes, that does, of course, follow," I commented.

He raised an eyebrow. I shrugged.

"Rumi was a Sufi saint. So was Omar's great-grandfather."

He nodded.

"Later when he was at university in Paris, he was quite the man for the ladies," he continued.

"That really does follow," I said.

"Only if you interpret Rumi's poetry in a secular vein."

"Shall we speak of the Song of Songs? Perhaps a young man's wild oats. And today? Is he still a man for the ladies?"

He looked frustrated. "That is a question I cannot answer."

I was surprised. "You, the fount of all gossip, don't know?"

"A few years ago it was said that he was very discontented, very unhappy in his marriage. His wife has not given him a son."

"But surely that's grounds for divorce?"

"It is, but his father forbade divorce, objecting to the scandal," he replied.

"Why? If he fails to have a son, the line will be cut off."

"Not so. Omar has a brother. So Omar asked his wife's permission to take a second wife, which she refused. She had a right to refuse, you know?"

I nodded.

"He was very unhappy, so unhappy that he moved out of his house into a flat in the Ville Nouvelle."

"Surely that's more scandalous than divorce."

"Yes, of course, but what could his father do? He could force his son to forgo divorce, but he could not physically force him to live with his wife."

"I suppose he could have, but people would be bound to notice."

He smiled. "After a while he ceased to be unhappy."

"A lover," I said.

He took a sip of the *crème de menthe*. "I believe so, but I cannot discover who his lover is." His discontent was massive. A failure like that went to the heart of his self-image.

"Rumors?"

"Oh, yes. It was a nine day's wonder, but after a while it settled down as other scandals emerged to attract people's attention. I'm sure everybody has forgotten about it by this time," he said in discontent. "Except me."

"And his wife. To change the subject slightly, are there any rumors about his Foundation?"

"What kind of rumors?" he asked.

"Money-laundering rumors."

He looked shocked. "But no, certainly not! What makes you ask that?"

"Somewhere Alicia Harmon got the idea that the Rashid Foundation was laundering money for terrorists."

"Terrorists!"

"I don't know where she got that idea. I thought you might."

He shook his head. "If there is some rumor like that, and I haven't heard it, I'm finished." He bowed his head sadly. "I might as well die and be done with it."

"You could ask."

He straightened his back. "Gossip comes to me. I do not go to it," he said haughtily.

"Ask," I encouraged. "Ask."

His head dropped down, and he started to breathe heavily. Should I wake him? He had drifted off before I could ask him about Zeynab Bentali. I decided not to disturb his slumber and left, making sure the lock caught as I closed the door.

After all, how important could she be?

Chapter 31

FROM THE MAN who knew all about people, I was going to the man who knew all about money.

"Bab Bou Jeloud," I told the cabbie.

If there was money moving, Mustapha Lahkim would know about it. Lahkim's shop was in the goldsmiths' quarter of the medina. Although the small crowded shop didn't look like much, Mustapha Lahkim's family was among the wealthiest in Fez. They had been in the jewelry business since caravans brought gold up from Sub-Saharan Africa. Mustapha was a jolly man, short and rounder than I remembered, with black eyes and a thin moustache. He wore a white *djellaba* of fine wool and, unlike most Moroccan men, was old-fashioned enough to wear a fez, a hat whose manufacture once bought the city millions. It looked as if business had been good. The shop was larger than I remembered it, at least three times the size of the other shops in the neighborhood, big enough for counters, big enough for customers to enter. Most of the shops were only wide enough for the merchant to sit on a pillow at the entrance and display his wares before him. Mustapha saw me as I climbed the two steps to the shop and, by the time

I was standing before him, had one of the loveliest baroque pearls I had ever seen in his hand.

"I see you recognize me, old friend," I said smiling and taking the stool he shoved toward me with his foot. If I ever go broke it will be from buying baroque pearls.

"A special price for a beautiful lady," he said and placed it in my unresisting hand.

I turned it over. Its irregular shape, its luster, its warmth in my hand were almost irresistible. I handed it back to him quickly. The longer I held it, the more likely I was to buy it, even though its price was likely near my yearly salary. I could always tap my rainy day fund, I thought, never mind that it rains every day in Paris in the winter.

"I didn't come for pearls," I said regretfully. "I came for information."

He clapped his hands, and a young man appeared through the bead curtain at the rear of the shop.

"Come," Mustapha said, holding out his hand to help me up.

The young man took Mustapha's place, and Mustapha led me through the curtain into the back room. Colorful pillows were scattered along the seating ledge that ran along two sides of the room. I took a seat just below an antique silk prayer rug that hung on the wall, its muted colors as lustrous as the pearl. Mustapha clapped his hands again, and a young girl appeared through a door with a tea tray, which she placed on the brass tray before Mustapha. He patted her head fondly.

"This is Ayesha, the youngest of my granddaughters," he said.

"Hello, Ayesha," I said. She executed a commendable curtsey and disappeared through the door.

Mustapha began the ritual for serving mint tea. I did my best to conceal my desire for haste. Mustapha was conservative enough to wear a fez, so there was no interrupting his tea making. When the tea was made to his satisfaction, he served it in a glass with sugar cubes in the saucer. Despite the fact that I like my tea unsweetened, I sweetened it, took a sip, and murmured the requisite compliments. After that, it was acceptable to discuss business.

"I'm looking for money moving out, Mustapha, probably new money and a lot of it. My colleague disappeared after reporting that she had found out something about terrorist funding."

"In Fez?" he asked in astonishment.

"Why not in Fez?"

"The Palace, the security forces, they all prevent such things."

"They didn't prevent a Pure Warrior of Islam from blowing himself up in the metal workers souk yesterday."

He looked uncomfortable.

"My colleague received death threats, and I don't know that she's still alive. I've been attacked since I came looking for her, which suggests that she was onto something."

He sipped his tea quietly for a moment. You had to wait for Mustapha to process things, but what he came up with was always good. Sometimes surprising, but good. He rubbed his chin, making a rasping noise.

"The money is from a new source," he admitted.

"The new source is?" I asked.

"I do not know, and I do not know where it is going," he answered, shaking his head mournfully. He poured us more tea. "I fear I am getting old."

That was the first time I had ever drawn a blank with both of my most knowledgeable sources.

"I do not understand the new ways. Once I moved a great deal of gold to South Asia. The people there keep their savings in gold." He looked at me through his eyebrows.

"I know. Wives wear the family treasure in gold. Is this no longer so?" I asked.

"Oh, yes. This is still so, and I still have a good portion of that trade, but of the other trade, transfers of funds to individuals, I no longer have a very large share, and I do not know who is now handling those transfers, or where the funds are going."

I was shocked. "Money doesn't move into or out of Fez without your knowing about it, Mustapha. There must be some new factor. Most goldsmiths move some money."

Mustapha nodded. "No goldsmiths here have increased their business, I'm sure of it. There is, however, a new *hawalador* in Crimson Alley."

Hawaladors move money in traditional societies like Western Union does in the West. You pay at one end and the money is delivered at the other end. The difference is that with the hawaladors there is no paper trail. Impossible to track and perfect for moving illegal funds.

"Who is he?"

"I can't find out anything about him. He is not Moroccan. I have only seen him once, but if I had to guess, I would say he is South Asian, probably Pakistani."

"Moving money to Pakistan, do you think?" I asked.

"It need not be so," he said, and his eyes weren't jolly then. "And it need not be illegal money if he does."

"Exactly," I said.

After getting directions to Crimson Alley, I began to disengage. It's no wonder Arab society is behind the West in development. At any given time, half of the population was uttering complicated farewells, and the other half was trying to get away. As I turned the corner into Crimson Alley, I saw several hawalador signs hanging over the alley. I couldn't see the new one at first. I strolled down the lane trying to look like a tourist. Halfway down the block, I found a newly painted sign in Arabic and something else that resembled Arabic. Urdu? Hindi? The solid doors had larger locks than the doors of the neighboring hawaladors. Is he natively suspicious, I wondered, or does he have more money to protect?

Tourists did not stray into Crimson Alley. It's too far from the tourist's medina of rugs and souvenirs. I was the only woman in the alley, and I was foreign. I needed to get out of there and fast. Halfway up the hill to the Bab Bou Jeloud, I came face to face with a little man wearing a three-piece suit and carrying a briefcase.

Chapter 32

HE WALKED RAPIDLY past me. I turned to watch. When he left Madame Verney's, I had assumed that he was carrying the gang's share of the take from the night before. What was he doing in the medina? I turned to follow, and he sped up. I sped up, but I got caught behind a bunch of black-veiled women, and when I got by them, he was gone. I walked a little farther, hoping to catch up with him, but it was no use. He was gone. As I turned, I saw a flash of tweed disappear around a corner to the left. I followed. He tripped and almost fell, because he was trying to walk faster and talk on his cell phone at the same time. He turned left again into an area of cheap jewelry shops. I continued following him. Then he turned left into a narrow alley. When I followed, two large men in traditional dress blocked my way. I tried to push past them, but one of them grabbed me. I stomped on his instep and whirled around to kick, but his friend grabbed me by the shirt and shook me. I started thrashing, struggling, yelling for help, and I heard someone run into the alley behind me, shouting. They dropped me and fled down the alley. There was no sign of the Man with the Briefcase, and I was in a part of the medina where I had never been before.

My rescuer was a middle-aged man with a neatly trimmed beard, his djellaba freshly laundered and spotless. He led me to a shop displaying garish paste jewels and sat me down a small stool. Now that it was over I began to shake. He looked concerned and tried to press a glass of tea into my hand. I shook my head and tried to get up. I sat back down dizzily. I drank tea after all and thanked my benefactor for his help. Then I returned to the alley, despite his protests. It was empty. I followed it to the next cross street and found myself in Crimson Alley. It was still crowded, but I could see no sign of the Man with the Briefcase. I looked around and followed the alley out to the main road, passing the new hawalador's shop as I went.

He wouldn't be collecting from brothels in the medina. He was European. Somebody else collected in medina. I lost him near Crimson Alley. He wasn't buying cheap jewelry. He must've been going to the hawalador's. I kept walking toward the gate. Why would he be using a hawalador? Surely the gang was local. Or was it? Maybe it was from Rabat, but Fez collectors wouldn't use a hawalador to transfer money to Rabat. Maybe the gang wasn't Moroccan. Maybe it was Algerian? One of the girls thought one of the breakers was Algerian. The whole thing made no sense at all. There were modern banking facilities to transfer money from Morocco to Algeria, but, of course, they left a paper trail.

If he was using a hawalador, he was probably sending money farther than Algeria. The jeweler thought the new man might be Pakistani. The sign over his shop had a script that was not Arabic. If the Man with the Briefcase was sending money to Pakistan he was sending it somewhere that didn't have banks. Like the Northwest Frontier or the Tribal Areas? That was the briar patch of the Taliban.

Brothel money to the Taliban? Why not? Al Qaeda smuggled drugs. There was no reason to suppose that the

Taliban would be tender about using brothel proceeds. Allah is very forgiving when the cause is right.

Did it make sense for two groups to be laundering money for terrorists in Fez?

My next stop was going to be the Rashid Foundation offices. Maybe Omar Rashid would tell me why Alicia Harmon thought he was laundering money for terrorists.

It was lucky I looked out of Bou Jeloud gate before I stepped though. The white Rover was waiting for me in a No Parking zone, one large Guard at the wheel and the other large Guard leaning against the door. I turned on my heel and went back down the hill as fast as I could. Which gate was closest? Jamal? I turned toward it. I could get a taxi there, couldn't I? After hacking across a medina that was not meant for crosswise traffic, I reached the Bab Jamal and found that, no, I could not find a taxi there, I had to walk a kilometer and a half to a boulevard to get one. I just had time to pat my hair into place before the taxi reached the Boulevard Mohammed V.

The Foundation offices were on the fourth floor of one of the new glass high-rises along Avenue Mohammed V. A pretty spiffy address for a charity, I thought as the elevator rose. The office itself was modest. Two glass doors each bore a small but tasteful Rashid Foundation logo. A pretty girl at the reception desk looked up enquiringly. I gave her my card, the one with Femme Aide Lebanon and a Beirut address on it.

"I'm sorry, but I don't have an appointment. Could Mr. Rashid possibly spare me a few moments?" I asked.

A cold call was a good way of getting to a subject before he had a chance to arrange a convincing story, but you risked not getting in. I wanted to know what effect a question about the news of Alicia Harmon's disappearance would have on Omar Rashid.

She read the card and asked, "May I tell him what this is in reference to?" she asked.

"It's about a missing person," I replied.

She looked startled and disappeared through the door behind her desk. It was opened by a breathtakingly handsome man holding my card between two long, slender fingers, a look of inquiry on his face. Possibly forty, he was tall and slender, with light skin and Arabic features. A mustache outlined his full lips. He wore a pair of beige slacks and a white shirt with no tie and the cuffs turned back, looking every inch the modern executive, but his true place was atop a galloping camel with his headdress blowing in the wind. Omar Sharif, eat your heart out, I thought, and hoped he was not guilty of anything. Prison would be such a waste.

He offered his hand to me. "Omar Rashid, Ms. Carruthers," he said.

How modern of him, I thought as we shook hands. He conveyed me into a bright office, and I stopped dead in my tracks, stunned by the magnificent rugs on the wall. They ranged from the best Berber I have ever seen to a silk Isfahan prayer rug that I would kill for.

He looked pleased. "I see you know something about rugs."

"A little. Enough to know that I have never seen such a collection in one room."

"My grandfather was a collector. These are the Foundation's financial reserve. They will keep us in business for a while if all else fails." He led me to a settee and waited until I seated myself before seating himself. "Now what can I do for you, Ms. Carruthers?" his English had a faint French inflection.

"My colleague, Alicia Harmon, is missing." I watched his face closely.

"Alicia Harmon?" he asked, his face giving no sign he recognized the name.

"She manages the Femme Aid Maroc Office here in Fez." I raised an eyebrow. "You know it?"

"Yes I do. It does some of the same work for women that we do for boys. But missing? This lady is missing?"

"Yes, she is. No one has seen her for least two weeks. I've come from Beirut to see if I can find her," I replied. "I found your name in her computer and wondered if you had seen her." Her report to Sidney must be in her computer, so it was only a fib, not an outright lie.

He went to his desk and flipped through his desk calendar. "Yes, I remember now. I see that she was here last month."

"If you don't mind my asking, what did she want?"

"She was looking for a place for two Tuareg women, a place where they could be trained." He looked again at my card.

"We do the same in Beirut, try to find places for orphaned girls."

"I had to tell her regretfully that we serve only street boys. That in itself is a task for Hercules. She was disappointed." He shrugged. "It is very hard to place women right now."

"It's hard to place women, at any time."

"There are simply more places for men and boys," he said.

"Always," I agreed.

I wondered if Alicia really came to visit to ask about places for the women in the house in the medina, or if she wanted to get the measure of this man. She certainly knew that the Foundation dealt only with boys.

The door opened, and a man entered. He gestured to his briefcase.

"I finally got it all in. There were a lot of five dirham notes. If you'll just sign the deposit slip, I'll run over to the bank on my way out." He saw me for the first time and skidded to a halt. "Sorry. I didn't know you had a visitor," he stuttered.

Rashid waved his hand. "No matter." He signed the deposit slip, and the man left quickly, almost running. I watched him leave. It was the Man with the Briefcase.

I rose and we shook hands.

"Thank you for your time, Mr. Rashid," I said.

"It was no trouble. I hope that you will be able to find your friend."

I left the office and sprinted down the fire stairs, hoping to beat the elevator. I ran onto the sidewalk. Dusk was falling, but there was enough light for me to see Briefcase Man go down an alley and enter a side door to the Credit Suisse. The Foundation was important enough to be taken care of outside regular business hours, it seems. I slid down the alley to wait. Following him in the dusk would be easier in one way because he couldn't see that I was European, always a problem in North Africa, but in another way it would be more difficult, because it would be easier to lose him.

I drifted into the shadow behind some garbage cans as he came out of the bank and turned toward the street. He stopped in the middle of the sidewalk to make a call on his cell phone. He nodded emphatically several times as if the listener could see him and returned the phone to his coat pocket. He continued on his way, with me treading softly behind him, trying to find enough light to photograph him with my cell phone.

It was entirely dark when I realized that I'd probably been burned, because he had led me in a giant circle. I slipped into the doorway of a shop and waited to see what he would do when he thought he had lost me. He scanned the sidewalk. When he failed to see me, sure that he had lost me, he made another phone call and waited patiently on the corner. Five minutes later a white Rover with a Fez license plate picked him up.

I flagged a taxi. There are a lot of white Rovers in the world, I thought, but too many are turning up around me. I photographed the car. The photo came out dark, but the license plate was readable.

"Follow that car," I said. I've always wanted to say that.

The driver gave me a strange look, and I gave him a fistful of dirhams, after which we drove sedately behind the Rover, all the way to the Bab Bou Jeloud. The Man with the Briefcase got out of the car and headed for the gate, past a white Rover with two large men waiting patiently, unwilling to go back to Kemal's without me.

Chapter 33

I HAD A few more things to do before I went back to Kemal's.

"Don't stop," I ordered. "Drive on."

The cabbie looked at me in confusion. "Take me to the Bab el-Marouk gate," I said.

After I paid the driver, I walked down the street looking for an electronics store. Moroccans are mad about cell phones. I didn't have to go very far before I found a shop and picked up some supplies, just in case. I went into a café nearby. Risking the annoyance of the men there, I sat down and ordered a cup of coffee. It was too early to do what I had in mind, so I improved my time by checking my e-mail on my phone. I deleted a bunch of offers to enlarge my penis, flagged some stuff from Baghdad, and went on to Mike's e-mail. He suggested we message, so I wrote him that he should be available in a few minutes. For messaging, I needed Internet.

"Is there an Internet café nearby?" I asked the waiter as he picked up my money.

He directed me to one over by the Bab Bou Jeloud where the tourists played. As usual, the café was full of young men checking their Facebook pages and playing computer games. They looked up when I came in and went back to their monitors. I snagged a table in the corner and waved to the clerk. He logged me on and brought me a cup of coffee. I looked at my watch. Mike wasn't long coming on line.

"Lee, it's about the Rashid Foundation. I scratched around trying to get under this stuff, but there doesn't seem to be anything under it. As far as I can see the Foundation is clean. I couldn't find any accounts other than the ones you found. If they're laundering money, they're doing it off the books."

I tapped off a message to him. "Mike, they seem to collect a lot of small donations. It wouldn't be difficult for Omar to skim some and send it anywhere he wants to. Maybe we can't find it because it's never been on the books."

"Could be. I couldn't find a thing about the brothel violence, not even in our own files."

"The Palace has managed to keep the lid on tight," I typed.

"Yeah, but we're an intelligence organization, remember? I should be able to find something. About Worldwide Entertainment Systems, I found something suggestive. Their website shows a map with a number of cities on it flagged. Rabat and Fez are just the beginning. The flags ring the Mediterranean: Cairo, Beirut, Istanbul, Naples, Toulon. There are a few in Northern Europe: Amsterdam and Hamburg," he wrote. "Suggest anything?"

"Yes," I replied. "With the exception of Fez, they're all ports."

"And get this. There are links to the offices, but none of them is hot. The home page is all you get. Want to bet what the entertainment they sell is?"

"Ports? I'd hate to take your money, Mike. And Sam Glover works for Worldwide. Interesting. Keep digging on him. His accent may be English."

"Right. All I could find about Zeynab, besides her genealogy, were records of her court cases. I'm having trouble identifying the defendants, but a lot of them seem to be members of the Truth and Justice Party."

"That's the fundamentalist group that works in the slums."

"Pro bono?" Mike asked, "Or is she a fundamentalist?"

"Nobody with eyelashes like hers," I typed, "could possibly be a fundamentalist. When I met her she had just finished defending a liberal newspaper editor. It must be pro bono." I looked at my watch. Time to leave.

"Gotta go, Mike. This time tomorrow?"

"Look at the time difference, Lee," he wrote. "I'll send you an e-mail unless what I have is earth shaking."

"Roger." I logged off and paid my bill.

I walked down the next alley and knocked on the back door of a grimy café. A dirty-faced kid opened the door and stared at me.

"I want The Knife," I said.

He continued to stare. I shoved him aside and went down the hall and knocked on the door next to the toilet. The noise from the café was too loud for anybody inside to hear anything, so I pounded on the door and opened it. Inside I saw a scrawny, wrinkled man embracing a woman twice his size. She looked at me and screamed. He squinted at me for a long moment and then recognized me.

"Lalla Lee, how nice to see you," he said sarcastically.

I jerked my head back toward the hall. The woman rearranged her clothing and picked up her shoes. She was so fat that I had to turn sideways before she could squeeze past. She popped out into the hall like the first olive from a bottle. By that time, Zafir the Knife had finished zipping his trousers. He was old when I first knew him and that was a decade or more ago. The grime and the wrinkles made it hard to see what color he was, but he was probably café au lait. Thin and wiry, he was invisible as he slipped through the crowd like a knife. He learned everything that was coming down and flogged what he heard to anybody with a spare dirham. I first met him when I came home from work one day and found him looking for something to steal. Since I was standing between him and the door, he couldn't get away. We looked each other up and down, and I decided we could do business. I had a mild bit of breaking and entering in mind, and he looked as if he could do it, for price. That was OK by me. I wouldn't expect him to do it for free. He proved to be a valuable servant, so long as I kept my eye on him. He didn't look any more honest than he had when I first met him, which was good. I would hate it if he got religion. He did look slightly fatter, as if business was prospering, but he didn't smell any better. You can tell a crook in Muslim lands by the grime ground into him. If Lahkim knew where the honest money in Fez was going, The Knife knew where the dishonest money was going.

"Not a social visit," he said.

"I don't do social with you, Zafir. I want something," I said.

"What?" he asked.

"I want to know about the money," I said, putting my right hand in my pocket. He flinched. I pulled a wad of bills from it, and he relaxed.

He looked at the ceiling. "What money?"

"The brothel money. You know who the new boys are, and where their money is going, and I want to know, too."

"What new boys?"

I switched the money to the other hand. He watched the money move. I put my right hand close to the pistol grip. He sat up and put his hands on his knees, looking at me through bleary eyes. Nobody knew what he knew. He sold it to the cops, and he could sell it to me, too. I rustled the bills.

"The new boys who trashed the houses," I said.

"I don't know nothing about that."

"Zafir, nothing happens in Fez that you don't know about. So who are these guys? They're from out of town, they've got to be. They're meaner, more organized than the usual two-bit criminals in Fez. The take must be enormous, and they have to do something with it. What?"

"There's a new hawalador in town." He looked away and scratched.

"I know there is."

"Maybe he handles it," he said to the wall.

"Look at me, Zafir," I commanded, and he reluctantly turned back to me. "You know he handles it. Where does he send it?" I put my hand back on the butt of the pistol.

"To a guy in Béni Abbès," he said hurriedly.

Cunning but not very brave.

"Algeria? That money is going to terrorists?"

"What do I know about terrorists?" He looked alarmed.

"To the Pures."

"Pures! What Pures?" He looked more alarmed.

"Don't tell me you don't know the Pure Warriors of Islam." It was a statement not a question.

"The Pure Warriors of Islam?" He looked from one side of the room to the other, anything to keep from looking at me.

"Zafir, you know what's coming down in the medina. You know where it's coming from, and you know where it's going. This new money can't have got past your nose. Money never does. Maybe you even get a little cut, eh? Tell me," I said, "And no one will ever know. Don't tell me, and I'll tell everyone you told me. What do you know?"

I leaned against the wall and prepared to wait. He did the eye thing again, and I rustled the bills again. I could see the wheels going round. Should he? Shouldn't he? This time I loosened the pistol in the holster.

He spoke in a rush. "There's somebody new."

"Well, I know that. Tell me something I don't know."

"A Westerner. They say he's a Westerner."

"Dealing in terrorist money?" I asked incredulously. "You mean a Western Muslim?"

"I don't think so. They say he looks like a tourist."

"What's his name?"

"I don't know," he said.

"You don't know much. Tell me something worth money. What does he look like?"

"I don't know. I've never seen him."

"Then how do you know he exists? I don't believe you."

This time I brought the gun out.

"I haven't ever seen him, but they say he's an Englishman."

"Who's 'they?' "

"Guys, just guys. You hear it around."

"Why would an Englishman be involved with terrorists in Fez? What does he do?"

"I don't know, but the money doesn't go the way it used to go before he came."

"What do you mean?"

"You know. The people who pick it up, the people who get a cut, they're all new. Not even the cops have been able to muscle in yet."

"Now *that* I don't believe."

"It's true, I tell you, it's true. These new guys are a mystery."

"To you."

"Even to me," he admitted and looked frustrated.

We went around on that a couple of more times, but he either didn't know any more, or he wouldn't sell me any more, so I changed the subject.

"There's been some trouble in the brothels—houses wrecked, customers beaten, like that. Who's doing it?"

He shifted nervously. "I don't know. I don't know."

"You don't know anything about the trouble in the brothels? Find out. It's worth more than your usual rates."

He actually looked pale under the dirt and started shaking his head back and forth. "No. No. I can't. I wouldn't do it for the cops, and I won't do it for you."

"I pay better than the cops do," I said and rustled the bills again.

"I can't," he said desperately. "I can't. They'll kill me. Anybody asks questions, they wind up in the river with their throat slit."

Zafir made his living by stealth for good reason. He wasn't the bravest villain in Fez, and I'd seen him afraid before, but now he was in a real panic. Terrified. Then I remembered what Abdullah in Rabat had said. Nobody there had felt like asking about them there, either, so I tossed him the money and left before somebody heard us and objected to my presence. He hadn't been much help. The breakers were Algerian. The money was going to Algeria. That was all. There was a man, a Western man. It didn't make any sense.

I had struck out with all three of my informants.

Chapter 34

AFTER I WENT through the el-Marouk gate, I turned left, and walked along the city wall far enough to be out of the lights. I squatted there and considered my options. I could go to the Bab Bou Jeloud and let the boys capture me. I knew they'd still be there. They'd be there until hell froze over, or I came back, whichever happened first. I thought about the money. Alicia Harmon thought Omar Rashid was laundering money for terrorists. The Man with the Briefcase picked up money from Madame Verney's. Why else would he be carrying a briefcase down the hall in a brothel? Why would she try to block me from seeing him if he was just there for a morning eye-opener? And why would he be in the medina with the briefcase?

He took it to the hawalador in Crimson Alley, if Zafir was telling the truth. If Zafir was telling the truth, that money went to Béni Abbès, Algeria. If Zafir was telling the truth. Would he lie to me just because I was holding a gun on him? Of course he would.

Later in the day, Briefcase Man took the Foundation's receipts and deposited at least some of the money in the Credit Suisse. He then went from the bank to the medina. Why would Omar Rashid need services other than those that Credit Suisse could provide, unless he didn't want to leave a paper trail? It could not be a coincidence that the little man took his briefcase into the medina twice after collecting money. Was the money from the Foundation going to Algeria, as well? I stood up.

Time to go and see.

I walked to where I could get a cab. At that time of night no respectable woman would be on the streets, so I dropped the gun in my pocket, pulled my T-shirt as tight as I could and pulled my jeans down as low on my hips as I could manage. I shook my hair loose from its confining pins and put on a ton of lipstick. Then I looked like the kind of girl who would be on the streets that time of the night. I waved my arm, and a cab screeched to a halt and backed up. When I asked to be taken to one of the big tourist hotels on Boulevard Mohammed V, the cabbie smirked and put the car in gear. When we got there, I gave him a big tip and went into the lobby, hoping the Morals Police had gone to bed. I slipped into the ladies' room to become a respectable woman again and tiptoed down a back hall and peeked into the kitchen. At that hour of the night, only two men remained, the cook and the room service waiter. I stole out the back door and down the alley to the Credit Suisse. I leaned against the wall and watched the building across the street that housed the offices of the Rashid Foundation. I could see lights flicking on and off in the windows as the cleaning crew went from room to room. Watching a building is hard on the feet. I looked at my watch. After half an hour, I sat down. The alley wasn't clean, but at least there were no banana peels.

After a lifetime, I looked at my watch again and found that my usual estimation of time was as good as ever. I'd been there for an hour. I crossed the empty street and squatted down behind a dumpster at the back of the building. After another half hour, several tired women came out, the last one pulling the door shut. After I was certain that all of them were gone, I approached the door cautiously. I could see no security. I ran my hand around the door frame and felt no wires. Good for me, if bad for the building's tenants, especially since the back door didn't lock automatically after somebody used it. The Rashid Foundation had its offices on the fourth floor. I crept inside and ran up the fire stairs to the fifth floor. I stuck my head out of the door and listened. Nothing. I walked back down to the fourth floor and stuck my head out. Nothing there either, so I walked quietly to the Rashid Foundation offices and looked around the door. Still no security. They were either stupid or had nothing to hide. I picked the lock and stepped inside.

I found the secretary's computer by the light from the hall and booted it. It began its interminable loading. Come on! Come on! I thought. It always takes forever. I kept looking at the hall. I hadn't been able to determine the guard's schedule, so I didn't know how long I had. It was too dark to see my watch. Constantly looking at it was counter-productive, anyway. Time is what it is. Finally it was finished. Just as I inserted the flash drive, I saw a sweep of light in the hall and knew a guard was coming.

Damn.

He found the door unlocked and came in muttering. The only place to hide was the knee hole of the desk. I crawled into it and prayed. Since I didn't pray very often, I feared that the deity wouldn't recognize me. I could hear the guard coming toward me, drawn to the receptionist's desk by the light of the monitor.

"Stupid woman! The second time this week. Probably left the door unlocked, too." he groused. "A looker all right, but she don't have the sense Allah gave a flea." He hadn't seen the flash drive. I heard him open the door to Rashid's office. I guess he looked around. Anyway he closed it. Then he swept the outer office with his flashlight, and I visualized doing time in a Moroccan jail. I pulled my legs up to my nose and sent another prayer up, reminding the goddess who I was. The light passed along both sides of the desk, and I closed my eyes, making myself invisible. Right. I also gritted my teeth. I opened my eyes and quietly shifted my position until my head and shoulders were to the front. If he found me, I had to come out fighting, not an easy thing to do from a pretzel position. He turned the computer off and stood watching it close down. He was so close I could have bitten his ankles. I was sure he could hear my heart beat. After about a hundred years, he grunted and left. I heard him go out and lock the door.

I crawled out and sat with my back to the desk trying to convince my body that it had not been folded up under a desk waiting to be discovered. It took a while. I counted to five hundred. It had been a mistake to boot the secretary's computer. The light from the monitor could be seen from the hall. If Rashid was doing anything shady, he wouldn't tell his secretary anyway. I removed the flash drive and stuck it in my pocket.

In Rashid's office, I fired up his computer. I didn't even bother to scroll down the files, I just inserted the flash drive and started copying them. I stuck my head out of Omar's door and caught a glimpse of light coming down the hall from the left. Why was he coming back? Rashid's computer kept feeding files into the drive.

He walked over to the secretary's desk and logged on to the computer.

"Got an hour," he said. Through a crack in Rashid's door I saw him pull up a game and begin to play. I watched as he killed zombie after zombie.

When Rashid's files had all been copied to the drive, I reached to eject it from his computer and hit a pencil can. When I grabbed at it, it hit the floor with a rattle, and I was sorry I hadn't shut the door all the away. I heard the squeak of the secretary's chair. The guard was coming to see what the noise was. I looked desperately around for a place to hide. The kneehole of the desk was no good. He'd see me as soon as he came in. The sofa. I couldn't get under it, and I didn't have time to get behind it. I spied a narrow door in the corner that I hadn't noticed when I was there before. I ran over and jerked it open. It was a closet. I stepped in and pulled the door to just as the guard came into the room. He must have looked around because he saw the closet door not quite closed. I heard him cross the room. He pushed the door closed and returned to the reception room.

There was a shelf in the closet that wouldn't permit me to stand without bending over, so I squatted on the floor. I couldn't see my watch. I couldn't hear a thing. After a time I began to wonder if the guard was still out there. I couldn't tell. I'd just have to go and see. I reached for the handle.

There wasn't one.

The closet was the size of a postage stamp, small and getting smaller every minute. No handle on the inside. I sat down and pulled my knees up to my nose. The room continued to get smaller. I discovered that if I put my arms out, I could reach the wall on either side. The walls were not moving. I didn't believe it. I held my arms in that position until they dropped. The room in the basement of the Palace was huge by comparison, but they were the same in one way. I couldn't get out. I couldn't get out! I got up on my knees and pounded on the door. I had to get out! Had to, had to! I lost it for a bit, flailing my arms around and pounding on the door. What did I care if the guard found me?

"Get a grip, girl," I said finally and put my arms around my body. I never knew the meaning of a cold sweat until then. I sat down again and began to tremble. I put my head on my knees.

I sat in the lotus position and tried to calm myself, but my mind continued to spin out of control. I don't know how long I sat there trying to control it. Finally, the spinning and trembling slowed. Eventually—a lifetime?—they stopped altogether, and I was able to assess my situation. I was in a small space. Don't go there! I was in a small space, and there wasn't any handle on the door. I knelt and felt the space where the handle should be and found just a metal bump. Was there a space along the door jamb big enough for me to insert the blade of my Swiss army knife? If there was I could move the dead latch with it and open the door. I pulled out my knife, almost afraid to try. I ran my finger along the door jamb and tried to insert the knife blade. The door was a nice tight fit. The knife wouldn't go in.

In frustration I kicked the door hard. It didn't move. The door's resistance threw me against the back wall and sat me down on my tail, which gave me an idea. I sat up and put both my feet on the door and shoved. And shoved again. I thought I felt some movement, but it might just have been wishful thinking. I drew my legs back as far as they would go and slammed my feet against the door. I heard a crack and saw a tiny line that was less dark than the rest of the door. I pulled my feet back and rammed it, hard. The door swung open.

I breathed the free air deeply. I stepped out of the closet, and suddenly my legs wouldn't hold me. I lay down on the carpet on my back staring at the city lights reflected on the ceiling and breathing. You never know what you'll miss until you don't have it anymore.

My watch told me I'd only been in the closet for two hours. My heart told me it had been ten years.

I left the office and locked the door behind me. It wasn't far to the fire stairs, but a light appeared behind me before I got there.

"Hey!" a man shouted.

I ran for the door and swung myself down the steps, around and around with him about a floor behind me. I burst out of the fire steps and ran for the back door.

"Stop!" he yelled. "Stop!"

Chapter 35

I KEPT RUNNING, out the back door and down the alley, praying that he wasn't armed. I am doing a lot of praying, I thought. I would probably run out of my allotment for some time to come. He followed me for a while, but I heard him gasping for breath. He stopped, but I ran on, zigging and zagging through alleys until I knew I was clear. I had not only used up my allotment of prayers, I had probably used up my luck for the night as well.

I might as well give the boys a thrill and let them catch me, I thought. I didn't bother turning myself disreputable again. I looked scruffy enough from my time in the closet. The cab driver looked disapproving, but he took me to the Bab Bou Jeloud anyway. As I started through the gate, I was grabbed and thrown into the back seat of a car.

I bounced around in the seat as the car sped away from the gate. I didn't need to see their faces to know my captors were unhappy. They had spent the whole day at that gate, and I was for it. Old Fez gave way to Fez el Jdid, the King's quarter, and soon we were driving up the alley in back of Kemal's pipe bar. When I got out, I saw Kemal waiting in the doorway, his hands on his hips. He was furious.

"I don't know whether to kiss you or beat you," he said.

I raised my face to him and said, "Kiss first, please."

That cracked him up. He put his arms around me, put his cheek on my head, and rocked back and forth.

"Where have you been?" he demanded.

"Here and there," I answered blithely. I suddenly realized that I hadn't eaten since breakfast. "I'm hungry. What's for dinner?"

We went down the hall to the office. Kemal clapped his hands like a pasha, and the boy with ragged jeans came in with a coffee tray.

"What do you want to eat?" he asked.

"Cheeseburger, Pepsi," I answered.

"What?" he asked.

I laughed. "Never mind. Anything."

He looked at me speculatively. "You've been in trouble. What have you been doing?"

"Let's eat first."

"Start now. You can talk while you eat."

I knew I was going to have to tell him. People kept trying to grab me, and there were three groups of people who might want me. Kemal might be able to help me with the Palace.

The boy came back with *shwarma* on flat bread, and I rolled it up and took a big bite. When my first hunger was sated, I began my tale.

"You remember I told you about Alicia Harmon's disappearance?"

He nodded.

"That she was asking about trouble in the brothels?"

He nodded.

"And about the Rashid Foundation and money laundering?"

"No, you told me nothing about the Rashid Foundation. Laundering money?"

"Somewhere Alicia Harmon got the idea that the Rashid Foundation is laundering money for terrorists. People keep trying to snatch me, and they did snatch my laptop. This can only be related to Alicia's disappearance. Somebody thinks I know something. But who? It could be either one of the groups. And what is it that they think I know?" I stopped for a sip of coffee.

"Today a new group showed interest." I finished off the sandwich and licked the yogurt off my fingers. "The Palace," I said.

"The Palace!" he exclaimed.

"The Palace. Yesterday I got an invitation I couldn't refuse. An equerry arrived to take me to the Palace for tea. I was received by Khalil el Hadid."

"Hadid!"

"You know him?"

"Yes," he said bitterly. "He's the head of the Palace Secret Service. Looks like a gentleman. Isn't."

"That's the man. He gave me a cup of excellent tea, some pretty little sandwiches, and told me that Omar Rashid was a friend of the King."

"Which means the Foundation could not possibly be guilty of anything?"

"Exactly. Then he turned me over to a different equerry, who took me to the basement and handed me over to the breakers."

Kemal looked alarmed.

"They knew I worked for the Agency."

"The Agency?"

"Somebody told them I worked for the Agency."

"Wait a minute! What's this Agency?" he demanded.

Oops. I had forgotten that Kemal didn't know that I worked for the CIA. I sighed.

"The CIA," I answered.

He digested that. He didn't look pleased.

"You told me you worked for Femme Aid."

"I did. Femme Aid belongs to the Agency. I set up the office here."

"The CIA is running spies in Morocco?" he asked angrily.

"We're following human trafficking, that's all. Femme Aid really does help women in distress, but the office keeps track of the slave caravans and sometimes arms smuggling. A security man in Rabat and one in Fez know about this. The government knows we do it. They haven't got the resources to follow the trade and don't seem to care about the brothels."

I looked at him, and he shrugged.

"We share information, but the slavers just keep working, selling women and boys into slavery, and nothing ever happens," I said bitterly.

"Anyway, the men at the Palace knew I worked for the Agency. As far as I know, nobody in Morocco knows I work for the Agency, except Hakim Ouzzat in Rabat and Driss Bouchta in Fez. One of them must have told the Palace."

"Not necessarily. The men at the Palace know everything. They probably knew about you as soon you arrived the first time. If they didn't interfere, it means the Palace doesn't care. But Hadid! He's treacherous, untrustworthy, cunning, devious, lying, immoral. They call him the 'King's Food Taster.' He will do anything no matter how dirty to see the King secure and on the throne."

"I can see you really like the guy."

"His 'breakers,' as you call them, tortured one of my men to get him to confess to a conspiracy he knew nothing about. Daoud was never the same afterward. It's one of the reasons I left the Guard. If the King's Guards aren't safe from the King's secret agents, then who is?" He took a deep breath. "Go on with your story."

"They seemed to think I had some connection with the Pures."

"Pures?"

"The Pure Warriors of Islam, the guys responsible for the suicide bomb yesterday. They seemed to think I had some connection to them."

"But why?"

"I have no idea. I told them that I worked for Femme Aid and refused to tell them anything else. Various interrogators came in and asked the same question: what was my connection to the Pures? They left me in the dark for a while. For a long time. I thought they would never come back. Nothing ungentlemanly but designed to get me to answer their questions. After some hours a new man arrived with a new question: why did I think the Rashid Foundation was laundering money for terrorists? I gave no answer. Even if I had been talking to them, I couldn't have told them that. It's what I'm trying to find out. But that's what they really wanted to know, I think. What I knew about the Foundation that made me think they are laundering money for terrorists. About the Pures, I just got here, and they're new. How could I have a connection with them? But they insisted the Pures had links with terrorists in Paris, and that I had contact with them there."

I got my cell phone out of my pack and showed him the picture of the man I killed in the apartment the night before.

"Know him?"

Kemal looked sick. "Yes I do. He's a Palace assassin."

Chapter 36

"I KILLED A Palace assassin?" I exclaimed, alarmed at the thought.

"Well, maybe not an assassin, but he's one of the men who do the dirty work for Hadid. He had a gun? Maybe he just wanted something."

"He had a gun, a nice 9 mm Glock like everybody else carries, probably Palace issue. What could I have that the Palace wants? Any way, they could search the apartment anytime I was out."

"Maybe it was something you had on you? You say that people are trying to snatch you. Maybe they want something you're carrying?"

"What? The car keys? They already have my laptop. Oh yes, he'd come to kill me, and he wasn't alone. Somebody followed me from the apartment. That's when I came to you."

"What did you do today—yesterday—that was so important that you had to ditch your backup?"

"My job, Kemal. I can't work flanked by two huge guards who look as if they're planning to break somebody in half. I went to Madame Verney's. She barely spoke to me. If they had been there, I would never have gotten in."

I told him the rest of it.

"Mustapha Lahkim knows that money is moving, but he can't say how or where. He did say that there was a new hawalador in Crimson Alley," I said. "He knows me well. He showed me the most beautiful pearl."

"Pearl?"

"A baroque pearl, the most beautiful one I've ever seen."

I looked off into space, visualizing the pearl, visualizing it on a chain around my neck. I shook myself. "Irrelevant."

"On the way back up the hill, I ran into a little guy I saw in Madame Verney's. He tried to pretend he didn't know me, but he did. He scuttled off, and I followed him. He must have seen me, because he led me in a circle and lost me."

"You're noticeable. You're a woman, and a Western woman, at that," he said.

He was right. I hate it when he's right.

"I was hacking back toward Crimson Alley, when a couple of guys grabbed me and pulled me into an alley. I kicked and yelled and escaped. Well, I was rescued. I went to Crimson Alley, but I didn't see him again. So I went back up the hill."

"And evaded—what did you call them? Heckle and Jeckle?—evaded Heckle and Jeckle."

"Uh, yes."

"You think he was collecting money from Madame Verney's and taking it to the hawalador's?"

"Maybe. I can't think what else could be happening. He didn't look as if he'd dropped in for a quickie. He doesn't look like he does quickies or anything else in a brothel. He could have been collecting from Madame Verney, but there's no way he was collecting in the medina. And there's more. My next stop was the Rashid Foundation offices. While I was talking to Omar Rashid, the Man with the Briefcase came in to get a bank deposit slip signed. He tried to pretend he didn't know me, but he failed. I left quickly and sprinted down the fire stairs just in time to follow him down an alley to the side door of the Credit Suisse. He must have seen me, because he led me in a circle again."

"I say again: you're too noticeable to follow people on foot in Fez."

I ignored him and continued. "When he thought he was clear, he went back to the boulevard and was picked up by a man driving a white Rover. I was lucky enough to get a taxi, so I followed him to the Bab Bou Jeloud, where your *associates* were waiting. I went to the next gate did some chores. Then I—uh—visited the Rashid Foundation and—uh—downloaded the contents of Omar's hard drive."

"Lee . . . ," he began. "Lee, I thought you had better sense." He was speaking quietly, reasonably. That was when he was the most dangerous. "They've presumably snatched your friend. She may not be alive. They are trying to snatch you. You're going to wind up dead."

I decided not to tell about the closet.

"Kemal, it was almost dark. I could have followed him to the hawalador's."

"You don't know that."

"He's the link between the Foundation and the terrorist money, I'm sure of it. The Foundation, the protection gang, and the terrorist money. They're all linked."

"You don't know that, either."

"And I never will, unless you get your people off my back. I need to see him go into that office. I need to find out where he's sending the money."

"Lee, there's no way you can follow him into Crimson Alley, if that's where he's going, even in the dark. You're conspicuous. Even overlooking the fact that you're European, women don't go into the medina at night. Few go into that area in the daytime. Not only that, but if you're right about the protection gang, the Foundation, and the terrorist money being linked, all three may be out to kill you. And then there's the Palace. You think you can handle that by yourself?" he demanded.

I looked at him grimly. "Kemal, I can't get any work done with two hulking guards behind me."

"Don't sulk. You know I'm right. Your manhood won't be revoked if you have backup for a change," he said firmly.

I went on sulking. I knew he was right. I hate it when he's right.

"All right, then I need someone else to follow him. If I'm lucky, and he goes to the hawalador's tomorrow, I need somebody who can follow him inside."

"I can follow him," offered Kemal.

I laughed. "Kemal, with that scar on your face, you're just as noticeable as I am."

"All right, I'll get someone."

"Someone small, Kemal, not the size of Heckle and Jeckle. They should take up sumo wrestling."

"I'll find someone," he insisted.

I was still sulking as we climbed the stairs to the European room, but he soon convinced me that we had more important things to do than sulking. He's good at that. When I took off my jeans to throw them across a chair, I heard something hit the floor. It was the flash drive I picked up in Alicia's apartment. I put it on the chest along with the one I copied Rashid's files to.

He held me close.

"This is too much cloth between us," I said. It was much nicer after we took care of that.

"Lovely body."

"Hmmm?"

"You have a lovely body," I said, "Strong and warm and very nicely put together."

"Lee, you say the strangest things."

"I'm not supposed to say you have a lovely body?"

"Women don't say things like that. At least in Morocco they don't."

"You object?" I asked.

He smiled at me. "How could I?"

"You like it. Lovely skin," I continued.

He laughed out loud. "You are one of a kind. Lovely rhinoceros hide. Now you, your skin is lovely."

He proved once again that he was a good kisser. He was good at other things, too.

After a while, he lit a cigarette and offered it to me.

"No thanks. This time I know my limits."

Sometime later I woke up and found him gone. I sat up. It was after 3 a.m. He was downstairs in the bar. I thought about reading Mike's second attachment, or scanning some of the files from the Rashid Foundation. I got up and dressed and reached for my gun. As I did I noticed the flash drive that had come from Alicia's apartment. It had been hidden there. Why had she hidden it? I felt excitement rising. I put on the holster, seated the gun, and ran lightly down the steps to Kemal's office.

His computer was booted, so I slipped the drive into a USB port and accessed it. Or tried to access it. It demanded a password. Encrypted, I thought disgustedly, and her key code is at the office, isn't it? I ejected Alicia's flash drive. All right, I thought, I'll do the files I downloaded from Rashid's computer. I was about to insert that flash drive when I noticed the keys to the rental car beside me on the desk. Alicia's key code was in the office. I closed down my e-mail, picked up the keys, and tiptoed down the hall. I struck lucky. Heckle or Jeckle had left the car in the alley. Covered by the sounds of music inside, I started it and drove down the alley, not turning on the headlights until I was out on the street.

Traffic was light at that hour, and it didn't take long to drive to the office. I found a parking place right in front of the building, which, I hoped, would give the bad guys no chance to drag me into the alley. The hall and the stairs were dimly lighted, the bulbs as small as the ones Ibrahim used, maybe smaller. On the fourth floor I avoided both the tears in the rug and was putting my key into the lock when I noticed the lights were on in Zeynab Bentali's office. A little late to be producing billable hours, I thought, so I didn't turn on the overhead light. I found my way to the computer room by what little light was coming in the window. Closing the door I turned on the light and found the mangled keyboard where I had thrown it. That's where they all keep the key code—on the back of the keyboard, and Alicia was no different. I copied it into my cell phone and turned off the light to go back to Kemal's. Crossing the room, I heard people talking in the hall. I opened the door a crack and looked out. There were three people, and I knew them all. With Zeynab Bentali stood Omar Rashid and Khalid el Hadid. An interesting threesome.

Hadid bowed to Zeynab, shook hands with Rashid, and went his elegant way, giving not the slightest indication that he was the most dangerous man in the realm.

Chapter 37

AFTER ZEYNAB AND Rashid were certain Hadid was gone, they embraced for a long moment. Then Rashid whispered something in Zeynab's ear, and they went into the office. I waited for a few minutes and then tiptoed down the hall, hoping they wouldn't hear me. I made it down the stairs and out of the building without attracting any attention. Outside, I drew my pistol and walked to the car. This time anybody who tried to grab me was going to get shot. Nobody tried to grab me.

I waited to see what would happen next. Hadid, Omar, and Zeynab. An interesting threesome. Their meeting at that hour could not be innocent. Hadid and Omar. Was that why Hadid had tried to warn me off at the Palace? Not because he was a friend of the King, but because the head of the King's Secret Service was conspiring with him to launder money for terrorists? Hadid didn't look like the ideological type. He did look as if he had expensive tastes, though. And where did Zeynab fit? The mistress Marcel couldn't find? Anything else? She didn't look like the ideological type, either. She still looked like an Egyptian belly dancer out of uniform. None of the three had the look of a fundamentalist. For a conspiracy, that would be an advantage. Who would suspect them? Except Alicia suspected Omar. Why? I was long on questions and short on information, as usual.

Omar came out of the building by himself and drove away in a white Mercedes. I pulled out behind him to follow, my headlights off. A good way to meet my ancestors, but the only way to follow him from the office. Three blocks away, I dropped back and turned my headlights on. We didn't have far to go. Omar turned into a parking garage under a high-rise apartment building in the Ville Nouvelle. I carried on around the block and set a course for Kemal's. Did Omar and Zeynab always meet at her office, or were they just there because of their meeting with Hadid? I wondered what Marcel would pay me for the name of Omar's mistress.

I parked the car in the alley behind Kemal's and slipped inside. No sign of Kemal. I went quietly down the hall to the office, hoping my absence had escaped his notice. When I opened the office door, I saw that it had not. Kemal was standing beside the desk, his face black with fury.

"Where have you been this time?" he demanded. "In the middle of the night, yet!"

"I'm getting damn well sick and tired of being treated like a child, Kemal." I threw the car keys on the desk. "I'll go out when I please. I'm a big girl now, and if you don't stop this, I'm going to a hotel!"

The scar on his face burned bright red. "What in the name of Allah was so important that you had to go out in the middle of the night? People out there are trying to kidnap you!" he shouted.

I shouted back. "What was so important? A flash drive I found hidden in Alicia's apartment. It's encrypted. It must hold Alicia's files, and I need to get into them. Now. So I had to go to the office to get her key code."

He wasn't happy to hear my explanation. "And this is worth risking your life for?"

"Yes, it is," I snapped. "It's my life, Kemal, and I choose when to risk it. I don't know what's going on. I'm stumbling around in the dark. People are attacking me, and I need to know who they are and why they're after me before somebody kills me," I said. "I've got to get into her files. The answer must be there."

He slammed out of the office. I put the flash drive in the USB port, accessed it and typed in Alicia's key code. With a whirr, the computer presented me a long list of files. She's never thrown a thing away, I thought. Or archived anything. This is going to take all night! Priority? Name? No. I organized them by date modified and went back two months. The first file there was the office bookkeeping from the first of the year, including all the trips she'd taken. I ran down the list. Nothing unusual. It looked as if there was nothing but Femme Aid business. The next file, labeled human trafficking, was huge. It included clippings on the topic for the last two years, updated just before she went missing, but nothing unusual. Her files were beginning to look like the filing cabinets, stuffed, hopeless to find anything in. I copied all the files I thought I needed to look at onto a new page. That didn't help a lot, but it made the task look less horrendous. It also made me focus on the names of the files. Some of them were made up: Oshkosh, Alcohol, and Byzantine. Others had only numbers for names.

This girl is going to achieve the world record for the fastest time for driving me crazy, I thought.

I opened random files and found nothing but ordinary Femme Aid business. I shook myself and began to open them methodically. There was still a lot of Femme Aid business, but Oshkosh contained Internet material on terrorism. The next file, number 4211, contained most of the open source stuff you could find about money laundering. She had most of what could be found on the Internet about both topics. The dates of the files suggested that she'd been turning the topics over in her mind for maybe six months.

There was a file on the Rashid Foundation containing much the same information that I had found. On and on I went, getting more tired and more frustrated by the minute. The only things I could find were things I already knew. I was about to close it down, and read Mike's second attachment in the morning, but I read one last file: her appointment calendar from the first of the year to the present. I scrolled down to the end. I ran the cursor up one more time and found an appointment with a woman named Aliya Rashid for June 14. Rashid was a fairly common surname. I thought I had found Rashid's mistress. Was it possible I had also found his wife?

Chapter 38

KEMAL CAME IN. "The bar's closed. It's time for bed."

"A tempting thought," I said. "One search."

He grimaced and leaned against the wall. I tapped in Omar Rashid and found a biography without personal details. I searched again.

"That's two," he said.

"OK. OK." This time his biography had his genealogy back to the Saint. And, bless its heart, his wife's name. Aliya.

"That's enough," Kemal said and took my hand. Why did Alicia have an appointment with Omar Rashid's wife? Kemal noticed that I was distracted.

"Pay attention," he said.

I paid attention.

I woke at a call to prayer, the taste of cinnamon in my mouth.

"Which one?" I asked.

From out of the tangle of sheets, he mumbled, "Noon."

I was getting used to the noon call to prayer. Of course if you stay up all night working on the computer, you're bound to sleep until noon. I got up slowly and stretched and smiled. No sleeping pill need apply. Then I remembered. Why *was* Aliya Rashid in Alicia's office?

I was getting tired of having olives for breakfast. I wanted eggs, sausage, fried potatoes—the whole cholesterol-laden thing. I had olives.

"How are you going to try to commit suicide today?" Kemal asked.

"Don't be rude. Do I try to stop you from running a house of assignation? I've got to work these files," I said. "And I need to follow the Man with the Briefcase."

I went to the office computer, and got into my e-mail. More stuff from Mike with attachments, long attachments. I felt myself sinking in a wave of information when only yesterday I was complaining of the lack. Either too much or not enough. Always. I went back to the previous messages and started through attachments. Omar Rashid—nothing I didn't already know. On Sam Glover he had struck out. Trying harder.

I e-mailed him that Glover worked for Worldwide, if that was any help.

Beside the computer lay the drive with Rashid's files. I put it into the USB port when Kemal came in with a little guy in a dirty *kurta* over dirty ragged pants. His sandals were coming apart and did nothing to hide his calloused feet and broken toe nails. His face was wizened and brown, his eyes squinty.

"This is Abdul," Kemal said.

I smiled. "He's perfect," I said. It was just about the time the Man with the Briefcase had left Madame Verney's the day before. I closed down the computer and got up.

Come on." I said. "Let's get Heckle or Jeckle and go to Madame Verney's.

"Not Heckle or Jeckle. I'll drive," said Kemal and picked up the keys.

I looked suspiciously at him. It's hard for man with a scar like that on his face to look innocent. Besides, I knew that he wasn't innocent. We adjourned to the car, me in front, Abdul in the back. Madame Verney's place was well into the Ville Nouvelle, but the traffic wasn't very heavy. I saw a white Rover parked in front of her place, the driver slouched down, dozing against the window.

I pointed. "That may be the Rover that picked him up yesterday."

"There are a lot of white Rovers in Fez," Kemal said.

There was a parking place where we could keep an eye on the door and the Rover without being conspicuous. It was half an hour before the little man in the three-piece suit came down the steps and got into the Rover. Kemal put the car in gear and followed along gently behind him all the way to the Bab Bou Jeloud.

"Does he know what he's supposed to do?" I asked.

"Yes," said Kemal.

Abdul got out of the car and walked slowly toward the gate, moving up to place himself in front of the Man with the Briefcase. The two of them passed through the gate and disappeared. We followed and took a table in the rear of the café on the right just inside the gate.

"And now we wait," I said.

"Yes" said Kemal.

A half an hour passed before the men returned. Abdul stepped inside the café and sat down at a table in front. The waiter was displeased at his scruffy look but served him his coffee anyway. The Man with the Briefcase got into his car and was driven away. Abdul threw some dirty dirhams on the table and left. We paid our bill and followed. Just outside the café we ran into Sam Glover.

"I'm glad I found you," he said. "I didn't know how to get in touch with you. I've remembered something about Alicia."

"What?" I asked.

"She has a boyfriend."

"You told me that."

"Yes, but I've remembered where I saw them. I saw them having dinner once, at Guido's, that Italian place over on Mohammed V. He was sitting down, but he looked like a tall guy, light brown hair. Mustache? No, I don't think so. Clean shaven. She introduced him to me as Jerry. I hope that helps."

"Bound to," I said. "Thanks."

At last, something from her private life!

We returned to the car and waited for Abdul. He drifted quietly up to the driver's side and looked shyly at me and then dropped his eyes.

"He went into the hawalador's as you thought," he told Kemal. "He sent 5,000 US dollars to Merinshah."

Kemal gave him a fistful of dirhams, and he wandered away, a wraith who could follow smoke through a fire.

"Merinshah," I said. "He's sending money to the Taliban. From whorehouses to terrorists. Allah is broad-minded when it comes to financing a jihad. We need to follow that guy tonight, Kemal. The money he sent just now was from the brothels in the Ville Nouvelle. If he goes tonight, the money will be from the Rashid Foundation."

Kemal looked at his watch. "It's too early to go to Guido's," he said.

I agreed. "Let's go back to the bar. I'll work the Rashid's files."

When I got into them, they were nearly as big a disappointment as Alicia's were, mostly letters and e-mails about placing boys in schools or jobs, nothing that wasn't Foundation business. There was a message to an outfit called Global that a shipment had gone astray. I searched his folders, but couldn't find out what that was. His bookmarks were instructive, though. At the bottom of a long list of unsorted URLs, I found a folder labeled "J." It proved to contain links to jihadi sites in Arabic: Al Qaeda, Taliban, the websites of miscellaneous imams with messages that were way over the top, some of them calls to arms, some of them just fulminations against the Crusader States. Some of them were new to me, but I was only interested in their money, not their ideology. Toward the end, I found sites with instructions for making bombs. I sat back in the chair. Why was Omar interested in making bombs? Did collecting terrorist URLs mean that he was laundering money? Not necessarily, but it made a good case for his commitment to jihad.

How would that lead me to Alicia?

Chapter 39

GUIDO'S, ON THE main stem of the Ville Nouvelle, Boulevard Mohammed V, was straight out of central casting, which probably explained its popularity with expats. Murals of Mediterranean villages produced by somebody painting by the numbers, red-checked tablecloths, even candles in Chianti bottles. The waiter wasn't up to the standard of the décor. He was a short, chubby Moroccan with tired eyes and feet that hurt.

"Might as well have dinner while we're here," I said. I decided to see what the Moroccan take on osso buco was. Kemal wasn't so adventurous. He had plain spaghetti and meatballs. Halfway through our meal, Kemal showed the waiter the picture of Alicia on my iPhone. When his memory had been suitably refreshed, he admitted that she had been there.

"Was she alone?" I asked.

He pretended not to understand my Arabic. They do that to me sometimes. Kemal never had any trouble understanding me. Well, Kemal was a special case, but failure to understand a woman's speech is just another way of making her invisible. I chose not to tell that to Kemal.

"Who was she with?" Kemal asked him.

He started to shrug his shoulders again. Kemal simply turned the scarred side of his face toward he man and asked again. "Who was she with?"

"A guy," he said hurriedly.

"What kind of guy?" Kemal pressed. "Black, white, European, Moroccan?"

"European," was the sullen answer.

"And?"

"And what?" Still sullen. He wanted more sweetening.

"What did he look like?" Kemal growled. "Short, tall, hair color?"

"Tall, maybe. Brown hair."

"Eyes?"

Two, I thought.

The waiter thought for a while, obviously not a familiar undertaking. "Maybe blue?"

"Or green?" Kemal asked.

"Or green," the waiter agreed.

"He didn't have two heads or a cleft palate," I said.

"Or one leg." Kemal nodded to the man, and we had a glass of the sour red wine. "Not a lot to go on. It fits half of the Europeans in town. Even Glover."

"His hair is blonde," I replied and remembered that Sam Glover lived across the landing from Alicia.

The spaghetti and meatballs were good, Kemal insisted, but I found the osso buco strange. I'm sure there's no saffron in it in Italy. There was flan, though. Every former French colony has flan. And good bread. I was showing signs of falling asleep in my dessert plate, so Kemal took me home. It was early for the bar, a couple of businessmen late going home, a college student with a textbook and glassy eyes. Obviously not tobacco. I wondered how he could afford it. The hard core wouldn't arrive until close to midnight and stay till dawn. This gave us a chance to have an assignation.

We went upstairs and ceremonially undressed each other, an anticipatory pleasure that I loved. He paused, and

I looked him full in the face. He reached around me and took a box from on top of my pillow. He opened it and slipped a chain over my head. I felt something cool and looked down. A baroque pearl was hanging lustrous between my breasts.

My first thought was to say, "You shouldn't have spent so much."

My second was, "That's a really bad thing to say."

"It's my pearl. But when? We've been together all day."

"While you were doing your e-mail before we went to Guido's, I went to Lahkim's. He knew exactly the pearl I meant."

"It's so beautiful!" I said. "I've never had anything so beautiful."

"A beautiful pearl for a beautiful woman," he said and kissed me.

I spent some time thanking him comprehensively and went to sleep nestled along his warm body. Sometime later, half awake, I reached to put my arm around him, and he wasn't there. I woke entirely and felt an enormous sense of loss. He came back when the bar closed, and the sense of loss was pushed into the back of my mind, but it stayed there. We weren't in love, although we cared for each other, and I knew I would return to Paris after I found Alicia Harmon, return to a lonely bed, with no one to warm me against the darkness of the night, but how could I stay? Wear a black suit for the rest of my life? And what would I do? Be the mistress of a man who ran a house of assignation?

When he returned, we made love, me with a kind of desperation, and I went back to sleep. It seemed only moments later when my cell phone rang. It was a woman, and she was so excited that I could barely understand her.

"She's safe! Alicia is safe! I just got a text from her!"

"Calm down. Calm down," I said. "I can't understand you. Who is this?"

"It's Zeynab. Zeynab Bentali. You remember, Alicia's

attorney? She's safe! She's safe! She's in Tangier! She's eloped. I knew she had a lover, but to elope!"

"When did this happen?"

"Just now. This minute."

"Did you talk to her?"

"No, it was a text. I didn't speak with her. I tried to call her, but all I got was her voice mail."

Curiouser and curiouser. "What did the caller ID say?"

"I don't know. I didn't look. Oh, Ms. Carruthers, she's safe!"

With that she cut the connection. Kemal struggled up from a deep sleep.

"What . . . ?" he mumbled.

"Zeynab Bentali, Alicia's attorney. She says she just got a text from Alicia saying that she has eloped to Tangier."

He opened both eyes. "This time of the night she texts her attorney? After being missing for two weeks?"

"Mmm," I said.

"Do you trust her?" he asked.

"Not an inch, but what if it's true?"

"And if it's not true?"

Chapter 40

HE THREW THE covers back. "It's three hundred miles, three hours or so to Tangier."

It wasn't as much fun getting dressed.

The quickest way to get to Tangier was to take the A-2 back to Rabat and then the A-3 along the coast, auto route almost all the way. The way Kemal drove it was a bit less than three hours. Were we on the verge of finding Alicia, of finally cutting through the tangled web? I hoped so, because I was getting really tired of her. I improved my time trying to figure out how to find them when we got there, since I didn't know the man's name. We stopped for breakfast just outside town at a hotel in an industrial park.

"How will we find her?" Kemal asked.

"By finding the hotel," I answered.

Tangier is not blessed with a multitude of fancy hotels. I searched the Internet and rejected the biggest and most expensive, a hotel-casino around the bay from town, as not suitable for an eloping couple, since it looked like Hotel Gigantique anywhere in the world visited by the Swiss. The Hotel Continental looked much more like it. It was a rambling, romantic old pile standing white on a hill in the medina overlooking the Mediterranean. From the pictures, it had Arabian Nights rooms, balconies, and splendid views of the harbor. It was perfect. I might elope there myself. It was ten a.m. when we parked in the lot down from the main entrance. The lobby was European and small, about the size of a reasonably large telephone booth.

"I am looking for a friend," I told the boy at the desk. "She has recently married, and I have forgotten what her husband's name is."

I showed him Alicia's photo in my iPhone and watched some strong emotion cross his face.

"I regret, madam, I regret." He looked as if he was going to cry.

"What is it?" I asked, my stomach knotting. We'd come so far.

Kemal asked him something in Arabic so fast that I couldn't follow it. The boy nodded. Kemal asked something else. The boy looked anxiously at me and replied. I caught the word "dead."

"Kemal?" Apprehension turned to anxiety.

"The boy says that they were staying here. He thinks they went for a sail and didn't come back."

The boy looked at me and then down quickly.

"He says we should try the morgue."

"But . . ."

Kemal put his arm around my shoulders. "I don't think he knows anything else," he said softly.

"So close," I said in shock. "So close."

Mourning a woman I had never met? In the few days I had been looking for Alicia, she had become a person to me. An annoying person, a rash person, asking questions that could get her killed, but a person.

"Kemal, do you think . . . ?"

"I don't know. We must go and see."

I don't know what I expected the morgue to look like, perhaps a combination of the eighteenth-century Medico-Legal Institute in Paris and Ducky's autopsy room in NCIS? This was just a room painted a flaking institutional green with a cement floor, some metal tables and a wall full of drawers. The medical examiner himself pulled out Alicia's drawer and showed us her remains. I turned my head away and tried to control my breakfast, which seemed to be trying to escape.

"The sea, you know," he said gently. "She was in the sea."

I looked at her again. The remains were very badly abraded, from the tumbling action of the waves, I supposed. Her face and hands were nothing more than meat. My breakfast threatened me again, and I turned my back on the body. I handed the doctor my phone with Alicia's photo.

"Is this that . . ." I gestured. "That?"

He looked carefully at the picture. "It could be. I can get no idea of her face from this, but it could be these remains."

I was about to touch the phone screen to switch to e-mail to ask Sidney to send Alicia's dental records to the Tangier medical examiner, when it dinged, signaling a new message. It was Mike sending me Alicia's most recent credit card charges. The last charge was a rental car in Rissani, the southeastern town at the head of the caravan trail. The one above it was a charge for a flight on Air Maroc. I showed the charges to Kemal.

"She didn't elope," he said. "She flew to Rissani."

Chapter 41

WE INFORMED THE medical examiner that the remains were not those of our friend and went back out into the light.

"We need to go to Rissani," I said, bringing up Air Maroc's schedule of flights from Tangier to Rissani. "There's a flight at three. A two-hour flight." I booked the last two seats.

"That woman was deliberately killed to end your search?" Kemal asked.

"I think she must have been. Her face and hands have been damaged. To prevent identification? I must be getting close to something, or they wouldn't have gone so far."

"You can't just throw a woman into the sea and expect nobody to miss her."

"Tangier is a vacation destination for secretaries and shopgirls on tours looking for a sheikh. One of them might not be missed for several days. If she found a man, she would keep him away from the tour, from the other girls. With any luck, by the time she was missed, the body would have been sent to the States as Alicia Harmon," I replied.

"But she was with a man."

"Who, you notice, hasn't come up from the vasty deep. I'm afraid our shopgirl found her sheikh, and it was the last thing she ever did."

The flight was miserably rough, as if every evil wind in Morocco had decided to plague us. The only landing I have had that was more terrifying was the time we did a combat landing at Sarajevo when the landing field was under fire. We came in on instruments in the middle of a sandstorm. We sat, quivering, until the storm passed and we could descend into Rissani's warm afternoon air. I was genuinely glad to be safe on the ground again.

Safe. If I had only known.

We rented a car and drove toward town. The Rashid tomb and zawiya were on the way, so we turned off on a narrow dirt road, and soon the buildings came into view. The tomb was a little white plastered building of one story, standing amid palm trees and shrubs. Plaster brackets ran around three sides of the roof, seven of them, giving viewers the impression that the simple structure was wearing a crown. A little one-bay porch protected the arched doorway. Connected to the tomb to the left was the zawiya, larger and also plastered white. In front of it was a tiled court with a fountain in a small diamond-shaped garden bed in the center. The windows and door were in the deep shade of a sheltering porch.

The door opened, and several heavily bearded men in traditional long white gowns, probably members of Rashid's Sufi sect, emerged and walked toward the fountain.

There was no construction that I could see.

"If there is no construction, I wonder what the extra money was for," I said.

"What extra money?" Kemal asked.

"The Foundation has a bank account in Rissani for the maintenance of the tomb and the zawiya. This is where it all started, with Omar's ancestor Rashid, who was a Sufi saint. It has received substantially higher amounts of money than usual in the past two months," I replied. "If there's no construction I wonder what it was for."

We drove back to the highway and on toward Rissani. There were four hotels in town. The best, the Hotel Kasbah Amaa, was just outside town, so we stopped there first. The desk clerk shook his head when I showed him Alicia's picture. The bills I gave him disappeared into his pants pocket, but he still shook his head. I considered taking them back, by force if necessary, but Kemal steered me back to the car.

The Hotel Sijilmassa was named for the fabled caravan city whose ruins lay just outside town. The clerk there hadn't seen her either. We took his word for it. It was cheaper. The el-Filalia and the Panorama likewise denied knowledge of her, but the Panorama had good pizza.

"She came to town," I said. "The clerk at the car rental desk recognized her, but, unless one of the clerks was lying, she didn't take a room in any of the hotels," I said.

"She can't just have disappeared," Kemal said.

That's what I loved about old soldiers. They thought the world was logical.

"She probably went to see Mehdi first," I told him.

"Mehdi?"

"Mehdi is an informant, one of the first I hired when I set up the office. He's an old camel dealer, works both sides of the Moroccan-Algerian border bringing herds of camels to be sold for meat in the market in Rissani. Also does a little gentle smuggling. If it's happening on the caravan trail, he knows about it."

We went to the camel souk looking for him. All we found was a scrawny camel searching in the dust for something to eat. Mehdi would be out of the sun in the café sheltered by the colonnade that ran around the souk. "Mehdi also arranges camel treks into the Grand Erg. That's why we've come looking for him," I said.

"Let me do the talking," Kemal said.

I looked mutinous.

He smiled. "Not for me. For them."

Grudgingly I nodded.

We entered the café and waited until our eyes adjusted to the darkness. All talk ceased abruptly. Kemal was OK, but women don't go into cafés in Arab lands.

"I seek Mehdi the camel dealer," Kemal said into the thunderous silence.

Nothing.

"He has arranged camel treks to the Erg for me in the past," he explained. "I want to arrange one for this lady."

A soft murmur greeted the possibility of tourist money. That and the few caravans of meat camels were the remaining sources of Rissani's income.

A middle-aged man in traditional dress sitting by the door said, "Mehdi has passed, may Allah give him rest. His son Selim now arranges the camel treks." He looked around the room. "Selim is not here today."

A murmur ran around the room as the men argued about where Selim might be. Finally a man with a long white beard spoke up.

"There are camel races today in Merzouga. Selim will be there."

"He has no camels racing today," one of the other men said.

At that, all of the men started talking, and it was only after some heated discussion that they agreed that Selim might be in Merzouga, so we went to Merzouga to see if Selim had seen Alicia Harmon.

It wasn't far to Merzouga, about thirty-five miles. The *piste* I had driven on my last trip had been blacktopped, so the only hazard was the sand blowing across the road. The way wound around little hillocks that sported the occasional palm, and brush showed here and there around rocks I wouldn't want to meet in the dark. The Ziz River had a new bridge north of the old ford. Then the brush began to disappear. Soon we were driving through a rocky plain with the dunes of the Erg Chebbi in the distance on the left. There were inns clustered around Merzouga, most of them trying to look like kasbahs, but Merzouga itself wasn't much more than a wide spot in the road with a tiny mosque, couple of shops, and an auto mechanic. That day there were multiple tracks leading south from town. Past the Auberge Ksar Sania, I could see vehicles parked every which way, and people milling around.

We pulled up alongside a bunch of trucks. When we got out of the car, five men came around one of the trucks, all but one in fatigues and carrying AK-47s. Sam Glover wore his usual pressed khakis.

Kemal and I started toward them. The middle one fired, and Kemal went down. I screamed "Kemal!" and covered him with my body. None too steady, I emptied my pistol at them, missing all of them, and, in the most futile gesture of my life, I threw it at them. I pumped Kemal's chest as hard as I could.

"Stay with me Kemal! Stay with me!"

But he left me.

I kissed him and screamed again, a howl of rage. I pulled the knife from my boot and jumped on the closest man, Sam Glover, to cut his throat. He bucked and squealed.

"Get her off me! Get her off me!"

I heard a sound behind me, and the lights went out.

Chapter 42

BITS AND PIECES floated in my brain. The acrid odor of unwashed male. A jolting ride. Men with beards outlined in dashboard lights. In between I dreamed. Kemal's skin under my hands, his lips on mine, his hands. I woke and realized he was dead. And I dreamed again. Hands, cinnamon kisses, laughter. And woke again. And realized he was dead again.

"I don't embrace women who wear guns."

"They won't revoke your manhood if you have backup for a change."

I fought my way up to full consciousness. If he hadn't been backing me up, he would still be alive. I closed my eyes. I would have to live with that.

After a while the ride became less rough. In the dim light from the dashboard, I saw that I was propped up in the corner of the backseat of some kind of vehicle. Not a car. Bigger. An SUV. I closed my eyes and tried to sleep, but Kemal kept getting in the way. Even with my eyes open, I could feel his hands moving over my skin. I forced myself to think. Kemal was dead, and I was alive, and I had to stay that way. I could mourn him later.

I was travelling in a SUV? I was traveling with three men. The one next to me wore fatigues and a turban. The men in the front seat wore turbans. A rifle was propped on the other side of the guy next to me. The next time I remembered that Kemal was dead, I remembered how he died and decided that I was riding with his killers. Why?

The vehicle jolted to a stop, and the men got out. They were outlined in the headlights as they knelt and faced east. As they performed their ablutions in the sand, I considered my plight. As they avowed that there was no god but God and Mohammed was his prophet, I tried, without success, to figure a way out of that plight. Escape? Even if I got away, where would I go? Tears formed in my eyes, but at that moment the men returned, and I stifled them. I would be damned if they would see me cry. Nobody had seen me cry since I was twelve and somebody had run over my dog.

The man next to me reached behind him and brought out a cotton sack from which he took a stack of flat bread. He passed that around and then passed us each a handful of dates. All it wanted was camel milk. After we had eaten, they passed around a water skin. I made a pure mess of drinking from it, and water soaked my shirt. My shirt already soaked in Kemal's blood. It clung to my body, exposing my breasts entirely too clearly.

Turning, the man in the passenger seat snarled, "Cover your face, woman!"

I doubted that it was my face that bothered him.

It was light enough to see by then. He was the man who killed Kemal.

"You go to hell," I snarled back.

He reached across from the front seat and slapped me in the face, hard. I turned to look out of the window, my cheek throbbing. I will kill him, I thought. Before this is over I will kill him. Maybe I'll torture him a bit first.

He threw me a long strip of cloth. An unwound turban? I draped it over my breasts and wound it around my face until it was covered except for my eyes. I understood viscerally for the first time how Muslim women could accept their traditional clothing. I felt almost invisible and marginally safer covered. If they put me in a burka, I might disappear entirely.

After we got underway again, it was light enough to see the men. The one beside me was young, slim, with skin burned brown by the sun. I couldn't see anything of the driver except his turban, but the man to the right, the one who had killed Kemal, had a round face, icy cold eyes, and some gray in his beard. His skin, too, was roughened by the weather. Above his beard I could see chicken pox scars or the remains of teenage acne. I looked out the window and considered the situation again. A coldness settled over me. They wouldn't have taken me with them unless they wanted something from me. Not knowledge. I didn't know anything they wanted to know. I was going to be held for ransom, and the Agency did not pay ransom. I returned to the thought of escaping. Looking at my companions I concluded that my chance of that ranged from slim to none. Maybe later? Not bloody likely. I represented money, and they would keep me in the vault.

We turned left through a break in the rocky hills and continued on another track which shortly narrowed and sank into a sand lake that looked as if it had once been a marsh. The man who killed Kemal walked ahead to guide our way, but the sand was packed enough for the cruiser to make it through with no problems.

I closed my eyes, and Kemal's killer began to speak. Was it good or bad that I understood Arabic? "The bomb went well, I thought."

The other two agreed, and the driver spoke. "I wasn't certain Amad could do it. He was frightened when we dropped him off. These new kids we're getting are not well-motivated."

"We have to increase our training," the man in the passenger seat said. "They're only at the training camp for a day. I do what I can, but it's only an hour before we have to start the technical training."

The driver said, "You should give the sermon out of the Quran. They know it by heart. Somebody just needs to quote the proper passage."

The young man beside me disagreed. "It's only that he was afraid. We all are. But when the time came he acted. We all know the King of Morocco is an apostate. He's allied with the Americans."

I opened my eyes, and they stopped talking. I closed my eyes, and they resumed the debate.

"Al Qaeda is angry that we left to form our own group. I think they will take some kind of action." The man in the passenger seat was older and spoke with authority. He must be the boss, I thought. "The emir doesn't agree."

"What can they do to us?" the driver asked. "They are tied down in Mali."

"Belmansur is the closest emir," said the Boss. "He might do anything."

"But he isn't in with them anymore," said the young man. "They threw him out, didn't they?"

"You think so? Maybe, maybe not. I still say he's dangerous. A loose cannon. Nobody can control him."

I opened my eyes and looked out the side window at the uninspiring scenery, which consisted of sand and rocks, relieved occasionally by rocks and sand.

We drove in silence for a while, and I dozed off. The Boss's next comment woke me up. I shut my eyes again quickly.

"What are we going to do with her?" the driver asked.

I thought I knew what they were going to do with me, but I was still chilled when the Boss replied.

"What do you think? Hold her for ransom, of course."

"They haven't paid for the other one yet," commented the boy.

"Maybe we'll have to send them a finger then," said the Boss, laughing.

I turned my face to the window. The Agency doesn't pay ransom. At least that's what they say. And my grandmother doesn't have the kind of money they'll ask.

"What'll we do next?" the boy asked. "I think we should attack the King. He's as bad as his father. He just smiles while he's jailing and killing people. Besides, he cannot be the Commander of the Faithful. He was not ratified by the Fez ulema."

Ah, peace and justice. Perhaps they could get the Caliph in Istanbul to do it. After they establish a new one, that is.

About midmorning, I saw four black tents some distance away. Bedouin camp? No. There were no sheep. As we drew nearer, I saw the well the tents were pitched around. I counted three Toyota pickups under a desert camouflage net and two camels hobbled and looking about for something to eat. We stopped by the well, and about two dozen men poured out of the tents to welcome us. They looked startled when they saw me, but the Boss assured them that I was just a foolish woman who would bring in some money. I looked away. I was just a cash cow.

The men went into emergency session in Arabic to figure out how to construct a woman's section in one of the tents. The issue had never come up before. They finally rigged the camouflage net from the truck park in one corner to save their blushes. It wasn't a good fit, but it would do. Maybe a satellite would see the trucks while they were out in the open.

My tiny apartment was stifling. Do the tents have to be black? Why not white ones to repel the sun? I lay down on the small rug and looked around. I dug under the tent wall and looked out. Other than the camp I could see nothing but the desert. Maybe at night? I wasn't much for celestial navigation, and I had lost my pack back at Merzouga, which meant no pen flashlight, and no compass. Or passport, money, or cell phone. The only tool I had left was the Swiss Army knife in my pocket, and my brain, and that was only marginally functioning. My emotions were clouding my thinking. Kemal was dead, and we'd never make love again. I had to find a way to push him to the back of my brain and focus. I had to stay alive long enough to kill the Boss.

Chapter 43

THE MEN CROWDED around were mostly young, slender men of the desert who wore faded and dusty *kurtas* with vests over them or djellabas that were equally worn. They clustered around the Boss, eager to learn the skills required by jihad. They sat on mats arranged in a semicircle around him. They had come to hear him, and he gave them a stem-winder of a sermon.

"You are Knights of the Faith who will defend the wounded Nation of Islam with your blood!" I heard him declaim. "As Sons of Islam, we were called by our revered leader, Osama bin Laden, may Allah give him peace, to the elevated, the exalted task of jihad against the Crusaders and their running dogs, the Apostate Rulers of our lands!"

His listeners began to respond to his words.

"Apostates! Dogs!"

"The Book demands it!"

"Yes!"

"The Prophet demands it!"

"Prophet! Prophet!"

"Allah himself demands it!"

"Allah! Allah! Allahhu akbar!"

He began to increase the pace.

"The world must be cleansed of these Devils!"

"Devils!"

"And Islam must return to its rightful place in the world as in the days of the Caliph."

"Caliph!"

"And a New Caliphate, a New Islam, must be forged by you Pure Ones. It is your task, you, the privileged Pure Ones, to raise our enslaved brethren and bring them back to righteousness! To rescue them from the degradation these Apostates have forced onto them and restore their unsoiled, their spotless, their immaculate spirit!"

He was certainly going it good, a real Islamic Elmer Gantry, but the break in the rhythm of his call had momentarily left his congregation confused. He returned to his style of short, punchy phrases, and his sermon was back on track.

"Forced, yes, forced onto us!"

"Forced!" They returned to the chant.

"By the machinations of those Engines of Infamy!"

Machinations was too much for them.

"Infamy!"

"The World Bank and the United Nations! Those international infidels' dens!"

"Infidel! Infidel!"

"Those partners of the Americans, the Great Shaitan!"

"Shaitan, Shaitan!"

"Who work to crush the Faithful!"

"Crush! Crush! Crush!"

"They must be destroyed!"

"Destroyed! Destroyed! Destroyed!"

By that time he had them jumping up and down and shaking their fists in the air the way you saw crowds of Muslim men doing on TV. I saw the rapturous faces of the congregation, and I wondered how he was going to bring them down now that he had got them up there. It was Come to Jesus Time, or rather Come to Allah. One of the men set up a table next to him with a sheet of paper on it, and handed the Boss a book.

"Come now and swear. Swear to give the last drop of your blood to destroy the enemies of Islam! Swear on the Book," he demanded.

The men pushed forward and, one at a time, they were guided to the Boss, laid their right hands on the book and swore, "By this Holy Book, I swear that I will give the last drop of my blood to destroy the enemies of Islam." Then they passed to the table, where each made a small cut in his right thumb and pressed it to the paper, leaving a bloody fingerprint. Those who could write signed their names. Those who couldn't signed with an X and the assistant wrote their names beside the X.

They said their noon prayers in ecstasy.

A meal of flatbread and goat brought them back to earth and prepared for the tasks ahead. They sat cross-legged on mats and waited for orders from the Boss. He divided them into small groups and gave each a teacher. In the shade of one of the tents, one assistant sat on a mat with one bunch and began instructing them in the use of a satellite phone. It was obvious that they had never seen such a thing, but many of them had cell phones, so they caught on rapidly. Another assistant taught another group how to strip an AK-47 and put it back together again. A third had several men off by themselves learning to fire the weapon. These two groups were not so uncertain; rifles were a part of their culture.

The next group the Boss had saved for himself. These were older men, browned and wrinkled by the desert sun. The Boss sat on the ground and gathered them around him. He was too far away for me to hear, but shortly he began to draw in the sand in front of him. Then he placed several small stones in his drawing and moved them about. He was giving them refinements on the art of desert warfare, a subject they had studied since childhood.

I was in one of the mobile training camps.

After a short break, the students in the phone class rotated into the AK-47 class, and the students from that class tackled the satellite phone.

The men in the strategy and tactics class remained the same. They had moved on to map reading. Few nomads had ever seen a map; they navigated by a mind map more perfect than any cartographer's, but if orders were to be transmitted by phone, they needed to be map literate. The Boss was using what looked from here like military maps of the area in his familiarization class. Was the Algerian army still using the old French ones? I'd have given my eye teeth to look at one of them.

Nearby, a group of middle-aged men who had come into the camp during the morning attended a class taught by a young, urban looking man in blue jeans and sneakers. He was a different kind of expert, and his students were a different kind of scholar. This was the graduate school, the school for bombers.

Class began with munitions familiarization. Each man was given the chance to examine a series of grenades, including rocket-propelled ones, and get a clear idea of their range and the circumstances under which they should be used. They progressed to learning to make bombs to be detonated remotely, the IEDs used in Afghanistan. It appeared that the group was training for both terrorist attacks and guerilla warfare.

With a kind of sick fascination, I watched the instructor assemble a suicide vest. First he cut into a block of plastic explosive and opened it out like a book. Then he spread ball bearings on one leaf like caviar until the whole space was evenly covered. Folding the explosive "book" back together, he carefully stitched the sides like a cobbler repairing a shoe, working delicately, precisely. He inserted the resulting package into a cloth bag with shoulder straps. He repeated the process and placed the second explosive package into another pocket at the end of a pair of heavy straps. He attached a package of batteries to the side of one of the bags, wired the bags together, and inserted a switch. He had one of the students model the lethal garment. It fit over his shoulders, one explosive package hanging down on his front and one on his back. It was unlike the more common vests of stiff green duck with vertical pockets, but it did the job. It was just as effective and a whole lot easier to make. The final touch was a long coat to hide the vest.

I turned my back on the display, lay down on the rug and put my hands over my face.

There was a roar. I was thrown to the ground. There was a moment of absolute silence, my ears popped; it began to rain bits of metal. And then the screaming began.

I saw the scene again in my mind's eye: chunks of metal and human flesh raining down, the uninjured screaming, the wounded moaning. People wandered in a daze among the blood and flesh and guts scattered over what had been a peaceful scene just moments before.

I tried not to vomit.

These men were learning how to inflict that destruction! I asked myself again: how could human beings do these things? Human beings? Monsters!

I had followed terrorist money for years, chasing it, seizing it, trying to find its source, but until the other day I had never seen the results of their abominable work on the ground. Pictures could not convey the horror! Watching that man construct that engine of evil—I couldn't bear it. Kemal's death was an evil thing, but a human thing, a thing I could mourn. But this, this was supremely wicked, and they were doing it every day all over the world. Unless they were stopped, it would go on and on and on, until all the humanity was leeched from the world, until blood covered the earth!

I turned my face to the tent wall and wept.

The next day, the students struck the tents after morning prayers, and we went our separate ways. Before the students dispersed, there was a little graduation ceremony. The Boss touched each man on the head as if anointing him and gave him a parcel of money. I wondered how much was in it. Jihadi's families usually got somewhere around 300 US dollars a month.

Each also got a plastic bag with a set of fatigues. Three of the men were given satellite phones to take with them. Platoon leaders? They all were bursting with pride. They were jihadi now, initiated soldiers of Allah!

Chapter 44

OUR WAY LED from the well through another rocky desert. I yearned for one of the maps they had been studying the day before; I had no real idea where we were, and I would need that knowledge later. If there was a later. We traveled silent and dry. The men stopped for midday prayers, and we had a water ration just before we turned north into the sandy dunes. I noticed the Boss looking at me over the seat. I dropped my gaze. Another lesson in being invisible. The more invisible one was, the safer one was. God! I'm becoming a Muslim woman, I thought. I sincerely hoped that my chance to kill that man came before I internalized this appalling feeling.

"Who are you?" he demanded.

I had no answer for him. I took a deep breath. "I ask you. What are your plans for me?"

"The emir has ordered that you be brought to the base camp," he said sharply.

So now I knew. Is knowing that you will die in a fortnight better than knowing you will die eventually? And only a few days ago, I had been making fun of Al Qaeda emirs.

In the late afternoon, we could see a palm-fringed oasis ahead, a lush green, the most beautiful color in the world. The stark desert fell away behind us, a bad dream. Here was water, the best gift of Allah. We passed tiny irrigation ditches with miniscule dirt dams to direct the water in one way or another. Vegetables were growing in the shade of the palms, and animals were grazing. I understood now why the Muslim paradise was alive with water. Here, I thought, was comfort. Here there might even be a bath. I was still wearing the shirt soaked with Kemal's blood. I thought with sensuous delight of clean clothes, and then I remembered that I was going to wear that shirt until I killed the Boss. All right, but I could still take a bath. We kept driving. The lush part of the oasis was soon left behind, its place taken by clumps of dispirited looking palms and piles of sand held in place by thorn bushes which wouldn't be there much longer at the rate the goats were eating them. We left even that, and my heart broke.

After a couple of miles, I saw a tent camp on a slight rise, a short radio mast in front of the first tent. This looked like a permanent camp. The radio mast had a circle of rocks around it, which made a kind of a central plaza. What was it with men and rocks? I wondered. Did men need precise boundaries? At least these weren't painted. An older man in fatigues and a turban stood watching as we drove up and parked under a camouflage net. We approached a tent, which had three sides rolled up to catch the breeze. The Boss embraced the older man. After a few words, the Boss came for me. We went into the tent, which was fitted out as an office with a camp desk and chair that probably went back to Foreign Legion days. A computer and printer sat beside a radio rig and a satellite phone on a table near the door. A generator, then. We passed the desk in favor of a section with rugs and cushions.

"Sit," the Boss ordered. I sat.

The man in fatigues looked me over as the Boss related how I came to be with them. I kept my eyes down. What they were saying was likely to have important effects on my immediate future, if I had one. Suddenly, the man spoke sharply to me. I jumped and looked up in enquiry.

"You are a tourist?"

"Yes," I answered. The Muslims permitted lying to infidels. They were infidels to me. Why shouldn't I lie to them?

The Boss knew better. He told the man so and poked me in the ribs. "Yes, *sir.*"

"Yes, sir," I murmured. I decided that simple tortures were not enough to use before I killed him. I need to think of something really bad.

"Do you know where you are?" the emir asked.

"We must be somewhere in Algeria," I replied. Next time I'll pay closer attention to geography.

He pushed his face close to mine. "Do you know who I am?"

It was manifestly a challenge, and my distaste for authority got the better of me.

"You must be some sort of guerrilla chieftain," I replied.

"I am THE commander," he asserted. "I am Abu Jamal, the emir of the Pure Warriors of Islam!"

"How do you do," I said. "I'm Lee Carruthers."

The Boss flinched as the emir glared at me. He poked me in the ribs again. "Be more respectful!" he hissed.

"How do you do, *sir.*"

The emir frowned fiercely at me. This close to him, I could see that he was older than I had first thought. There were flecks of gray in his beard; the wrinkles around his mouth spoke of a bad temper, his face burned as brown as the rest of them.

"Where did you get her?" he asked.

"She and a Moroccan man came to Merzouga. The Glover man said she'd come from Paris asking questions about the other. We shot the man . . ."

"His name was Kemal," I shouted. "And he was worth ten of you."

The Boss reached over and slapped me across the face. "Shut up!" he said.

I began to visualize ways to torture him. I didn't think I would have a car battery. Pity.

"So we get a ransom for her, too?" the emir asked.

"Or we kill her," the Boss replied.

"We ransom her, and then kill her," the emir ordered.

"Have they paid for the other yet?" he asked.

"Not yet," the emir replied. "We're going to have to send them a video soon. She's fair-skinned. Bruises will show well."

"I'll bruise her some tomorrow. Then we can photograph her."

I said furiously, "You're the kind of men who blow up women and children and say Allah requires it! The old gods demanded sacrifices. I've not yet heard that Allah does."

The Boss reached over and slapped me. They weren't going to have to go out of their way to bruise me for my video. I bared my teeth and glared at him. He slapped me again.

The emir looked at me contemptuously. "You Western slut! Do not say the name of Allah!" He turned to the Boss. "She needs to be taught a woman's place. See to it."

The Boss smiled at me menacingly. "It will be a pleasure!"

My mouth is going to get me killed some day. Possibly today. The only thing I would regret would be not killing the Boss first.

The emir clapped his hands, and a small boy appeared. He gestured toward me and told the boy gruffly to take me away. I followed the boy to a small tent at the back of the camp. He pointed, and I entered.

Across the tent, I could see a figure in black, and as my eyes adjusted to the subdued light, I made out a slender woman. She had a perfect oval face, but there was no sign of kitten in it. Her blonde hair was drawn back so tightly that I thought her eyes must hurt. She backed against the tent wall.

"Alicia Harmon?" I asked. "Sidney sent me to find you."

Chapter 45

"DID YOU BRING the money?" she demanded.

"Money?"

"The 100,000 euros they want for me," she said.

I stalked toward her until she was backed up against the tent wall.

"You stupid bitch!"

She looked frightened. "Who are you? What do you mean?"

"My lovely Kemal is dead, and you're alive! I may kill you," I raged, nearly out of my mind with passion and grief. "Did you think waltzing around Fez asking questions about terrorism and brothel violence wouldn't have any blowback? You stupid, stupid woman!"

Without conscious orders, my hands reached toward her face. My fingernails weren't long, but they would do the job. Was it having my face covered that made me act like a stereotype? Lord knows what I would do if I had on a burka. I snatched off my head covering.

She was alarmed by my attack. "Who are you?" She looked at me more closely. "You're covered with blood," she stammered.

"You bet I am!" I looked down at my shirt. It and the pearl still bore bloody marks. Kemal's blood. All I had left of him.

I looked at her grimly. "And I will be until I kill the son of a bitch who shot Kemal. I may kill you, too."

She flinched. "Who *are* you?" she demanded.

"I'm Lee Carruthers. Sidney Worthington sent me to find you. Because we didn't know what you had been doing, I had to go around town asking the same questions you did to find out what happened to you. Well, I found out, didn't I?" I sat down on the rug that filled the ground under the small tent. "Kemal and I followed you to Rissani and then to Merzouga."

"Who's Kemal?"

"Never mind who Kemal is. Why were you in Rissani?"

"I went to Rissani to see Selim. There was something new going on, and I couldn't find out what it was. The girls I took to the house in the medina spoke of two groups of men in fatigues, fighting. When it was over a new set of guards took over the caravan. The dates of the slave shipment coincided with the first time anybody ever heard of the Pure Warriors of Islam. I wanted to ask Selim if they had taken over the escort duties."

She stopped abruptly. "Sam Glover," she whispered. "We were lovers."

"Of course you were, you silly cow! Who else could be your lover without going past Ibrahim? I'll bet you told him everything you knew after you had sex." The rage was cold now, a cold fury unlike anything I'd ever felt before. "How could you be so stupid?"

"He said he loved me," she said through clenched teeth.

"Well he would, wouldn't he? That was his job."

"You've never been in love," she said, picking on her black gown.

I stared at her. "I loved Kemal. He was protecting me when he died, and all because of you! You brainless, dim-witted, thickheaded, incompetent ... You're an analyst!" I spoke with deliberate slowness, as if I was talking to a mentally deficient child. "You find things out, and try to figure out what they mean. You report them to Sidney, and he sends an agent to do the rest. A trained agent."

"But I wasn't *certain* ..."

"You report even *rumors*. Somebody else takes it from there. Somebody who knows what he's doing. Somebody who won't go around asking dumb questions. About terrorists! Were you insane?"

She put her hands on her hips. "I think you about exhausted the topic," she said angrily.

I snorted. "So how did you get here?" I prodded.

"I ran into Sam Glover in Rissani. I don't know why he was there."

"I don't either, but he was with the terrorists who shot Kemal."

"He was with these people? But why?"

"Well may you ask. Go on."

"We had lunch at the Sijilmassa, and he took me to my car afterward. I got very dizzy. We had wine with our lunch. I don't drink much, so I thought that was what it was. The last thing I remember is him kissing me. I woke up here." She cut her eyes at me. "Judas!" she said angrily.

"You must know he is in with them."

"He betrayed me!" she glared at me.

We were interrupted by a woman in a black gown and hijab who brought a black gown and hijab for me. She pointed to my bloody shirt. I shook my head violently. She pointed again. I shook my head more violently. She shrugged and handed me the gown. She waited until I put it on and helped me with the hijab before she left. That made two of us. Alicia was wearing a burka and hijab, too, a fashion statement that was just the thing for the unit's yearly group picture.

"And so Glover kissed you and handed you over to them, and they want somebody to pay to get you back."

She sat up straight, glaring at me.

"How long has Sidney known that you are a prisoner?" I asked.

She pulled a string from under her gown and counted knots like rosary beads. "Ten days."

Ten days after they started looking for her. Two days afterward he ordered me to Morocco without telling me of the ransom demand. He would hear about that. I stood up and began to pace.

"He sent me in with no briefing at all," I said almost to myself. "He's going to pay for this. All I knew was that you were missing. Knowing that you were in the hands of terrorists might have been useful." I punched the tent pole hard enough to hurt my hand. It shook the tent.

"Why the *hell* did he send me in alone?"

"When a team of SEALS might have been more practical?" Her voice rose in volume.

"Shut up," I whispered.

She cleared her throat and brought her voice back down.

"So now there are two of us. Is he going to send them out one at a time until the whole unit is here?" she asked sarcastically.

"I imagine he expects me to do something."

"And what you going to do, Wonder Woman?" she demanded, pushing back.

"Oh, doubtless something will suggest itself," I replied, turning away.

She snorted. Our touchy conversation was interrupted by the arrival of the woman in black who was carrying a lamp. She went back outside and brought in a tray of rice with meat and a jug of water which she placed on the rug. We'd just begun to roll some rice around a chunk of meat when the Boss arrived.

"Cover your faces!" He ordered.

Alicia covered her face. I popped the ball of rice into my mouth.

"It's goat, but it's good. Have some," I said and began making another ball.

Boss smacked it out of my hand. Two points to me, I thought. How long before this game becomes dangerous? He waved a satellite phone at me.

"Who would want you back alive?" he demanded.

"Sidney Worthington," I said. Alicia gasped. "He's the trustee of my trust fund."

His eyes glittered. "Trust fund?"

I popped another rice ball into my mouth. He contemplated smacking again, but instead he asked for the phone number. He punched it in impatiently. It took a while before the call went through and was shunted to Langley. Finding Sidney took another while.

"Worthington?" the Boss asked. "We have Lee Carruthers. If you want her back alive, you will pay."

We could hear the squawk from the other end.

"Fifty-thousand US dollars."

I was mortified. Half of what they wanted for Alicia, and in dollars, too. He handed me the phone.

"Lee?" Sidney said.

"In the flesh," I replied.

"Well?"

"Mission accomplished."

"You found her?"

"Yes, I did, and I will have something to say about that when I get back to Paris."

The Boss jerked the phone from my hands and went outside.

"Are you trying to get us killed?" Alicia hissed.

"They'll kill us anyway," I answered. "Do you think the Agency will pay ransom for us?"

Alicia shifted uneasily on the rug and looked away.

"So what have you been doing while I was out there looking for you?" I asked. "Filing your fingernails?"

"Trying to escape!" she retorted.

"Right. Name, rank, and serial number, and it is your duty to escape." Perhaps I would escape and leave her behind.

She jerked her head up. "I tried to escape the second day I was here. They caught me. I should have waited longer. That junk was still in my veins."

"What junk?"

"The junk Sam Glover put in my drink. Four days ago I tried again. They caught me that time, too. As you see. Then they started guarding me."

I looked outside and saw a dumpy guy wearing a cheche and fatigues, armed with an AK-47.

"How did you get here?" she asked.

"By following you to Rissani. I thought you might be going to see Mehdi."

"He's dead."

"So we discovered."

"We?" she asked.

"Kemal was with me," I answered.

"Who's this Kemal that you keep talking about?"

"A friend," I whispered. "Just a friend, a dead friend." I raised my voice. "We went to Merzouga to find Selim and found these terrorists and Sam Glover instead. They killed Kemal." My voice went up sharply, and I fought to control my emotions. Tears sprang to my eyes. I looked down and balled up my hands so fiercely that my nails cut into my palms. She wasn't going to see me cry either. Finally, I shoved my emotions into a separate compartment of my brain for another day. There *would* be another day.

"Do you still have your own clothes?" I asked.

She lifted her gown to display the jeans under it.

"Why?"

"Because we're leaving here tonight."

"Leaving tonight?" She began to laugh, up the scale until she was nearly hysterical.

I slapped her in the face. It relieved my feelings, and she stopped laughing.

"That's very funny," she said. "Do you know where we are?"

I shook my head.

"The Talmine oasis, that's where!" she retorted.

"So? There must be a gendarmerie down the village."

"Oh, there is. Bought and paid for. The Talmine oasis produced the largest crop of poppy in Algeria last year. Grew a lot of kif, too. The local people produce nearly as much as the area around Tetouan. The gendarmerie. That's a laugh! And you're just going to walk out?"

Her laughter was derisive that time.

Chapter 46

"THAT JUST MAKES it more difficult," I said.

She just snorted and turned her back to me. At sunset the guard let down the tent flap, closing us inside. I got up and started walking back and forth, back and forth, trying to suppress an urge to scream. It was a little space, hot, and even with the lantern, dark. Larger than the closet, but still small. I couldn't stand being cooped up. I had to walk free. I had been deprived of that for two days. I was used to walking free. I *had* to walk free. With the flap down, the tent wall seemed to move closer and closer. It was becoming intolerable to be shut up without even a view of the outside world. It *was* intolerable, and I was afraid that pretty soon I was going to lose it.

"Oh, for God's sake, sit down," Alicia sat. "You're driving me crazy."

I lifted the tent flap and looked outside. The sun was going down and had turned our rocky hill a soft gold with touches of lavender and rose. It was in Algeria, I recalled, where the Impressionists learned that shadows aren't black. Impossibly beautiful. Impossibly far from help.

I sat down by the flap and breathed in the cool air. That helped a little. The dusk turned into evening and then into night. In the dark, the stars were so low you could almost touch them, beautiful and cold and aloof.

What I needed was a do-it-yourself escape plan.

About every twenty minutes, a guard went by, circling around the tents in front, and disappearing from my view. The parked vehicles. Does the guard go under the camouflage net, or does he just walk around it?

As much to take up the time as anything else, I asked, "How did you learn that Rashid was laundering money for terrorists?"

"From his wife."

"His wife? Where did you meet her?"

"At a reception at the *Alliance français*. She wants to keep up her French. She wanted to talk about her marriage, but she didn't want to come to the office. I don't know why."

"I do. Zeynab Bentali is her husband's mistress."

She looked shocked. "Zeynab? But she's my attorney. His mistress? How do you know?"

"I saw them kissing in the hall one night. Careless of them, but I suppose they didn't expect anybody else to be in the office that time of the night."

Her shoulders drooped sadly as she considered the perfidy of men.

"There's more. She sent us to Tangier. They hoped to end my investigation, I think. Killing me in Fez would be noticeable, but they had to get rid of me before I learned that you were right. It wasn't just the money laundering, it was the whole human trafficking scheme, too. She called me and told me that she had a text from you saying that you had eloped to Tangier and were deliriously happy, knowing I'd go there. When Kemal and I—" I stopped. Because he had my back. Don't go there. I resumed, "When we got there we were told that you were dead. We went to the morgue to identify you and found a corpse with face and hands too abraded to recognize because she had been in the water."

"But—" Alicia began to ask.

I went on. "I would have identified the girl as you, and gone back to Paris. End of story. But just then I got an e-mail from Langley saying that your credit card bill said you'd gone to Rissani."

"But who was the girl?" Alicia asked.

"I don't know. Some girl who was enough like you for me to identify as you. I'd never seen you, and they knew it. A girl they killed to stop me."

"That's horrible!"

"Yes it is. A lot of money involved. Why should human traffickers balk at killing one girl if it made them safe? These are not nice people, Alicia. Go on about his wife."

She stared at me. Shaking herself, she went on. "Anyway, Aliya and I had lunch and talked. She's trained as a pediatrician, you know, but Omar won't let her practice."

"Sweet man," I said.

She shrugged her shoulders. "Muslim husbands are like that."

"She could leave him," I said. "I understand her family is wealthy."

"Her father won't let her," she said.

"He leaves her, but she can't leave him."

"That's the way it is; you know that."

"Yes, I do. I never know whether to laugh or cry about women's rights in Muslim lands."

"I know, but there's no point. I told her she could support herself as a doctor. She said she couldn't leave the children, Omar wouldn't let her have them. The courts wouldn't either," she said.

"He comes to see them and takes them out. Lee, she told me he was teaching them bad things. Evil things. Terrorism, maybe. Since he left, he's become more and more secretive. He began to wear traditional dress outside the office, and he prays all the time. She said he never used to.

"She has a cousin in Rissani," Alicia continued. "He wrote her that there were new people at the zawiya. They forced the brothers to stop doing the dancing ritual. They said it was pagan."

"Jihadi attack Sufi wherever they find them. While Al Qaeda held Timbuktu they destroyed the ancient tombs of Sufi saints," I said.

"Well, whoever they are, they don't allow visitors anymore, either. They always used to let people pray at Rashid's tomb. The family supported itself and kept up the buildings with the visitors' gifts."

I remembered the sudden increase in funds in the Rissani account. "When was this?" I asked.

"About the time I first began hearing there was a new terrorist group."

"And you neither reported this to Sidney nor recorded it in your files?" I asked harshly.

She looked down at her hands. "Sam convinced me that they were all down in Mali fighting the French. But when they posted their manifesto, I knew he was wrong. I didn't suspect he was in with them. I just thought he was wrong. He was laundering money, wasn't he? Omar?"

"Yes, he was. Some of it was going to Pakistan."

She put her hands over her face. "Oh, God. Oh, God! I knew it. I should have done something about it."

"Right. You should have reported it to Sidney. It's a job for Clandestine. They might have been able to use it."

I didn't tell her that the way they would probably use it was to leave the network in place and manipulate it.

I couldn't stand to talk with her anymore. Even then I knew it was irrational, but she had caused pain and destruction and maybe the loss of our lives. Passionate about slavery. Passionate!

I was leaning against the tent wall dozing, maybe, when I heard footsteps. A new guard. I looked at my watch. I made the shift four hours. I hope it isn't shorter at night, I thought, as I lifted the tent flap.

"Where are you going?" Alicia demanded in a whisper.

"Out to have a look at the vehicle park," I replied.

"Are you crazy?" she whispered fiercely.

"Probably. We're stealing a car and leaving."

"You'll never get away with it."

Disgusted with her, I snapped, "Alicia, we're never going to get away if we don't know what's out there."

"We're never going to get away, period."

"No wonder you're a prisoner. You have just enough initiative to get into trouble," I said.

"You're here too," she snapped.

"Not voluntarily," I stepped back.

"You think I am?"

"You trusted the wrong people," I replied.

"And you have never trusted the wrong people?"

Chapter 47

I ROLLED UNDER the side of the tent and ran silently after the guard. There were eight tents in the camp: the emir's command tent in front, our small tent in the rear, and six larger tents in a double arc between the two. There had to be a woman's area sectioned off somewhere. I knew there were two women in the camp. There must be more. Somebody had to do the work.

I waited until I saw the guard round the tents in front of ours. I had to get to the vehicle park before the guard's next round. I squatted beside the emir's tent and watched the guard pace from the parking lot and start back. Heading to the park to see what I could see, I stopped at the sound of voices coming from the emir's tent. I heard three voices, one I knew to be the emir, the second was the Boss. The third was a stranger.

He was speaking. "You will return to the command of Al Qaeda in the Islamic Maghreb! Your desertion will not be tolerated! Dividing Allah's forces is a crime against jihad! Abu Hassan, I order it!"

"You give no orders in this camp, Belmansur!" said the emir. "You disgrace the jihad, you disgrace the Prophet, you disgrace Allah himself. You are nothing but a criminal! You spend your days selling drugs, arms, women."

"Allah's war requires funds. You do none of these things because you're not strong enough! How many men do you have? Fifty, a hundred?" he sneered. "You are a joke!"

"Al Qaeda itself once had fifty men. We are growing, we're growing every day. Every day new men flock to our flag, the black flag of jihad! I repeat: You spend your days selling drugs, arms, and women."

"Because I have sold drugs, arms, and women, Al Qaeda in the Islamic Maghreb is rich and strong."

"Strong enough to attract French troops to Mali, but not strong enough to defeat them. Allah has taken his hand from you. Al Qaeda in the Islamic Maghreb may be rich, but you are richer. You steal Allah's money. You are a thief!"

Belmansur snarled, and I risked peeking around the tent flap. He was a tall man with a thin and lined face burned by the sun. With his one eye, he glared like an eagle preparing to strike. He leaned over the emir, his hand on the hilt of his dagger. The Boss drew his knife, and thrust the point of it to the other man's throat.

"You forget the laws of hospitality," Belmansur grated and pushed the knife away. He turned his glare on the Boss. "You would kill me, a guest in your camp?"

The emir responded, "You are safe until you leave my camp. After that, look to your safety. There are few people here who would give you sanctuary."

The three men rose. Belmansur turned to the emir.

"I have warned you. I will use force to return you to your duty if necessary, and the deaths of your men will be on your head!"

He turned and started away but stopped and turned back. "I have warned you."

I watched him stride into the night. The two men watched him go. Would this help our escape or make it impossible?

"He is not alone," remarked the Boss.

"No, he is not. We must move the camp," replied the emir.

"Into Morocco?"

"Perhaps."

"There is a good place to the east of Hamid," the Boss said. "There is a road, a bad road, but it leads to the Tindouf-Hammaguir highway. There's also a road that intersects the Rissani road at Merzouga. We would be closer to the rendezvous point."

"The Moroccan gendarmerie has reinforced that border and patrols it in strength. We could be vulnerable there."

"If we intend to confine our operations to Morocco, the gendarmerie would be no problem after we cross the border. All we have to do is lie low in the hills and move quietly to our target. The radio mast would give away our location. We must leave it behind and use only the satellite phone."

"I don't know. We must send someone to look for a site."

"We could just slip away," the Boss offered. "We know this place better than he does. If we move now, we will surprise him, for he expects to attack us at dawn."

"Going now will not make any difference. He will follow. If we go now we will have to leave everything behind—the money, the arms, the explosives—everything we have amassed these last months. We may get away with our lives, but we will have to start all over. If we try to move now, he will catch us in the open with our baggage. It will be better to fight here," the emir replied. "He is arrogant. He has brought only a few men with him; otherwise, our scouts would have observed them. We can defeat a small force and then move to a new camp. You must wake the men. We have several hours until he attacks. Everything must be packed and ready to leave, except for striking the tents."

"Shall I send a man to Hamid?"

"Send Faisal. He's from that area. He will know where to look for a secure place."

"And what of the American women?" the Boss asked.

"They will be in the way," replied the emir.

"It wouldn't be much trouble to take them with us. They're worth a lot of money, and we're going to need money after we move."

"They are a distraction," the emir ordered. "Kill them."

Chapter 48

I RAN BACK to the tent.

"Get your stuff. We're leaving. Now," I ordered.

"I'm not going anywhere with you. You're insane!" she replied angrily.

"Suit yourself," I said. "They're going to kill us in the morning. I'd rather die on the run than be executed in a filthy terrorist camp."

She looked mutinous.

"Come now or not at all," I ordered. "Wear the burka. The black will camouflage us. We have to get to the vehicle park before Faisal comes to get a truck. We can hide from him, but we have to get there first."

"Who is Faisal?"

"Oh, for God's sake, Alicia, move! We haven't got time."

Was she waiting for an engraved invitation? I stuck my head carefully around the tent flap. Nobody yet. Soon the camp would be like a disturbed ant heap as they packed to leave. I crept down to the emir's tent, with Alicia right behind me, breathing hard, her face like granite. Not a pretty little kitty now, if she had ever been. The Boss was striding toward the first row of tents behind the emir's, talking to two men as he went. "Everything must be packed and ready to move out." He turned to look back at the emir, and his gaze swept the area. I hurriedly turned my face to the tent wall. My burka would hide my body, but my skin was light enough to be seen even at that distance in the dark. I could only hope that Alicia followed suit. Soon the whole camp would be awake. We had to get to the vehicle park before that.

I sprinted down to the vehicle park and swung myself under the camouflage net with Alicia on my heels. I had no idea where the sentry was. There were three Toyota trucks parked behind the Land Cruiser I had arrived in. We would take the Cruiser and disable the trucks.

"We have to get away now!"

I gave Alicia my Swiss Army knife and set her to wrecking tires. I was pulling handfuls of wires from under the trucks' dashboards when I heard boots coming our way. Faisal? I picked up the jack handle from the truck I was working on and waited until he was just past me. I ducked out from under the net behind him as he swung under the net and saw Alicia.

"Wha—?"

He grabbed her. She kicked and struggled, but he was too strong for her. When he opened his mouth to shout, I hit him hard on the back of the head. He went down, and Alicia rolled out from under him. We ripped strips from his cheche with his knife and bound and gagged him. He snorted a little when we shoved him under the middle truck, so he was still breathing. I couldn't find it in my heart to care. After she stopped shaking, Alicia took his knife and went back to tire-stabbing. It was a much better weapon for the job. The AK he was carrying I put into the Land Cruiser. I had just reached for the wires under the dashboard of the last truck when Alicia whispered, "Ssst!"

I heard the crunch of boots on the gravel outside and looked through the net. A man in fatigues and cheche was approaching, his rifle slung over his shoulder.

"Faisal, where are you? The emir wants you," he called.

Alicia and I looked at each other.

"You go up front and shake the net," I whispered and crawled to the edge. Alicia moved the net, and the guard's head went up at the unexpected motion. While it was up, I hit him in the neck with the jack handle, and we pulled him under the net. We bound and gagged him, too. His weapon went in the Cruiser. That gave us two. And two men under trucks. They would be missed soon.

"Finished with the tires," Alicia reported.

I heard the sound of gunfire up behind the tents. The Boss was wrong. They didn't wait until dawn.

"They're here," I said.

"Who's here?"

"Alicia, there's no time for that. Just do what I tell you." How many men did Belmansur have? "We've got to go now, before the battle comes this way!"

Alicia stood nervously outside the net just in front of the Cruiser, and I lay under the dashboard trying to hot-wire the engine in the dark. The noise of the battle increased and seemed to be moving our way. It's amazing how the knowledge that you are going to die concentrates the mind. The engine finally caught, Alicia lifted the net, and I drove the Cruiser out from under it. We headed toward the oasis below. Armed men rushed out of the houses, drawn by the sound of gunfire. A man in fatigues stepped in front of us and pointed his rifle. I gunned the engine and lurched forward, hitting him squarely. He bounced off the windshield leaving a smear of blood. Alicia gasped.

"You just ran over that man!"

"I'm sure Allah will regard him as a martyr," I replied.

I spritzed the windshield and turned on the wipers. It only smeared the blood, so I did it again.

"How could you do that?" she asked.

"Alicia," I snapped, "these darling men sent a suicide bomber to blow himself up in the metal souk in Fez a couple of days ago. Got a lot of people. Almost got me. You can weep for him tomorrow, if you like."

I drove quickly through the village, listening anxiously to the sound of the battle. The only good thing about the attack was the fact that nobody was paying the slightest attention to us. The road had been paved within living memory but it had not been repaired since, which made driving on it more treacherous than if it had not been paved. We bounced into and out of the ruts, shimmying dangerously. As we passed the gendarme post, men in combat gear ran out, sparing a brief glance at us before running north to the sound of the guns. We drove on, the sound of battle growing gradually fainter. After an hour driving on that wretched road, my shoulders were in knots. I was about to turn onto the highway when a large truck, the kind the French call a *camion*, hurtled past us, running without lights. Alicia caught her breath. I slammed on the brakes, and we skidded for fifty yards before they caught. After I stopped shaking, I got out of the Cruiser slowly and rolled my shoulders to loosen the muscles there. Being on the run is hard on the nerves.

"Your turn to drive, but ditch the burka first." I took mine off and threw it in the back.

Alicia did the same and slid into the driver's seat. The highway had a decent surface, so she floored it. It was important to get as far away from the camp as possible before the battle ended, and one side or the other found us gone. We might have disabled their vehicles, but we could do nothing about the sat phones, and we had no idea where they had allies. Soon every vehicle we encountered might belong to friends of the terrorists.

Alicia was a good fast driver, much better than I was, so I wedged myself into the corner between the passenger seat and the door and worried. Suddenly Alicia swerved and slammed on the brakes, sending me flying toward the dashboard.

"What is *that*!?" she exclaimed.

Chapter 49

WHITE WISPS SWIRLED and drifted across the road. Alicia had driven into it before she saw it. She slammed on the brakes and sat there shaking. I pulled myself off of the dashboard.

"It's a *sebka*," I said. "Drive on."

She started forward and pulled to the side of the road trying to escape the white cloud. The right wheels teetered on the edge of a ditch.

"Get back on the road. Now!" I shouted.

"I don't know where the road is!" She yelled back.

"Drive to the left before we go into the ditch! Carefully. Very carefully!"

She crept to the left until she felt solid ground under us, and she stopped again.

"What *is* it?"

"It's a *sebka*," I said.

"Well that tells me a lot!"

"It's an ancient salt lake. When it rains in Oran or the Atlas Mountains, water flows down to this lake, and a cloud rises. After the rain ends, the water sinks and another layer of salt is deposited."

"Great!"

She still looked like a deer in the headlights.

"So what do I do now?"

"Drive on, and pray nobody is coming the other direction."

"I can't see!"

I wouldn't be able to see any better. I got out of the cruiser, got one of the AKs out of the back, and dropped the clip. Walking to the front of the cruiser, I yelled, "Can you see me?"

"Yes," she shouted in reply.

I used the stock of the rifle to find the right edge of the road. When I found it, I moved close to the cruiser and put my left hand on the right fender.

"Follow my lead and drive carefully forward."

"But what if . . . ?"

"Just do it!" I shouted. "NOW!"

She pulled slowly forward inch by inch, with me tapping the stock like a blind man with a cane. I *was* a blind man with a cane. It seemed forever before we ran out of the cloud. When we did, Alicia stopped. She was shaking, and I was breathing hard. I got back into the cruiser and leaned back in the seat. Reading about *sebka*s in a book was one thing, running into one in the dark was another. The sky was getting lighter, but it was still dark down where we were.

"We've got to get off the road," she muttered. "We've got to get off the road."

"It's not far to Béni Abbès. That's a good-sized town. They can't have bought all the gendarmes from the oasis to the Moroccan border."

"I don't see why not. They have enough money."

Suddenly, a dark shape appeared in the lane ahead of us. Alicia slammed on the brakes and skidded. Two of the wheels went into the ditch, but she recovered. In front of us was a rickety horse cart riding without a lamp on the rear. The driver looked curiously at us as we drove around him.

"Slow down," I ordered. "If you don't, you'll wreck us."

"We've got to get off this road."

"We've got to live to do it," I retorted.

Not long after that a green Toyota truck like the ones the terrorists used met us going the other direction. We watched him carefully in the mirrors. He kept going and was soon out of sight. Fifteen minutes later another pickup appeared suddenly behind us. He rode our bumper for a while, and we braced ourselves, but he passed us with a rude gesture.

"It's getting light," Alicia repeated. "We've got to get off this road! They're going to think a woman driving a Land Cruiser is odd. They'll talk about it."

"Alicia, there's *hamada* on the left," I said, pointing to the solid wall of rock along the road to the left. "And the ditch and the desert to the right. There's no place to get off the road."

She gave me a mulish look. I slapped the dashboard. "OK. Get out. I'll drive for a while."

We exchanged places and started off again. It was full daylight now, and we could see for miles on the flat road. Just as we could see a sandy trail through a break in the hamada, a Toyota truck passed us going the other direction. I looked behind us. The truck rolled to a stop, and I pulled on the hand brake and reached behind me for an AK, but the driver got out and went around the side of the truck. He was facing the hamada in an unmistakable pose. Just taking a leak. I turned left off the road onto the track in the hamada.

Driving in sand is never fun. Driving in sand while on the run is hell. Sometimes the trail was packed hard, and driving was easy. But when the sand was loose and drifted, it was important to drive slowly forward without cutting the wheels to the left or right, otherwise you'll bog. Digging the Land Cruiser out of the sand was not my idea of fun under any conditions. With terrorists probably right behind us, the possibility of having to do it made my blood run cold. The trail twisted and turned, on sand now solid, now soft. It was impossible to see forward or backward for more than fifty yards, so besides the difficult driving, I was seriously worried that they would catch up with us before we knew they were upon us. Alicia twisted and turned too, unable to sit still.

"Sit still, Alicia! You're driving me nuts!" I said.

"Are we having fun yet?"

"One more sneer, and I'm going to kill you!"

"Oh, kill me and get it over with, or stop talking about it!"

Chapter 50

"IT'S NOT MY fault!" she snapped.

"It's not your fault? How can you say that? If you hadn't been stupid, if you hadn't been kidnapped, I would be in Paris right now happily chasing laundered money." And Kemal would still be alive. Kemal would still be alive. "Just shut up!"

The driving was nerve-wracking because the soft spots were difficult to see. My shoulder muscles were in knots, and my hands were sore from clutching the steering wheel. The scenery wasn't much either. Little stones and big stones, big stones and little stones. For miles, just sand and stones. The hamada was built, seemingly at random, by a giant and his son, the father with the big stones, the son with a little stones. The stones were somber gray and brown colors which did nothing to improve my mood. Neither did the sense of claustrophobia I felt when the trail narrowed. It felt as if I was driving through a tunnel with a huge wall of stone looming over me, threatening to topple and crush me. After a couple of miles, the track widened and led to a wide space, like a town square. I stopped for a minute and wiped the sand from my face. It felt as if somebody had run an emery board over it

"What's that?!" Alicia demanded.

That woman thinks in exclamations, I thought crossly.

Across the valley to the right was a stone tower rising tall against the sky.

"It's a *ksar*, one of the old fortified villages," I replied.

"A village? Why would there be a village here? There's nothing for miles."

"In the old days life was dangerous in the wild places, so extended families built fortresses against other families and bandits, who would capture people and sell them into slavery. Even the government was a player, only the government called it taxation. Every once in a while the Sultan would bring his army and sweep through the area collecting back taxes. Until the French came, there was no law south of the Atlas mountains and precious little later."

"But out here? Surely this place is uninhabitable."

"Now it is, but then it was not. I wonder how long ago?"

As we got closer, I saw that the fort lay in ruins, just another example of stacked up stones, this time by a giant with a taste for architecture. Perhaps they were the bandits? Perhaps what they were defending against had disappeared? Perhaps they were wiped out?

"But what could did they do for a living in this barren place?" Alicia asked.

"I don't know. Rustle camels? They couldn't possibly raise food. Even grazing stock looks impossible," I said. "Maybe it was wetter then."

Driving on, I saw another ruined tower on a hillock facing the first across an expanse of sand.

"Looks like the Hatfields and the McCoys. Maybe they destroyed each other, and there was nobody left to tell the tale."

Alicia shuddered. "You're terrible," she said.

"There's a distinct shortage of rainbows and puppies in the desert, Alicia, not for them and not for us," I said bitterly.

I stopped the car and got out to stretch. I saw no way of getting any relief, and I didn't trust Alicia to drive in the sand, so I got back in the car, put it in gear, and drove on. In the endless loop of sand and rock there was nothing to see, nothing to do but drive on. My instinct told me to drive faster, that they were just behind this, and we wouldn't see them because of the bends in the track. My head told me that slow and steady won the race. We would surely be caught if we got bogged in the sand.

About noon Alicia looked back. "I see dust!" she cried. "There's dust behind us!"

I looked in the mirror and saw that she was right. Instinctively, I pressed harder on the accelerator, and the wheels slewed to the left. I held my breath and steered gently into the skid, hoping that what worked for snow would also work for sand. I only breathed again when the tires found a stony surface to grip, and the car steadied.

"How close is the dust?" I asked. "Is it getting closer?"

"No," she said.

"Can you tell how far away it is?"

"No," she said nervously. "The wind is blowing it sideways."

The wide spot was by the first ksar then, I thought. Maybe five miles behind us? We were on solid gravel, so I sped up. Looking in the mirror, I saw that we were throwing up the dust plume, too. If we knew where they were, they knew where we were, too. The track grew wider, and the sense of constriction I had felt lifted. Suddenly the hamada ended, and we emerged to see a graveled road, running east and west as far as the eye could see in the flat land.

"It's a road!" exclaimed Alicia excitedly.

She must be feeling better, I thought. She's back to exclamations. I moved to cross the road.

"But you're not taking it! It's a road. Why aren't you taking the road?"

"If you were the Pure Warriors of Islam, supposing you survived the battle with Belmansur and his men, where would you expect to find us? We're city girls, not used to the outback. We would stick to the roads at all costs, wouldn't we? We have to stay off the road. Besides, we don't want to go east or west. We want to go north, north into Morocco where we might be safe."

She wasn't happy with that answer. A few miles to the east, I could see a trail going more or less north. I fancied it was traveled mostly by goats, but Toyota says a Cruiser will go anywhere. If it went up that track, I would personally film a TV commercial for Toyota. I turned east and then gingerly urged the car onto the track. I put it in four-wheel drive and started up slowly.

"The dust is getting closer!" Alicia said.

I pressed the accelerator harder, and the engine began to sputter. Then it quit.

We were out of gas.

Chapter 51

"WE'RE OUT OF gas," Alicia cried.

I pounded the steering wheel. So close. We were so close. I looked back toward the hamada. The cloud of dust was almost to the road. They would see us very soon.

"We've got to get away from the car!" I ordered. "Now! Get the rifle and come on."

She looked uncertain.

"Your choice," I said and got out of the car.

She followed me, and I paid no further attention to her. The track led straight up a dry water course into another hamada. I climbed as fast as I could, but I knew we couldn't get far enough away from the car. There was no cover, unless we could hide under a pebble. I kept on climbing, struggling for breath.

"They're going to catch us!" Alicia said.

"Probably," I said. "Keep moving."

I looked back, and, like Lot's wife, I nearly turned to salt. Three trucks had emerged from the hamada, one of them with a 50-caliber mounted on the cab. I'm honored, I thought, as I resumed climbing. There were fifteen or twenty men in those trucks. All for us? Were they Al Qaeda or the Pures? Did it matter? We'd find out when they caught us. Alicia was bent double, trying to catch her breath.

"We have to stop. I can't go any farther," she said.

I looked back and saw that they were gaining on us. I could not go much farther either. About fifty yards ahead, I saw a little pile of rocks, marbles the giant's son had left behind.

"Come on," I said and ran behind the stones.

She crouched beside me. I unslung the rifle and looked down at it. Once. I had fired one once. At least I knew where the moving parts were. I looked at Alicia.

"Do you know how to use one of these things?" I asked.

"You point it and pull the trigger," she said uncertainly.

Oh great, I thought. The blind leading the blind. Whoever the guys in camouflage were, they were going to die laughing before we managed to kill any of them. I showed her the selector switch and moved it from safety, past full automatic to semi-automatic.

"You have to pull the trigger for each shot," I said without any hope that she could do any good. Maybe full automatic? Set on full automatic she might shoot me. She might shoot me anyway. If I could keep her pointed outward, she might not hit anything, but she might be able to scare them. God knows she scared me.

The crowd of men began to advance slowly. It was like Fort Apache, without any hope of rescue by the cavalry.

"Don't fire until they're in range," I ordered. How did she know what the range was? I amended the order. "Don't fire until I do."

They had seen our rifles, so they advanced slowly, ever nearer, but we were only women after all. What did we know about rifles? I wondered that myself. I waited, forever, it seemed. They were still out of range when they split into two groups and moved to flank us. Alicia could stand the tension no longer. She fired several rounds, and I fell on my face. She did more damage to any low-flying birds than to the men attacking us.

"Stop that!" I ordered, getting up on my knees.

I grabbed her rifle and pushed her down. She cried out when she landed on the stones. If we get out of this, I will strangle her with my bare hands, I thought.

"Get up! And pull the trigger *once*. Pointing it toward them!"

"I'm not stupid," she said.

"There is a difference of opinion about that," I said.

"I've never fired the thing before."

It was impossible to defend against the flanking movement, and she was more of a danger to me than she was to them. I held my fire, and the men came closer, tightening the noose around us. I had only about twenty rounds plus whatever Alicia had left. They worked closer. I gave Alicia's rifle back to her. They were getting close enough that she might actually hit one of them, if she didn't kill me first.

Quite soon they were very close, and I had my choice of targets. I identified the Boss among the men climbing toward me. Pures, then.

"Oh well," I said. "Some of us are going to die."

"Lee!" Alicia yelled in protest.

I fired several rounds at the Boss and missed him each time. I set it on full automatic and fired in a sweep. It was hard to control the rifle. It was too heavy for me. Good. A fine time to be a weak woman. When my magazine was empty, I grabbed her rifle. Fort Apache was never defended by one person, I thought. Somewhere in the back of my mind I knew that if I killed any of them it would go hard with me when they captured us, but I went on firing. All I could do was keep them off of us. When I fired the last round, we were dead. How do I get into these things anyway? I'd rather die fighting than be executed in a filthy terrorist camp. They were nearly on us, waiting until I ran out of ammunition. They slowly tightened the noose around us. I ran out of ammunition. I dropped the clip and clubbing the rifle, prepared to swing it.

"Oh, well," I said out loud. "Today is as good a day to die as any."

"Lee!" Alicia protested.

I gritted my teeth and swung.

I heard a satisfying "clunk" as I hit one of them in the head. Out of the corner of my eye, I saw Alicia go down under a pile of camouflaged bodies. Then a guy grabbed my rifle and jerked, and I went down, too. The last thing I remember was a boot coming toward my face.

Chapter 52

THE HEADACHE CAME first. Then the smell of goat. Goat? Gradually other senses surfaced. After a while the pain localized in my left cheekbone. I moved my mouth, and pain shot through it. I felt something warm trickle down my cheek and off my chin. Other parts of me woke and demanded attention, too. I opened my eyes. The sun hurt them, so I closed them. I hurt. My face hurt the most, followed by my shoulders. I did a status check looking for something that didn't hurt and couldn't find a single one. I was lying on my side, and when I tried to move my arms, I couldn't. Couldn't move my legs either. Puzzled, I tried to turn on my back and found I couldn't do that either. A man in fatigues nearby shuffled over to look at me.

"She's awake," a man said as he bent over me.

I shifted so I could look at him. A thin desert man with a straggly beard. Wearing green fatigues and a turban. He was talking to a colleague, also in green fatigues. I was slipping and sliding and bouncing on the floor. The odor of goat reclaimed my attention. I opened my eyes again and saw the green metal side of a truck. That explained the bouncing. Also the goat, probably. I couldn't move because I was tied hand and foot. I remembered then. The Pures had us. We were captives.

Again.

I should have played with the dollhouse my mother gave me for my eighth birthday instead of going out and buying a cap pistol. Maybe baking cookies in a rose-covered cottage wouldn't have been so bad. A non-Muslim Kemal would come home from work, and I would bring him crackers and beer. The only violence in my life would have been cutthroat bridge.

I would hate it.

The bouncing of the truck didn't help my head any, and the sun shining down on me made it worse. I pushed very hard and turned all the way over. Beside me was Alicia, also bound and not yet conscious.

It was past midafternoon when the truck started climbing at a steep angle. We reached the top of the incline, and afterward the ride was not so bad because we were driving on the flat. I couldn't see a thing but Alicia and the side of the truck. The one with the scraggly beard came to look at us from time to time as if we might be going somewhere. I couldn't turn onto my back, but I could get sort of forty percent there. When I did, all I saw was the sky. A yellow, cloudless, hot sky. The sun was low in the sky when we turned through a gate into some kind of courtyard. The crumbled remains of a tall ksar, one of the ancient, fortified villages, rose dark against the lavender and gold of the setting sun. We drove to the left, swung around in a wide circle, ending up facing the gate, and the driver cut the engine.

Alicia began to stir. She opened her eyes and saw me. "What . . . ? Where are we? Lee, where are we?"

"With our old friends the terrorists. We just drove into the courtyard of a ksar. I don't know any more than that."

"But what . . . ?"

"I told you I didn't know any more than that," I said sharply.

She gave me a wounded look and subsided.

One of the men with us in the back of the truck opened the tailgate, and he and another man jumped down. The Boss and the driver got out and slammed the doors of the cab. I scooted myself up to the back of the cab and tried to sit up. After several tries and some lost skin I succeeded. I could see the courtyard, a large unpaved area with bits of paper and other junk scattered around. On closer inspection, I could see that the ksar was more than crumbled. The irregularly spaced windows had no glass in them, and the fourth floor had subsided onto the third. The wall of the first floor had collapsed into a line of rubble, which would be a good place to fort up, if we could get there. I could see that there were only four terrorists, the Boss, the two who had been riding with us, and the driver. The Boss and the driver stood near the gate waiting for something. The other two stood beside the truck. To guard us? Three were carrying AKs, the Boss had a big pistol on his hip, and the two by the truck, besides carrying their AKs, had automatics stuck in the backs of their belts. Glocks? Probably old Makarovs. Like AKs, Makarovs were on the street everywhere. Russian ingenuity. Since the Boss was there, the Pures had us, if it made any difference. I remembered his boot coming toward my face. I will kill him for that, I thought. He killed Kemal. Maybe I'll torture him a little first. There were three trucks when they caught us. Did that mean they had won the battle with Belmansur's men or were the men in those three trucks all that were left of the emir's force? Where were the other two trucks and the rest of the men now? There had been at least thirty men in those trucks.

"What's going on?" whispered Alicia from the floor. "I can't see."

A second truck arrived, a two-and-a-half-ton army job with a canvas top. It swung around until it was near the middle of the courtyard wall, facing the gate on the right. I saw an African face peep out of the back. A woman's face.

It looked as if Alicia was going to get to see a slave trade go down after all.

The sun was nearly down when I heard a car outside the gate, and Sam Glover sauntered in, as pressed as ever in his khaki safari clothes. He certainly didn't look like a villain, but that's the best kind, isn't it? Alicia moved restlessly. As if his arrival was the signal, the headlights of both trucks came on, lighting the courtyard as if it were a stage. Glover stopped when he saw the Boss, and they locked eyes. The lights from the trucks cast long shadows, making both men look taller and thinner than I knew they were. Glover shrugged and carried on until he could look inside the truck. He turned away smiling to see a small man, looking rather like the White Rabbit, coming through the gate. He wore his three-piece suit even in the desert. This time he was without his briefcase. This time Glover had it. He glanced briefly at Glover and away nervously. Glover smiled ironically. Buyer and seller, I thought. Sam Glover did coordinate things for Worldwide. He bought women for their brothels.

If the men were focused on the women, we might have a chance. I slumped back down on the floor and pulled Alicia with me. I turned my back to her. "Untie me," I whispered.

"What with?" she asked irritably.

My voice rose. "Your teeth, damn it!"

Had she never seen a prison movie? I backed up to her and felt a tug on my bonds. Fortunately it was some of that rotten plastic stuff they use for rope in the Middle East. After a good bit of pulling, the rope was loose enough so that I could free my hands. I rubbed my wrists and used my Swiss Army knife to cut Alicia's ropes. Freeing our ankles, we peered over the side of the truck to see what was happening. We saw the women and children lined up in the truck's headlights, Glover walking along the line like a field marshal reviewing his troops, except that a field marshal doesn't grope his troops. Glover had the briefcase in one hand, but all he needed was one to squeeze a woman's breast, run his hand lingeringly over another's stomach, or pull another to him, grinding his hips against her.

Alicia gasped. "Oh, I will kill him," she said grimly.

"Be my guest. If you miss him, I'll have a go."

The Boss barked at Glover, who turned away from the women. The Boss strode closer and held out his hand for the briefcase. Glover shook his head and moved back. The Boss's sidekick circled around to box him in, and the Boss moved closer again, well inside Glover's comfort zone. Glover backed again but stopped before he ran into the second terrorist. The Man without the Briefcase scuttled away from the confrontation, then squared his shoulders, and joined the group claiming the briefcase. I couldn't hear what was said, but from their gestures, the Man and the Boss were both demanding it.

"That's not the way the girls said it happened when they were here. The terrorists got only a part of the money," whispered Alicia.

"These are a different bunch, and I suspect they need all the money they can get," I whispered back.

"But they don't own the people, they only protected the truck."

"God is on the side of the biggest battalions," I replied.

"What battalions?" she asked in confusion.

I shrugged. She didn't do quotations very well.

The confrontation had turned into a stalemate. The Boss and the Man without the Briefcase were standing close to Sam, hands on hips, red in the face. A chance, maybe. I looked around the truck bed for some kind of a weapon and saw some short metal poles, possibly parts of tent poles. They would do. I picked two up and handed one to Alicia.

Our guards had their backs to us enjoying the show.

"We're going to jump on those guys and whack them in the head. You see the pistols in their belts? We're going to steal them."

"But Lee . . . ," she said nervously.

"Alicia, they're going to kill us. Remember? We're going to steal their guns and run over there," I pointed to the ksar rubble. "and hide."

She looked uncertain, but she followed me anyway. We moved quietly to the side of the truck, and, at the count of three, we jumped on the men. We bowled them over, and they went down. We hit them as hard as we could in the head with the metal poles, and they stayed down. We snatched the pistols from their belts, sprinted to the ksar. and took refuge behind part of a wall. Alicia might make quite a good little criminal with some practice.

The argument over the briefcase was now intense, and the Boss had drawn his pistol. Glover drew his. The Man without the Briefcase darted hurriedly out of the line of fire.

Alicia took no notice of our need to remain hidden. She wanted to kill Sam Glover, and so she fired. From the movement of the Boss's hand, I thought that he fired, too. Either way, Glover went down.

"I killed him!" exclaimed Alicia.

I thought it more likely that it was the Boss's round that took him down, but why shouldn't she think so? Glover had fallen on the briefcase, and the Man was struggling to pull it out from under him. A shot rang out, and the Man fell on top of Glover and the briefcase. I looked around. Out of the rubble on the other side of the courtyard stepped Khalil el Hadid, as impeccably dressed as ever, claiming his share. He held a gun on the Boss while he tried to pull the briefcase out from under Glover and the Man. He couldn't keep his eye on the Boss and rummage for the money at the same time. I saw him decide to simplify his problem. He raised the gun into firing position. I wasn't having any of that. The Boss was *mine.* I fired three times, and hit him three times, the last a head shot. I turned aside and vomited, but only bile came up. I hate head shots. I spun around and turned my gun on Hadid. I fired just a fraction of a second faster and hit him in the right shoulder, spoiling his aim and sending his bullet astray, but far too close to my left ear for comfort.

At the first sound of gunfire the women and children began to scream and run around the courtyard. The driver jumped from the large truck and ran for the gate. Alicia screamed, and a nightmare in black swept through the gate.

Chapter 53

GENDARMES. GENDARMES IN riot gear.

I put my gun on the ground and raised my hands. Alicia just stood there frozen, holding her pistol, her knuckles white. Alicia Harmon still needed more practice in the matter of lawbreaking.

"Put the gun down, Alicia," I instructed.

She turned toward me, and I went down. So did every man in the compound. The captain of the gendarmes stepped forward pistol in hand.

"May I?" I asked. When he nodded, I said, "Point the gun up, Alicia." She continued to look at me with blank eyes.

"Alicia!" I yelled, and some intelligence came back into her eyes. "Alicia! Take your finger off the trigger, and point the gun up," I said slowly and clearly.

Gradually, she took her frozen finger from the trigger, but her knuckle was still white, and she still aimed at the men.

"May I?" I asked again. When he nodded again, I stepped behind Alicia, forced the barrel up, and snatched the gun from her.

"Get down on the ground," I ordered. She complied. I put the gun down on the ground beside mine and slowly joined her.

The driver had chosen the wrong time to try to flee. He ran straight into the arms of the gendarmes, who promptly cuffed him and dumped him by the wall for further reference. Two of the men were dealing with the injured—our two guards and the Boss's sidekick. I looked around and didn't see Hadid. He was a man who would always land on his feet. Bleeding or not, he had gotten away in the confusion. Several were trying to corral the women and children. One was shouting at them in Arabic. When that didn't work, he tried Berber.

I sat up. "Try Tuareg," I yelled. He looked blankly at me. "They're probably Tuareg."

The captain barked, "Anybody speak Tuareg?"

Nobody replied.

"Sheep!" he ordered, and seven men circled them, and began to drive them into a cohesive bunch. That accomplished, a sergeant put his hand on one of the boy's heads and pushed. The boy sat down abruptly. Finally all of them were sitting down. The captain phoned for an ambulance and a truck and a Tuareg speaker, if they could find one. Vehicles came and removed the dead. But they hadn't been able to find a Tuareg speaker. Using gestures, one of the men tried to get the women and children to get back in the truck. They were frozen in terror. After everything that happened, the men in black were too much.

The commander turned to me.

I propped myself up on an elbow. "Maybe she can get them to move?" I suggested.

He looked at Alicia. She seemed to be almost as afraid of him as the women the children were.

"Get up," he ordered.

She just lay there and looked at him.

"Get up, Alicia," I said.

She looked at me.

"These are the good guys, Alicia. Get up and get the women and children into the truck." I said.

She looked at him.

"Get up," he ordered again.

She got up shakily.

"Go over and get them into the truck," he ordered.

She moved slowly toward the truck, motioning the women and children to get in. They remained frozen in place. She looked at me. I shrugged my shoulders. She climbed up in the truck and motioned them to follow her. They began to move very slowly. When they saw one of the men in black get into the cab and start the engine, they began to scream and try to get out of the truck, but Alicia held them back. Alicia looked at me forlornly as the truck pulled away.

The commander of the gendarmes turned to me. "Get up!" he ordered, and I rose wearily, surprised that I could stand. "We got a call that somebody was out here making a revolution. Just what happened?" he demanded.

I shook my head wearily. For a minute I thought he was going to hit me. It looked as if he thought so, too. Then he sighed and gestured me into one of the vans. I went to sleep wedged into a corner by a window and woke only when we stopped. I was taken into a building under guard. It's the same the whole world over. The desk man put my belongings in bags and gave me a receipt. I was installed in a standard-issue interrogation room and sat waiting to see what delight the evening still held in store for me. The gendarme looked at my chest. Why do they always look at your chest? I looked down and saw Kemal's blood crusted on my T-shirt.

"What are you doing here?" he demanded roughly.

I shook my head. I wondered where Alicia was and what she was saying. As for myself, I refused to say anything.

We looked at each other for a bit. "American?" he asked, and I nodded. Apparently, he expected Americans to do anything.

He made a phone call, and we were joined by a captain. He looked hard at me and called for another chair. The room had been crowded with two chairs. The third filled all the space. To keep from looking at them, I looked around the small room. No windows, of course, and institutional paint. Why was it always green? Why was it always dirty? The odor of fear permeated the room. I'd been in better interrogation rooms, and I'd been in worse, but I understood the fear. Nobody knew where I was, and nobody was going to come and get me. The captain slammed his hand on the table.

"All right, what happened out there?"

I shook my head.

"Lady, we found you in a compound with a bunch of corpses."

"Phone call," I replied.

We went back and forth like that for a while. It had been a long day, and I was having trouble keeping my head up. I really wanted to put it on the table and go to sleep.

"Phone call," I said for what I had decided would be the last time.

He slapped his hand on the table again.

"All right," he growled and pulled out his cell phone. "American embassy," he said and started dialing.

I shook my head. "No," I said. "Driss Bouchta in Fez."

That startled him, and he stared at me. "Why do you want Driss Bouchta? You can't be working for him. He wouldn't have any agents in my territory unless I knew about it."

I just looked at him. I knew enough about interservice rivalry to know that Driss could have any number of agents in his territory. Redundancy was the name of the intelligence game. He wasn't happy about it, but he really wanted to know about the Shootout at the OK Corral, so he began calling around until he got Driss' home phone number. I could hear Driss complaining at having been awakened.

"Captain Bashir, Rissani Gendarmerie. I've got . . ."

"Lee Carruthers," I said.

"Lee Carruthers. It looks like she shot a bunch of people."

"Only two," I said modestly.

He glared.

"I found her with a bloody shirt and three dead men and three wounded. She won't talk to anybody but you."

The loud noises I heard were coming from Driss. The captain handed me the phone quickly.

"Lee?" he said incredulously.

"Driss, we're in jail in Rissani. Come and get us," I said. "We?" he asked.

"Yes. I found Alicia Harmon," I replied.

"And this resulted in three dead and three wounded?"

"It's complicated."

"I'll bet. I wish you'd go home." He sighed. "It'll take me a while to get there."

"That's all right," I said. "We're not going anywhere."

Eventually the captain agreed to hold us for Driss, and I was taken to a cell. I hadn't had anything to eat in over twenty-four hours.

"Food?" I asked.

"We don't have room service," replied the sergeant.

I shrugged and took off my boots. I took the bottom bunk and went to sleep. I woke up when Alicia was shoved into the cell, marks of tears on her face, and that mulish look in her eye.

"What happened?" I asked.

"I thought you said these were the good guys," she said bitterly.

"What happened?" I asked again.

"They just kept asking the same questions over and over again."

"Did they touch you?"

"No, they just kept asking the same question. I thought they'd never stop," she answered. She was more annoyed than frightened, as if the interrogators had breached some obscure rule of etiquette.

"Alicia, we shot up a bunch of people on their turf. You have to expect them to want to know why. What did you tell them?"

Now she was annoyed with me. "Nothing. Nothing. What could I tell them?"

"Nothing they'd believe. Go to bed."

"You've got the bottom bunk."

"I got here first," I said.

She grumbled all the way up. Alicia Harmon was a strange combination of Girl Scout with attitude and Susan B. Anthony. What forces shaped her, I wondered, besides the family slave trade and abolitionism? With that background, you'd figure a girl like Alicia would never think of going to work for the CIA, even if she did meet Sidney at an American Anti-Slavery Society meeting. None of the New England women I knew were quite so wide-eyed in the way they looked at the world, but then most of them worked for the CIA. So did Alicia, come to think of it. Why? Why didn't she see the Agency as an evil tool of the state? The next thing I knew the cell door was being opened, and I saw Driss smiling at me.

"What happened to your face?" he asked.

"It met an Al Qaeda boot," I answered.

"And the shirt?"

I shook my head.

"Body count of three dead and three wounded, eh?"

"Four, if you count Kemal."

Driss looked at me. I just shook my head again. We were taken to the captain's office, which was much better appointed than the interrogation room had been. Through a mouthful of flat bread and cheese, I told Driss the story.

Driss shook his head and smiled at certain places in the tale. The captain's mouth was hanging open most of the time. Alicia sat there eating sullenly. After I finished, Driss took us to the desk and got our property back.

"Send me the transcript, and I'll get her to sign it," Driss said. "We've just got time to catch the afternoon flight to Fez."

There wasn't much to do in Fez.

Pack Alicia up and send her on her way. She went to the bedroom to pack her things, and I sat on the couch staring into space. I would be profoundly glad to be rid of her. Thoughts of Kemal flashed across my mind, across my body, and I tried to wall them off, but it didn't work. Now that the crisis was over, he flooded my senses and nearly took me down. Cinnamon kisses. Bleeding out under my hands.

"Don't go there," I whispered. "Don't bloody go there." I put my head in my hands. "Oh, God."

Alicia. I couldn't get my head around her. The thought of ending sex slavery is irrational. All you can do is shoot one of the slavers off the tree sometimes. Like the rest of crime, eternal. She was so inexperienced that she couldn't see the risks? She was so obsessed that she didn't care about the risks? Fine for her if it was only herself that she was risking. Kemal threatened to overwhelm me again, so I jumped up and went into the bedroom. Alicia had the file drawer open and was looking inside it.

"How much of this junk do I need?" she asked drearily

"None of it," I replied. "If you need to, you can get copies. You better destroy the credit card bills, though."

She put those on the bed, and I began to shred them and throw the pieces in the trash can. She put the suitcase on the bed beside me and began throwing things from the chest of drawers in, helter-skelter. When she came to the teddies, she took a large breath and her shoulders began to shake. I knew I should try to comfort her, but I'm no good at that sort of thing. I have enough trouble dealing with my own tears. She threw the unused teddies into the trash as hard as she could and turned to glare at me. I looked away and crossed to the bookcase.

"You want any of this stuff?" I asked.

She shook her head violently and opened the wardrobe. She threw all of the navy and brown things in the suitcase. I wanted to fold it, but I didn't think she'd like that. She tossed the shoes in on top of the clothes. When she came to the beaded dress, she bent over, clasping her stomach with her arms. She flung herself on the bed weeping, and I jumped up like a scalded cat. Whatever doesn't kill you makes you stronger. Yeah. Right. I sat down beside her and tentatively patted her back. She jerked away from me, and I felt a tiny bit of sympathy for her. It grew. I had lost Kemal, but he hadn't betrayed me. I went to the wardrobe and pulled out the beaded dress.

"No!"

I looked back at her. She had pulled herself up. Her face was blotched, her eyes red from crying. She came and snatched it from me.

"That's mine!" She crushed it to her face for a long moment and then threw it into the trash can. The spike heels went next.

I stood at the bathroom door and watched as she popped each and every birth control pill out of its case and threw it in the toilet. Then she flushed them down. I could only hope that it wouldn't stop it up. She grabbed her pitiful supply of makeup and threw it in the bathroom trash. She returned to the bedroom, closed the suitcase, and rolled it to the living room, tears still streaming from her eyes. She looked over my left shoulder, her lips quivering.

"I don't know how to do these things."

No, she didn't, and it was a lesson she shouldn't have had. I put my arm around her.

"It'll get better."

She shrugged my arm away.

"Time wounds all heels?" she asked caustically.

I took her to the airport and put her on a flight to D.C.

Packing up my stuff was more difficult. My stuff was at Kemal's. I took a cab to the house of assignation and knocked on the door. A man I'd never seen before opened the door. He was a tall, straight, heavily muscled man of late middle age. Darker than Kemal, he had wavy hair and dark eyes. He was a Guard, I could tell.

"You are Miss Carruthers," he said, a statement, not a question.

"Yes. And you are?" I asked.

"I am Kemal's brother, Karim." He led me to the office and sat me down. The small boy arrived with a bottle of raki, and two glasses. He poured out the raki and handed me a glass.

"What happened?" he asked gruffly, grief engraved in the stiff lines of his face.

I sipped the drink. Raki was a good anesthetic. "I was sent here to find a colleague who was missing. Kemal and I—" I stopped. He poured me another glass of raki and waited. I drank it and resumed. "We followed her to Rissani. We were ambushed by terrorists, and Kemal was killed. They took me hostage to hold me for ransom. They also had my colleague; she and I escaped." I looked him in the eye. "I killed the man who killed Kemal."

He nodded. "Good."

"But Kemal is still dead."

He nodded again and poured us more raki.

"Revenge only evens the score. It doesn't change anything."

I looked into my glass, and for a moment the liquid swam before my eyes. Then I shook myself and raised my glass.

"To Kemal," I said and let the tears flow. His brother deserved to be the person who saw me cry.

With unshed tears in his eyes, he raised his glass. "To Kemal," he said.

We drank into the night, but neither of us ever felt anything. It was one of those nights when you couldn't get drunk to save your life. Finally, I went upstairs to pack my things. I sat on the bed and looked blindly at the wall. Kemal was dead, and we would never make love again.

I heard the dawn call to prayer. I needed sleep desperately, but I couldn't bear to sleep in that bed. Karim drove me to the Hilton, where they looked at my face a little strangely but rented me a room. Karim took me up to the room and hugged me. I saw him out, and threw myself on the bed and wept.

The next day, Driss came and took me to the airport in time for the afternoon flight to Paris. He hugged me, too.

"I'm getting too old for this kind of adventure, Driss," I said. "It's time to quit."

Chapter 54

I CLIMBED THE worn stone staircase to the flat. I unlocked the door and turned on the light. A tall thin figure stood in front of the French windows.

"Well, if it isn't my esteemed mentor, Sidney Worthington," I said. "Just the man I want to see," I said coldly.

He sat on the sofa.

"What happened to your face?" he asked.

"It met an Al Qaeda boot," I replied. I didn't have the bloody shirt on anymore. That was packed in the suitcase.

He crossed his arms over his chest, one of his favorite poses. He's going to cross his legs now, I thought. He crossed his legs.

"Lee . . ."

"Sidney, you knew Alicia Harmon was being held for ransom before you sent me out there," I said.

"I could use a drink. So could you. You're overwrought."

"The next thing you're going to say is that I'm having my period."

"Don't be coarse."

"I'm feeling coarse. I always feel coarse when I come back from nearly being killed. There's nothing but gin."

"So make me a martini."

"There's no vermouth," I said.

"So what do you drink?"

"Gin."

He rubbed his face with his hands. He looked old and tired. I relented.

"There's some brandy, I think."

I went into the kitchen and found the brandy pushed back on the top shelf in the cabinet over the sink. I didn't have any brandy snifters. He was going to have to have it in a vulgar Manhattan glass. I poured myself some gin over an ice cube and took both drinks into the living room. He raised an eyebrow when I handed him his brandy.

"It's that or nothing," I said. I sat beside him on the couch and sipped my drink. The cold gin felt good against my teeth. Then I got up and sat in the chair next to the sofa. Somehow I didn't feel like sitting next to him. That was too friendly.

He swirled the brandy around in the glass and took a sip, "What happened out there?" he asked.

The room smelled musty, so I went to open the French windows. There was no sun in the street. There never was. There was no sun in the case either, unless you counted the bad guys who were dead. I turned back to him and wearily told the story again.

After listening to it, he began to ask questions.

"Hadid. What happened to him? Was the Palace in on it?" he asked.

"He got away in the confusion after the gendarmes arrived. I don't think the Palace was in on it. I think he was just in it for the money."

"What will happen to him?"

"Nothing. He's the King's food taster." When he raised an eyebrow, I translated. "He's the head of Palace security.

He's the most dangerous man in the kingdom, and he can do virtually anything he likes."

Sidney nodded. He was used to people who could do virtually anything. "And Rashid? He was doing what?"

"He was laundering two streams of money. His man was collecting protection money from the brothels and taking it to the hawalador, who sent it to the Pures on the Talmine Oasis. As for the rest of the money, Rashid got it by skimming from donations from the saint's tomb. The money never went on the Foundation's books at all, which is why they were so clean. The Man with the Briefcase took the skimmings to the hawalador, who sent it to Miranshah in Pakistan."

"The Northwest Frontier Province. That will go to the Taliban. What will happen to him?"

"Nothing. He's dead. They put the whole thing on him, and he can hardly deny it. As for Rashid? He's a Friend of the King and is untouchable."

"And—what's his name—Glover. Where does he fit in?"

"He was employed by Worldwide Entertainment. They own the brothels in Rabat and Fez and in several other places around the world. His job was to buy the women and children for them. He enjoyed groping the women in the slave shipment, so I imagine he enjoyed doing other things, too."

Sidney grimaced.

"It's a tough trade, Sidney. Alicia is right to despise it," I said.

"The trafficking?"

"The Pures will wait until the heat dies down, but they'll be back in business inside a month. They need the money. They may have trouble getting a shipment through Al Qaeda in the Islamic Maghreb. They're still sore about the Pures defecting. They're pressing them hard to come back into the fold, and they don't want to. The Pures are moving into Morocco, I think. So I think the rendezvous point will shift close to wherever they move, but the trade itself will go on, and on, and on. Men use women, and brothels need a fresh supply regularly."

"Lee," Sidney protested.

"It's simple. Supply and demand. Or, in this case, demand and supply. Sometimes, I feel like the boy with his finger in the dike. There are more leaks every day, and I'm running out of fingers."

I went to the kitchen and got us new drinks. When I returned, Sidney asked, "What will happen to the women and children?"

"I don't know. Even if the authorities could determine where they originally came from, they can't go home. Their parents would only have to send them back. The labor recruiter paid for them. The payment was disguised as a long-term loan, but the recruiter actually owns them, and I'm sure the outfit has enforcers."

"Does Morocco have a place for them?" he asked.

"No," I said, "it doesn't." I looked out the window. It was raining. I took a deep breath and—again—asked the question that had been haunting me.

"Sidney, why did you send me out blind? Knowing she was a captive might have helped," I said. "It would have prevented me from asking stupid questions around town. They thought that Alicia had reported her suspicions and that I had been sent to do something about the situation."

"But she hadn't reported anything," Sidney said.

"They didn't know that. They took the hard drive from the office computer. When they found the files on the drive were encrypted, they thought the files might be on my laptop, so they snatched that, but they didn't find them there, either. That meant either I didn't know anything or I knew everything."

"You would have done something if you had known."

"Not necessarily. In either case, the simplest solution was to kill me. If they could kill me, all the information Alicia had would disappear." I stopped to consider. "That's why there were so many attacks on me. They needed to know what I knew, and I knew nothing," I said. "Nothing. How could you not know she was a captive?" I asked harshly. "They took her ten days before you sent me out."

He looked me in the eyes. "I did not know they had her. The call went to Beirut. That fool Riley in the station there fiddled around for days trying to figure out what to do. It was only when he got a phone call threatening to send him a finger that he finally reported the situation to me. By that time you were in deep trouble in Fez."

"Believe it. I was hot the moment I got there."

He looked away. "All my calls to you went straight to voice mail, and, after a while, they stopped going there, probably because the mail box was full. I had no idea what happened to you until I got the call telling me they had you."

I began to pace back and forth in front of him. "And what did you do then? Send in the Marines?" I asked sarcastically.

"We had to wait for a second call to zero in on your location."

"There was a GPS in my phone."

"We got nothing from it. They must have taken your phone."

"They did."

"And destroyed the GPS. We had no way to locate you. All I could do was count on your instinct for self-preservation and your ability to get out of tight spots. I didn't know they had her until he called about you."

I stopped pacing. "This is what working at that place does to you, Sidney. Failure is not an option. Results required no matter what you have to do the get them."

"You know that's not true. I'm making allowances . . ."

"Well, kill somebody else for a change. I've been quitting for a long time. This time I mean it."

"Lee, you're exhausted. You need some rest."

"Don't patronize me, Sidney. I've been a big girl for a long time."

"I did not know they had her, Lee," he repeated.

"I don't believe you," I said bluntly.

He looked at me over his glass. "Suddenly you don't trust me?"

"I don't feel very trusting at the moment. I had no information other than the fact that she was missing."

"You knew that she had mentioned terrorist funding."

"Sidney, I had to go stumbling around asking the same questions she asked. The same questions that got her sold to the terrorists got me sold to them, too, and got my backup killed. Kemal's dead because of this.

"Yes, she'd found a new money-laundering operation, run by a man with such an irreproachable reputation that no one could possibly suspect him. That's probably why she didn't tell you the details. You wouldn't have believed her. You sent me into the mouth of the beast, blind and deaf and dumb, with no briefing at all."

He slammed his glass down on the coffee table. "That's enough, Lee! She was missing. I knew you could find her."

"Your faith in me warms my heart. I've known you to do rotten things before, but I have never seen you do anything like this. I never thought you'd send me to my death without a briefing. After all, you were my father's best man. You're even my godfather."

He speared me with ice blue eyes. "I have never sent anyone into the field without a briefing. You knew all I knew. She thought she had found some new source of terrorist money. She did not say where. She did not say who. When I asked for more information, she didn't answer. I know now that was because she was already in their hands, but I didn't know that then," he said.

I resumed pacing. "Drug smuggling, arms smuggling, human trafficking, terrorism have all increased, and they will go on increasing. There is nothing you or I or anybody can do. The flow of dirty money is endless. It's like playing whack-a-mole. Hit one on the head and another pops up the next day. Get somebody else to do the chasing. And while I'm at it, stop sending greenhorns out into the world without supervision."

"I sent you out when you were green."

"Yes, you did Sidney, and I've always wondered why."

"Because you had the best Arabic in the office."

"Bill's Arabic was better than mine."

"But he couldn't have done the job."

"Oh, I did the job. I always have, haven't I? Once, I was proud of doing things most analysts only read about in reports. I learn fast, and, fool that I was, I was proud of that, too. You sent me into situations I was only marginally prepared for, and I thrived on it. The Beqaa Valley in Lebanon was no place for a greenhorn. Bill was right about that. It wasn't a safe place for a trained agent, much less a green girl, but I did the job, always. I'm really good at it, but after a while it gets old. I'm alive because I have a strong sense of self-preservation, but one day I'm going to be just a little too slow, a little less sharp, and I'll die in some God forsaken alley in some God forsaken town where you sent me to do a little job for you in the interests of national security. I've given my life to national security, Sidney, and it's not perceptibly better."

"There has been no perceptible decline, either," he replied.

"We are not amused. People with obsessions are dangerous. Me, I'm not obsessed with anything but self-preservation. Send a girl like Alicia Harmon, who is obsessed with slavery, out to track it without supervision, and she's bound to go off half-cocked sooner or later. That idiot woman went to Rissani because she wanted to see the purchase go down. To see women being sold into sex slavery with her own eyes. I guess after seeing that, she might have told you there was a new bunch running the trade, or she might have told you about the trouble in the brothels, about the new men there, new men she thought were terrorists. She might have reported any of these things, but she didn't, and it took me several days and several attacks on me to figure them out for myself.

"In any case, they knew she worked for the Agency. If she hadn't gone to Rissani, they would have killed her in Fez for asking all those questions. Even if she didn't discover the answers, someone might eventually have listened to her. They had no idea she was so stupid that she hadn't reported everything she knew. They assumed I'd been sent to deal with what she had found out, so they had to find out what I knew, which was precisely nothing." I was so furious that I kept repeating myself. "Sidney, if Alicia Harmon belongs in the Agency at all, which I very much doubt, she belongs at Langley, where she can't get into any trouble."

"I need somebody in Fez," he said stubbornly.

"Do you need somebody like Alicia? Do you really need any of those offices? I've read her reports. If all of the offices I set up produce reports like that, you might as well save the money and spend it on drones. All of the work of your unit can be done at Langley and at less expense. These offices exist only to support your budget."

"I need people in the field to tell us which way the money is jumping. I agree, it could be done at Langley, but at Langley you get cubicle think, brains in boxes, and nobody can see anything that has never been done before. Your brain is not in a box. You're an original, Lee, and that's the kind of person I need. Maybe the Femme Aid offices aren't that important, but I still think what they do is necessary."

"Oh, it is, Sidney, but whether it's related to our mandate or not is another question. The Agency can't do everything, especially if they're going to spend all that money on drones."

"Stop harping on drones. They're beside the point. What you in Paris and Charles in Geneva and Mary Lou in Singapore do is more important than just chasing black money. Unlike those of us who work at Langley, you live in the real world. You get the feel of what money is going to do before it does it, the kind of feeling you can't get if you're shut up in a cubicle at Langley. It's that feel that we need to have to figure out what the bad guys are going to do next."

"That's what embassy analysts are for," I said.

"That's State Department. They're focused on other things."

I stopped in front of him, my hands on my hips. "I know. I've always wondered what they do. Even Agency stations have other priorities. They're all out chasing Al Qaeda."

"You found the gold sector deal last year before it was on anybody else's radar."

"I'm not sure that justifies the expense of keeping me in Paris. You only need people in the field to support your budget," I said bitterly. "Real estate at the Puzzle Palace is cheaper than a fifteenth-century building in Paris, cheaper than all the other real estate, too, but you need that real estate, Sidney, need it to keep yourself at the table with the Big Boys, especially since Special Ops is getting such a big cut of the pie these days."

"Lee, I know you're upset about . . . What's his name?"

"Kemal, Sidney, his name was Kemal," I said through my teeth. "Haven't you been listening? Kemal's death is just the last straw. We weren't in love. We cared for each other, but we weren't in love. There is no way I would move to Fez and set up housekeeping with a Muslim man, and we both knew it. Can you see me as the mistress of a man who runs a house of assignation? But if I hadn't gone to Fez—if you hadn't sent me to Fez—Kemal would still be alive. I keep saying that Alicia Harmon killed him, but I know she didn't. I killed him as surely as if I had pulled the trigger myself. If he hadn't been protecting me, he would be still alive."

I looked into my glass and saw nothing there, not even gin.

"Lee, the best way to get over a fall is to get back up on the horse," he said.

"This isn't just a fall off a horse," I said sharply. "This is desolation! I've seen it coming, and I've told you it was coming, but you wouldn't listen. You never listen. I'm burned out. I'm through."

"Lee, take a few days off. Then I need you to go to Dubai. George Branson washed up on the shore there carrying a false passport. I need to know why."

I clenched my teeth in cold rage.

"Sidney," I enunciated very clearly, "You. Haven't. Heard. A. Word. I've. Said."

"I need you to go to Dubai."

"I'm not going to Dubai or anyplace else for you, Sidney. I'm finished."

I sat on the porch of a shack in the Caymans wearing a bikini bottom, drinking gin, and watching the sun go down. I'd been there a month, and I thought I might stay. It was so peaceful. I hadn't shot anybody in a whole month, and I liked the way that felt. I heard the buzz of a mosquito and slapped at it. In the Caymans the mosquitoes are so big they carry five hundred-pound bombs. Pretty soon I was going to have to go inside and get a shirt.

The pearl on the chain around my neck still had Kemal's blood on it. I had stopped feeling his hands on me and his lips on mine, but I would never rid myself of the guilt I bore for his death. Like so many other things in my life, I would just have to live with that. I finished the gin and put the glass down. Maybe I dozed a little. When I woke, the stars were out. They weren't as close or as crisp as they were in the desert, but they were just as enigmatic.

Why *was* George Branson carrying a false passport when he washed up in Dubai?

Coming Next

DEAD IN DUBAI

Out of the Agency and looking for work, Lee Carruthers accepts an appeal from Cynthia Branson to find her husband, George. Lee knows where George is, but what does the mysterious key he sent his wife open?

About the Author

Marilynn Larew was born in Omaha, Nebraska, and after living in a number of places, including the Philippines and Japan, she finally settled in southern Pennsylvania, where she and her husband live in a 150-year-old farmhouse. She has taught courses about the Vietnamese War and terrorism at the University of Maryland and traveled extensively in Europe and Asia. She likes to write about places she has been or places she would like to go. She has published nonfiction about local history, Vietnamese history, and terrorism. This is her first novel.